HOLDING OUT
FOR A
HERO

HOLDING OUT
FOR A
HERO

ORDER OF OLYMPUS
❊ BOOK 1 ❊

MARIA SHIELD

ISBN: 978-1-7343533-1-0 (Paperback)
ISBN: 978-1-7343533-0-3 (Ebook)

Any references to historical events, real people, or real places are used fictitiously. Names, characters, and places are products of the author's imagination.

Book cover and design by Damonza.com

First printing, 2020.

www.maria-shield.com

This book is for my own personal hero, who encouraged me to pursue my dreams with support and love. Thank you, Nate.

"Tell of the storm-tossed man, O Muse, who wandered long after he sacked the sacred citadel of Troy."

—Homer, *The Odyssey*

I

"IT IS TRULY a mark of the gods that after centuries you are still great in bed."

The words were delivered in a lover's complimentary tone, but that didn't stop the agony of a spear to the heart. Argos let the sting wash over him as he collected his breath. It was best not to let immortals know when their aim struck true. "It is a curse," he panted, eyes fixed on the stone ceiling, where a mosaic stared back at him. The collection of dyed pebbles did not do Circe justice in their imitation of the Sea Witch.

"Indeed, a curse." Circe leaned her perfect body across his to caress the chain that tethered him to the wall. She was not flushed from the exertion of sex like a mortal woman would be. Instead, her skin shimmered as if it had been kissed by both ocean and sun. "We are both forsaken by the gods, that is why we are perfect for each other."

Argos nearly bit through his cheek at the sentiment. The smell of sex and shame clung to the limestone walls of his exquisite dungeon. Pillars carved from pure marble, animal furs thrown over chairs—all of it was an attempt to recreate the old days. Circe had taken few things from the outside world to make the room comfortable. The bed was certainly grander than anything Argos had slept on in either the thirteenth or fourteenth century. She had bragged years ago of stealing it from some foreign princess or prince from gods knew where, with four towering posters and enough room for an entire harem of lovers to make use of it.

"We are a tragedy," Circe continued, her voice faraway, as if there was something romantic about their predicaments.

She moved to stroke him, slow and sensual, but he was quicker. His hand snapped forward and captured her small wrist at the base of his cock. Circe's cold eyes met his. In the firelight, they were as dark as the River Styx. "Afraid of coming too soon?" The question was a double-sided blade, all innocence if not for the lingering threat underneath. In truth, she did not care if he came. Circe had only taken pleasure from him these past centuries, never sparing him an ounce of the same consideration.

"My love," he said, surprised by the softness of the words. "If we are going to do this again, I will need some fruit and wine."

Circe stared at him for a long moment, face unreadable. He worried she might suspect, but then a smile cut across her lips as she laughed. "Dear Argos, whatever for? Does my island not keep your body free from hunger and thirst?"

"Of course, I don't mean to eat it," he answered, meeting her stare. In his old life, breaking eye contact had been a sign of weakness, and showing weakness to a creature such as Circe could mean death. On her island, though, it would mean something worse than death. Endless torture in a place that would never let him die.

But Argos was a quick study; his old ways would not serve him on Circe's island. So he'd adopted a new way to fight. Soft words and pleasurable touches had gotten him the littlest rewards. A day of rest, a hand free from the chains restraining him. Now, he licked his lips to emphasize the lie, noting how her eyes tracked the movement. "I wish to lick the wine from your body. I wish to worship you in ways that will make even the gods blush."

Those words got a reaction. Her eyes sparkled with something that was no longer just lust. "That would please me very much." She sat up slowly, her long legs sliding over the edge of the bed. She didn't bother wrapping her body in a silk robe. Instead she strolled towards the doorway, hips swaying with the confidence of a woman who owned everyone and everything on her island. "I shall gather food for your sacrifice."

Argos gave her a well-practiced look of longing as he watched the curtain fall behind her. He held his breath for the span of three footfalls before she was out of earshot, then he sat up.

Many heroes had fallen to tragedy; he would not be one. It was time for his escape.

Twisting his body on the bed, he grabbed the steel chain that bound his wrist to the stone wall. The cold metal was thick and heavy in his hands, reminding him how weak he had become.

Long ago, he had been one of the strongest men in the known world. Now, his muscles had grown lax from centuries chained to a bed. He tugged at the chain, but it did not fall from the connection against the wall.

There was no time to lock pick or chisel at the stone. If Circe caught him in this escape, he would face the same fate as so many men before him. He would have to resort to more gory means, but for the sake of his freedom, he would do it. He wrapped the chain around the narrow part of his wrist and pulled. The chains bit into the skin, drawing blood and rubbing the spot raw. Gritting his teeth against the pain, he desperately tried to call upon the strength he had once taken for granted.

A low growl echoed from the shadows of the room as a large cat stepped through the blood-red curtain hanging over the doorway. One of Circe's many Pets. It bared its fangs at him; the part of the animal that was still human knew exactly what he was doing.

Her Pets hated him, hated any man who took away the attention of their mistress. He could see it in their bright yellow eyes. When Circe left him alone, they would claw at him, tear at his skin and wait for him to heal before doing it again. The Pets had been sailors once, before Circe's magic had turned them into her own personal menagerie of animals, binding them to her forever.

Argos gave the cat his own feral smile and held out his hand, urging it to step forward.

The jaguar stared at his injured hand, licking its lips.

"Come on," he hissed, voice barely louder than his own drumming heart. The promise of his escape was the only thing that kept him from thinking of the pain that was about to come. He shook his hand, tightening the chain and getting a few blood drops to fall to the floor. "Come on, come on."

With a violent hiss, the cat lunged, aiming for his upper arm. Just in time, Argos managed to move enough that its teeth fell on his hand. He clamped down on a scream, knowing it would alert Circe. Instead he closed his eyes and repeated the gods' names in his head, cursing every one of them as the jaguar tore his hand apart.

Zeus, Hades, Demeter...

They did not come in any order. Just old names that he repeated to himself every now and then. Names that he had once shouted at the top of his lungs, hoping for mercy.

Hera, Poseidon, Apollo...

But no one answered. He had once been favored by the gods. A hero. Now, he was a prisoner, forsaken and forgotten by all.

Hestia...

Hestia, the goddess of the hearth. Out of all the gods, she had been his favorite, and he had been hers. When that favor had disappeared, though, she had thrown him to Circe.

The pain was still raw from that betrayal. He gritted his teeth at the memory, opened his eyes, and stared at the broken stump of meat that the jaguar was still gnawing on. It was enough.

Yanking back his bleeding arm, the chain snagged against the small lump and then fell free. The jaguar looked appalled that its meal had been snatched away, but then its golden eyes lingered on Argos's body as it realized there was a bigger meal to be had.

The hero smiled at the cat, swinging his feet to the floor and attempting to stand up. His legs wobbled, weak and forgetful of their proper purpose. He reached out to steady himself, but his hand was gone. The miscalculation cost him as he fell against the wall, leaving a bloody smear against the stones. The jaguar saw its opportunity and pounced.

Compared to the league of monsters he had fought in the past, a giant cat was nothing. Even in his weakened state, with his arms free he knew he stood a chance. Argos caught the cat around the throat and did not even blink as its claws desperately sunk into the flesh of his good arm.

Gathering all the strength he could muster, he slammed the cat's head against the stone wall. A dying howl from the Pet was cut off with a twist of its neck. Shit. Circe surely would have heard that.

Argos dropped the body to the ground. He did not flinch when the skin of the jaguar shifted; long feline limbs shrank, morphing back into the man the animal had once been.

He would not remain dead for long. Already the broken neck was beginning to heal itself, thanks to the island's magic. Lifting his stump of a hand, Argos found the bones of his fingers mending themselves; in a few more minutes it would be as if he had never lost the hand at all.

Those minutes would have to be on the run, though. A wolf's howl from outside assured him that the jaguar's call had been heard. Circe would be back soon, and her monsters would be with her.

He quickly moved to a wooden chest across the room, feet stumbling awkwardly as he forced them forward. He was shaking like a newborn foal, embarrassing for a man who wanted to sprint when he could barely walk. Every second mattered.

Inside, he found a collection of trinkets—drachmae coins and silver beads from men of the heroic age. Newer, shinier items from the fools after—a silver flask, a well-tailored coat, and a necklace with a loved one's image inside. Argos discarded them until he found what he was looking for. A gold coin connected to a hardy piece of string. His thumb smoothed over its bumps; on one side was the faded face of Zeus, and on the other a word was written in a language long dead: κόσμος.

Order. Those who brought purpose to a world that knew only chaos.

His fingers lingered over the coin, brushing it with care as he waited for the coin's magic to light against his skin.

It did not.

He had dreamt of this moment, of the warmth that came with the coin's touch, for so long, and now it was not there.

Something was wrong, but there was no time to dwell on it. He tossed the coin around his neck and grabbed a few of the items from the chest that would ensure his survival. Once he left the island, he would be mortal again, but at least he would be alive. Then he followed the smell of the ocean just outside the stone walls.

Towards his freedom.

II

SOMETIMES A GIRL just had to get away.

Claire sighed at the thought. This was supposed to be relaxing. *She* was supposed to be relaxing. Under the bright summer sun, with the easy bounce of the waves against her boat rocking her to sleep, it should have been easy to forget all her troubles. But for a woman up to her eyeballs in debt, relaxation didn't exist when there was a restaurant to open.

All her life Claire had been the girl to play it safe. She'd always had money in savings, always had a steady job. Then one day that girl decided to take a leap of faith. Turns out, following your dream was both more expensive and more work than she could have imagined.

At least you have a home, she told herself in a valiant effort to stay positive. *Not everyone can say that.* It was a tiny room above the kitchen that held the few things she hadn't sold off to purchase furniture for the restaurant. But that had been a strategic decision, she told herself again. Moving out of the apartment in D.C. made sense. Besides, her commute was reduced to a single staircase—a perk that would come in handy when she was working day and night to pay off the bank loan and "gift" from her mother.

That was another headache for another day. The voice-mail notification was still glaring up from her phone. The fourth one this week. *"Oh, hello Claire, just calling to see how the renovations are going. I know the plan is to open next week, but I just finished talking to Roger and his Italian restaurant is hiring. I couldn't help but drop your name, you know, so you can have a bit of income while your restaurant is getting off the ground. Call me back."*

No way, Claire told herself stubbornly. A call back would only result in a fight. Luckily, out on the water, her phone had no reception. There would be no unwanted phone calls during her relaxation time.

She took a deep breath and looked out onto the water. The only thing she had left that was worth any money was the tuckered-out old fishing boat her father had left her. Selling *Sebastian* was not an option. Despite his aged appearance and sputtering engine, there was no place she'd rather be.

Relax, she told herself for the hundredth time, and for a second her muscles listened.

Her first time out to sea had been on the 1988 Dyer. She remembered the sharp smell of seawater encasing her entire body, even after they'd returned home. Remembered the moment her dad had allowed her to steer the boat, even if just for a second. The way they had laughed at the baby trout he'd caught but cooked it for dinner nonetheless. Even at the age of six, Claire had been the better cook.

A total and complete daddy's girl, she clung to the few

things that he had left behind with an almost obsessive frenzy. *Sebastian* included.

The boat was an essential part of the Claire Winters' Life Dream. *Sebastian* had a place of honor tied up at the part of the pier right outside her future restaurant, where Claire could look outside her window every morning and see the boat along with the sunrise over the bay.

Her eyes closed at the thought. The boat's flooring warmed her summer-touched skin, and she hummed happily. *The little things*, Claire reminded herself. *Life is about the little things.*

A harsh scraping noise suddenly echoed through the boat, and Claire jumped to attention. She'd been around boats long enough to know that noise.

Sebastian had hit something.

Carefully she took in the water around her. She was anchored at least a couple miles south of her home at Edgewater. Nearly half a mile of water lay between her and the edge of Kent Island. No one was around.

Another harsh noise interrupted her observations, kicking Claire to her feet to investigate *Sebastian*'s sides. A look portside yielded nothing. She turned to peek over the starboard railing and froze. A small worn rowboat bumped anxiously against the side again. The structure was unlike anything she had ever seen before. The elegantly curved bow was made from a rich wood she didn't recognize.

She didn't pay the strange boat much attention after that. Her eyes focused instead on the body taking up its entire length. Muscular limbs stretched and dangled from one end to the other. It was a man, no doubt about that. Claire tried not to dwell on the scrap of cloth hanging around his waist and instead zoomed in on the rise and fall of his chest. From where she peeked down at him, he looked as if he was taking a late-afternoon nap.

"Hello," she called. "Are you alright down there?"

No response, but he was breathing. That was a relief. His brazened skin looked dry, almost leathery, and his short, rapid breathing didn't bode well for his overall health. A silver flask was clutched between his fingers, clearly empty from the precarious way it was held. The man had been out in the sun for far too long. Summers on the Chesapeake Bay could be humid, and any amount of time without proper hydration was dangerous.

The scruff along his chin and the length of his hair suggested only one thing—a castaway. Who knew how long he'd been floating in the waters with no help or food? That was a strange thought. The Bay wasn't that big, and they were far enough north that someone should have spotted his boat. Concern overrode logic for now. The man needed help, and there would be time for questions later. She threw a rope ladder over the railing and prepared to board the small vessel.

Years of living in the city and the warnings of a paranoid mother urged her to stay cautious. As she grabbed two water bottles from her cooler, Claire also picked up the small pocketknife she had stashed under the steering wheel before tucking it into the back pocket of her khakis. She had never used the knife for anything but cutting rope and peeling the occasional apple. She hoped that didn't change today, but just in case she reminded herself: *stick him with the pointy end.*

Poking her head back over the railing, the man was still where she'd left him, unmoving. The waves brushed the small rustic rowboat against her own. There was no choice. She scaled down the rope ladder and struggled to place her feet somewhere that wasn't already taken up by bulging muscles. She wrapped the chain around the bow, successfully connecting the two boats and ensuring that the rowboat wouldn't be wandering anywhere. Then she concentrated on the stranger. Getting him up the ladder and into shade was an impossible task on her own.

"Hey, wake up." She brushed her fingertips along the closest part of his body, his bare legs. Her touch started as a gentle poke before shifting into a firm shake when he didn't respond. Worry clawed up her throat at the idea that he might be seriously injured. She needed to get him awake and get water in him.

But the small boat barely had enough room for the two of them. Claire planted her feet on one side of him, but the waves threatened to send her into the water. Clenching her teeth, she searched for an alternative way to aid the man that didn't have her fumbling over his naked body.

There was only one option.

"I'm sorry," she whispered, gently straddling his upper body. His breathing didn't waver under her weight. For a moment, Claire just took in the stranger. Besides the loincloth, the only thing on his body was a web of scars decorating his skin. One danced up his left pectoral muscle and over his shoulder; another sliced across his waist. Others were nothing more than light lines across his dark skin. A necklace made from braided thread with a dull gold coin settled along his collarbone. At least if he had any weapons on his person, he wouldn't be able to hide them.

What are you talking about? said an awed voice in the back of her mind. *Do you see his arms? If those guns aren't weapons, I don't know what is.* She ignored her own misguided thoughts and opened a water bottle. Her fingers brushed long dark locks out of the stranger's face before tilting his head up. Water dribbled over the side of his mouth before his throat worked to swallow. His body jerked in response before he began to enthusiastically gulp down the water.

"Whoa, slow down," Claire said, pulling her arm back. Too much water too fast could be just as dangerous. The bottle was nearly empty, but one large hand shot up and snatched it from her. "Hey!"

The man gulped the last of the water, even licking at the inside of the bottle for another drop. Claire clutched the spare bottle close to her chest as she watched the stranger come to life.

Slowly, startling green eyes opened and stared at her, taking in her position on his stomach, the mess her hair had become under the gentle gusts of wind, and finally the water bottle between her breasts. Without saying a word, he reached out to take the bottle. Claire leaned back despite the fact that his arm could easily reach her. At least her movement got him to pause.

"You're awake, good." A sigh of relief escaped her as she pinned him with a look. "I'll be happy to give you this water bottle, but first do you think you can climb the ladder?" She pointed at the rope behind her and watched as his gaze fell onto it. He looked dubious.

"Why do I need to? Are you taking me captive?" His voice came as a surprise. Smooth and deep, rolling over her like thunder and making the hairs on her arm stick up. The thought seemed to amuse him, and once again his eyes took her in, this time with more awareness of different points of her features and the loose clothes that hung off her body. He eyed her breasts the same way he eyed the bottle of water.

Claire scoffed, quickly shrugging off his gaze. "Look, there is more of this"—she waved the bottle in his face, pulling back just as he attempted to grab it—"up there. Not to mention shade. How long have you been out here?"

A considering look crossed his handsome features. "The last time I fell asleep I had counted three suns."

"Oh God. You really are a castaway." An enormous amount of sympathy hit her with the realization. He simply blinked in response, looking confused. "How did you even get lost? Did your boat sink?"

No one heard of real castaways anymore. She couldn't even remember hearing of any plane crashes or boat accidents in the last week. Not in their neck of the woods, at least.

He looked solemn as he answered. "I escaped the Sea Witch's lair after centuries of captivity. I cannot remember the last time I ate or drank anything." His voice had a reflective depth to it, but after a pause it returned with a new, slightly musing tone and an upward curl to the corners of his mouth. "But it seems Poseidon is finally smiling on me by delivering one of his daughters to my aid." The curl broadened into a sober smile, but there was no humor in his words.

Dear God, she thought. *He's delusional!*

Claire took a deep breath and thrust the second water bottle into his chest. "Water. You definitely need more water." Maybe after he hydrated, he'd start making sense.

Four days at sea had nearly destroyed his mortal body. Over the years, Argos had forgotten what true hunger felt like. The stabbing pain that made a man's gut clench like an angry fist. The weakness that settled over the body, leaving one immobile. His cries to Poseidon had been useless; the ocean had been silent company.

He wondered if Hestia had poisoned her brother against him. It would have been a wise move for her. Without a god to give him a new quest, he would be forever stuck as a mortal. Fragile and soft. His skin crawled at the sheer thought of it.

He could have easily *died*.

Never in all his years had Argos even considered that word. Not when he had been littered with arrows or when he had almost drowned. His death had been torn out of the threads of fate the moment he had become a hero for Olympus. And now, lying on a boat, he felt defeated and broken and mortal.

Maybe that was why Poseidon had finally answered his prayers. Another one of the gods' games. He would have cursed them for their carelessness, but he did not have the strength and the gods' gift was too good: the sweet taste of cold water and a nymph sitting on his chest. At least, the woman looked like a nymph, with small hands and nose contrasting nicely with plump pink lips. She was finicky like a nymph too, the way she had taken away his water so suddenly—taunting and flirtatious.

While strength had leaked out of all his muscles, the days on the water had also robbed the curse of its devastating effects. He should have gone mad without a woman's touch, but there had been no women to entice him. Instead his body had other needs; food and water had taken priority.

Despite his hunger, it had been bliss not feeling his cock throb for a few days.

The nymph must have known how she was affecting him as she slid off his chest to sit at the opposite end of the boat. A sharp sword of disappointment slashed him at the sight. Already his body was stirring, responding to having a woman's flesh so close after four days of being denied it. He sat up, desperate to have her touch him again.

Just as quickly as the disappointment reared its head, it fell away as the nymph handed him more water, muttering under her breath, "Just drink, okay? Don't say another word until you finish this bottle."

He continued to watch her as he drank. The woman wore the strangest garb he had ever seen. Cloth the same color as her skin only covered half of her legs, showing off the rest of the smooth shapely limbs. Meanwhile, her upper half was clad in loose draping that showed him none of his favorite assets on a woman.

She must have read his mind, known the right areas to cover just to tease and pluck at him. Nymph.

One thing was certain, though—she had fine sea legs. Feet planted in the only free spaces of his boat, the nymph managed to keep her balance as she stood. Argos was not used to a woman towering over him, but as he looked up at her, drinking in the sight of the sun playing against her soft brown hair, his body rumbled in response.

The bottle of water was finished in seconds. For the first time in years he felt almost satisfied.

"You probably need something to eat. I have some fruit up on the deck," the woman said as her fingers curled around the rope. "I can't carry you up, but if you can make it there yourself I'll make it worth your while."

I bet you will. Argos smiled at the thought and once again the nymph must have read his mind as she flushed.

"I mean… I'll feed you. Fruit. I'll feed you fruit. And there's shade, so…" Her voice trailed off as heat flickered across her face. She turned away from him abruptly and practically stumbled up the rope ladder. "Come on."

Despite his weakened state, he managed to climb up after her, staring up to appreciate the view until she disappeared over the side with a firm glare and a muttered, "Even half dead and delusional, a man is still a man."

Pulling his body up was not difficult, but his muscles still burned from his escape. There had been a time before all this, before Hestia and Circe, when he would have been able to pull his entire body weight with two fingers. He had been one of the strongest men to sail the uncharted seas. Others knew his boat and crew on sight and stayed clear. That time felt like another life. A dream he would often revisit to escape the hell of reality.

Now here he was, free but weak, weaponless and mortal. Not to mention with a strange woman. After both Hestia and the Sea Witch, he was ready to swear off women for the rest of eternity. They were too much trouble. But the damn curse made him ache for them. His shaft became hard as steel just thinking about them. His rescuer was nothing like his past lovers. She did not have Circe's curling lip, nor her sense of seduction. Everything Circe did was with a purpose. The nymph was more like a butterfly—delicate, unaware of its own beauty. A creature that would surely be crushed if he dared to do more than look at it.

At the top of the rope Argos staggered to take in the sight that greeted him. Architecture like he had never seen in his life. The boat had no sails, and a low growling that reminded Argos of a sea monster seemed to be coming from the ship's belly. He stared at the deck of the boat, unable to place what it was made of. As promised, a small overhang provided shade with seating. Most surprising, though, was the fact that there were no men, only this tiny leaf of a woman. How could a single female effectively handle a boat so large?

Small hands pulled him forward. Argos moved in the direction she ordered without a word as she brought him under the shade. The temperature drop was noticeable, and he could feel his skin relax once it was out of the sun's heat. A third bottle of water was shoved into one hand as another was placed against his forehead. The biting chill of ice tickled his skin and he turned to move his head away when the woman shushed him. "You need to bring your body temperature down. Just hold this here, and don't chug the water like last time."

She moved away, back to a small blue box, which she picked through before pulling out an orange. His mouth watered. Blue eyes looked up, caught and held his stare. "So, do you have a name?"

"Argos," he stated, "and what is your name, nymph?"

"Nymph?" she snorted, smiling for the first time since he had laid eyes on her. It was a nice smile. Shy, like those women used to give him when he walked through a marketplace. "My name is Claire."

"Claire…" He tried out the word. "That is a strange name."

"So is Argos," she said before pulling out a small black rock from her back. With a flick of her wrist, a knife appeared. It shined in her hand, a deadly weapon held in the soft grip of a woman. Claire noticed his eyes on the knife and waved it around with narrowed eyes, daring him to try and take it from her.

A laugh bubbled out of his throat. Fiery. He liked that in a woman.

He shrugged his shoulders to show her that he would do her no harm, but her body remained tense. She cut the orange in fourths and threw two pieces his way. "You think I'm going to hurt you, Claire?"

"No." Though the knife suddenly moving out in front of her said the opposite. "I just wanted you to know that it's here."

Her grip was all wrong—the thumb needed to be under the fingers or risk being broken—and then there was her stance. She might have nice smooth sea legs, but the way she was standing would not protect her if he charged. None of that surprised him, though, and most likely she knew it all as well. She was spirited, and he liked that, but not enough that he would risk the same mistake twice. No matter what his body demanded, he would not fall under another woman's spell.

III

"ARE YOU FEELING better?" Claire asked, looking over her shoulder from the steering wheel. Her castaway was sitting by the cooler. Empty water bottles littered the deck around his feet, along with the remains of the lunch she had packed. Breadcrumbs clung to his messy beard even as he combed a hand over it.

His bright green eyes had followed her every move as she'd weighed anchor and were now transfixed on the control panel as she started *Sebastian*'s engine. A thick blanket hung around his shoulders to keep him warm and prevent shock. Not to mention it served well to keep his nearly naked body from being a distraction.

She pushed up on the throttle and turned *Sebastian* in a sweeping arc towards home. The wind startled him out of his trance. His eyes shifted from the control panel to the water, watching as the wake rippled along behind them. "Then why don't we try this again? What happened that you got stuck out at sea for four days?"

"I've told you," he said with an aggravated sigh, smile

dropping. "I escaped Circe's island. The only boat I could find was the one in which you found me. I had no need for food or water on her island and forgot that as soon as I left my body would regain mortality."

"Right…" Claire rolled the information around for a moment.

Argos's green eyes pinned her with a stare. "You do not believe me."

"Look, the Chesapeake has islands, but none of them belong to a Circe. And, not to boast or anything, but I know these waters pretty well and I've never seen an island like the one you've described. The places around here don't grant the power of immortality." She took a deep breath and combed her fingers through her hair in frustration.

"You are an Atheos, then." He shook his head, looking grim. "They grow in numbers every year."

"A what?" Claire pinned him with a look, but he didn't elaborate. Her frustration mounted. "You've probably got amnesia or dementia or… something. As soon as we get home I'll take you to the hospital."

"Do not bother," he ordered. "My brothers will come for me now that I am away from that Sea Witch's temple."

"Brothers?" Claire raised a brow at him and quickly noticed his fingers rubbing the small medallion around his neck. "So, you have family?"

"None living, but Barcus and Xanthus are like blood. They will be interested to know that I am alive and well."

Well was probably a loose term, she decided. "So where do they live? I'd be happy to take you there, if you'd like." It wasn't as if she had enough things to do. Her food shipment came in a few days and she had résumés to look at before she hired a staff. Not to mention all the maintenance work that still needed to be done before The Saucy Leg opened.

"I was born in Iolcuson the west side of the Aegean Sea. The same homeland of the great hero Jason," he boasted. "Barcus hails from there as well, but we have not been back in a very long time."

Claire stared at him, unsure of what to say. "The Aegean Sea? Are you telling me you're from Greece?"

"If that is what you call it now. Our land has been called many things. For a long while we were a part of Macedonia, but the Ottomans were expanding their empire before I was imprisoned."

"Er… I meant around here. I probably should have emphasized that. Is there anywhere around here that you or this Barcus guy live?"

He blinked at her and Claire sighed, turning back to the blue waters in front of her. "Never mind…"

Finding out he was Greek didn't surprise her at all. Her work in D.C. meant she had cooked for plenty of tourists and foreign professionals; she knew an exotic-looking man when she saw one, and Argos was the definition of exotic. He had the dark eyebrows, and his long hair had just the right about of curl in it to make him look like a movie star instead of a caveman. A perfectly straight nose and strong jawline made him look like he'd been cut from marble. Then there was his accent; it was beautiful and very sexy. It would explain his strange name, and maybe even the stranger things he was saying.

"Claire." Even the way he said her name made her toes curl, the thick accent rolling over it with careful enunciation.

She hummed at her name. "What is it?"

"You're holding the wheel all wrong."

Her eyes snapped back at him, realizing he was dead serious. The delusional man whom she had found in a rowboat was telling her how to drive. "Excuse me?"

He motioned to her hands, set at the nine o'clock and three o'clock. "They're too low. Your hands should be up, like you are grabbing a bull's horn."

"*Sebastian* isn't a bull," she told him in all seriousness, though sometimes the boat needed to be handled like one. Turning was harder on the aged equipment; she kept her hands low for a firmer grip, so she could put her whole weight into it if need be.

Argos's sharp brows narrowed on her. "Who is *Sebastian*?"

"My boat," she explained hotly, feeling a blush touch her cheeks.

"That is a person's name." Argos seemed genuinely confused at the notion. Which was strange for a man who clearly knew a thing or two about boats. Most boat owners named their vessels; traditionally it was a feminine name, which was exactly why Claire had made hers a boy. Of course, at the time she'd been six and really hadn't been thinking about gender stereotypes for boats. In her case she'd just seen *The Little Mermaid* and had a fondness for a certain singing crab.

"It's ironic," she explained. At his green-eyed stare, Claire sighed. "It's funny."

"I am not laughing."

"Well, then maybe your sense of humor sucks," she said before hunkering close to the steering wheel and concentrating on the shore in the horizon.

"Women are allowed to captain with no crew. What

else has changed since I've been away?" the strange man muttered behind her.

Oh dear. Claire managed to keep her mouth shut about the women captaining part and focused on sailing. Argos might be attractive, but there was baggage there, and she couldn't deal with any more problems at the moment. Her life was already a chaotic mess.

At the time, taking a quick break on the water had seemed essential for her sanity. It was the only time she felt close to her father, now that he was gone. With opening only a week away, Claire didn't know when she would get another opportunity. It was much-needed therapy before things got too crazy. One last chance to relax and what does she find? More problems.

She hated when things didn't go according to plan, even though that seemed to be her entire life since she had taken this gamble. Over the months since getting her loan and quitting her job, she'd discovered the best thing to do when it came to unexpected chaos was to deal with it as quickly as possible and not to get rattled.

It would be best if she just brought him to a hospital where some professional would take care of him and help find his friends.

Yeah, that was the plan and she was going to stick to it.

She didn't have time for delusional men. Her to-do list was long and taped to the counter above her stove as a constant reminder. The need to do right by her dream, her father's dream, was a burning sensation in the pit of her stomach.

But her father wouldn't want her to put herself first and abandon someone in need.

That thought made her frown as she steered the boat to

shore. The bright summer's day was quickly disappearing, replaced with strong wind and clouds pregnant with rain. Claire sent a silent prayer that they'd get home before the storm hit. She hated being caught in the rain, not just on land but especially out on the water. Storms were unpredictable, and a boat could easily get out of control. "Looks like a storm is brewing," she commented softly.

She glanced behind her and found him staring dubiously at the clouds. "Don't worry, big guy, we're almost there," Claire said, attempting to reassure them both.

Of course, it was at that exact moment that the rain poured down upon them.

꽃

A storm was brewing, but not the kind that Claire was referring to.

Argos was not afraid. If Circe wanted him back on the island, she would have to drag his dead mortal body there herself. He would not go willingly. Not like the first time, when Hestia had sent him there on another one of her quests. He should have known something was strange when she requested he go alone. Pride was a trait known to lead men to danger, and he had been no different.

But he had been foolish and in love. Even then. Even when he knew Hestia was angry with him. Every man knew that nothing could protect you from a god's wrath. Not even love. But his immortality and innumerable victories had made Argos think otherwise, and look where that had gotten him.

Not again.

He watched as Claire stared down the storm, her body tense as she fought with the wheel. She was so different from any other woman he had met. Commanding and competent, even now she faced the storm with a fierceness that reminded him of an immortal. There was no way she was an ordinary woman. She was a nymph. A stubborn one, who no doubt would lash out at him if he dared to do something she saw unfit.

Claire's boat—*Sebastian*—had a roof to protect them from most of the rain. Thank the gods for small blessings. He watched the nymph struggle to turn the boat in the right direction. Her hands were still located at the wrong points of the wheel as she pushed all her weight into the turn. The waves batted against them and were growing bigger by the moment, delaying any progress towards shore. Behind them, the small rowboat he had escaped in bumped against the ship's hull.

Claire gave the rowboat an anxious look as it battered against her own ship. Argos knew what she was thinking: a storm raging around two ships meant increased chances of damage. Without a word, he stood and walked to the metal rail where Claire had secured the connecting rope. He did not need to think twice about his actions. Untying the rope and letting the small boat drift off was a relief. His last physical reminder of Circe and her island. He watched as an aggressive wave swallowed the boat whole.

When he turned back, he found Claire watching him in both appreciation and surprise. It was only for a second, but the distraction was long enough for her to lose the battle against the wheel. It jerked in her grip, throwing her off-balance as the ship jerked in the opposite direction.

Claire shot to her feet, a curse falling from her pretty lips as she threw her entire body against the wheel. Argos was already on his feet. He took position behind her, hands falling instinctively into place where hers did not cover. He followed her lead, pushing in the same direction as Claire. Together they brought the boat back on track. Even with both their strength, the wheel trembled like an angry cat, fighting against them as they tried to correct it. Claire shot him a look but didn't say a word as they worked together.

"I told you to adjust your grip," he said.

A scowl pulled at her lips. "Don't boss me around on my boat."

Argos did not say anything. He had learned to choose his battles and this was one he would not win. This was the reason women should not be allowed to steer their own boats. Claire's strength was not enough to do much in a storm. Especially on a boat that fought back so viciously.

They were slightly off course, but he could see the dock to which Claire had been trying to steer them.

Claire stood close to him, both hands gripping the wheel, refusing to let him take on the full breadth of the burden. Stubborn woman.

Her clothes were completely soaked, but none of that diverted her focus. Every part of her body was posed to get them back to the pier in one piece. "Help me get it to those two poles there. That's my dock."

He nodded; the dock was not much but at least it was visible. He had done harder tasks in the past. Once he'd had to navigate a fleet of six boats through a narrow passage with cyclopes chucking boulders on every side. Beating out the storm would be one last defiant act against Circe. That thought made him smile.

They came up to the dock faster than he intended, the waves pushing them towards shore. Claire handled the boat well now that she braced herself to fight against the waves.

Argos hesitated to step away in case she lost control again, but someone had to ensure the boat didn't ram the dock. He moved to the railing, bracing against it when another strong wave rocked the boat.

Sebastian hit the side of the dock with minimal impact, but it was wedged into place, that was all he cared about.

Claire moved like the wind after that. She bustled around the ship, gathering things and throwing them into Argos's open arms, hardly fazed at all by the jerky rocking of the boat. The box with her water supply and food was thrust into his arms and the blanket he had worn earlier was flung over his head. "Take these and head down the dock," she told him, turning to pick up one more item lying on the deck. It was a long, thick piece of white rope. Claire tucked her body over the boat's side and fell the short distance to the dock, where she skillfully tied the rope to a tall wooden pole on the side of the dock.

Her fingers were quick as they wrapped around the wood and pulled the rope tight before she moved on to the next pole. Argos watched in fascination; even some of his old crew could not tie a knot that fast.

She whipped her head back, surprising him by how calm she looked with a storm pounding around them and a boat still loose in her grasp. "Hey," she yelled, straining to be heard over the rain. Her head jerked in one direction. "Come on."

He was not a fan of being bossed around by a nymph, but he also was not keen on standing out in the storm. He jumped off the side, feet hitting the wooden dock with a thud that rattled his muscles.

The pain was a reminder that he was still mortal and weak, but it was nice to be able to step onto solid ground after days on the water. Barcus and Xanthus would laugh if they knew of his state, and Argos would not even mind. His muscles, his old skill with the bow and sword... those could come back. Even his immortality could be won back with the favor of the gods.

That was what he loved about living. It was something a man worked at, always pushing his body and his skills to new levels. When he had been immortal, there were decades of training put into a single weapon. Now, his abilities were soft, his muscles softer.

Claire's dock was big enough for two boats at most. It was unlike the ports Argos remembered, where nearly a thousand ships could be kept docked at one time. The wood under his feet was sturdy enough. The ground sloped up a small hill where a house stood out, its white walls a beckon, offering shelter from the storm. In four long strides he hit land. Soppy, muddy land, but land nonetheless.

He looked down at his bare toes in the cold mud, felt it move around his skin, coating it black like the eyes of a chimera. The storm darkened the world, but Argos embraced its mystery. He remembered dreaming of far-off lands meant to be discovered, new sights to behold. Then he had gone to Circe's island, contained by the same four walls for hundreds of years. Now he inhaled the smell of fresh earth and rain.

Freedom.

He had done it. He'd defied Circe. He'd defied the gods.

A soft rumble echoed in his ears, thunder or maybe the rain, but after a moment he realized it was his own laughter. A sound he had not heard in so long it was foreign to his own ears.

With that realization his laughter boomed louder.

Argos threw his head back as a rush caused his heart to pound rapidly against his chest, Hephaestus's hammer hitting against the steel of his rib cage.

A bird's soft wings fluttered against his shoulder and he turned to find that it was the gentle touch of Claire's fingers. The boat was anchored and the woman was drenched from standing in the rain. Her loose shirt now clung to her body as if becoming one with it. Her eyes were wide with concern as she looked at him. "Are you alright?"

His joy was overpowering, though, still pumping through his body with the adrenaline of a fresh fight. It had been centuries since he had felt so alive.

Another feeling bubbled to the surface as he smiled and dropped the items in his arms in favor of grabbing the nymph around the waist and swinging her around. Another whoop of joy escaped him as a yelp of surprise left Claire.

"What are you doing?" she asked, grabbing his arm tightly. "Oh God, please don't tell me you're going to kill me."

"Kill you?" Argos laughed. "I am indebted to you." He set her down and watched as Claire took a few shaky steps back, a dubious look set in her eyes.

He did not like that.

Nymphs were usually cautious creatures, never enjoying when a man got the upper hand on them.

After all she had done for him, he could at least let her be at ease. He calmed his emotions down, biting back the growling animal that was his curse. He would not harm this woman. He refused to become the monster Hestia saw him as, a sex-crazed animal that was to be added to Circe's collection like a stray sheep to a herd.

Slowly he raised his hands. Like approaching a startled

horse, his movements were slow and deliberate. Her face contorted in a strange expression that he could not read, but it did not matter.

He cupped her cold cheeks in his hands and brought her attention back to him. "Whatever you want," he told her. "My treasure, my loyalty, my property I will give to repay you for what you have done."

"Oh…" Her pink lips parted in the single syllable as she stared at him. A shiver caused her body to shake under his touch before she looked away. "Why don't we discuss this inside? When we're dry."

Yes, there was plenty of time to discuss his repayment to Claire after his fellow heroes found him. Once his brothers arrived, he would be able to access the collection of gold he had amassed over the years.

He would repay Claire and then set about getting his vengeance on Circe.

IV

"THIS IS A tavern," the big hulking mass of muscle and chiseled features said as soon as Claire walked them into the restaurant.

"It's a restaurant," she corrected taking in the large wooden foyer around them. Sure, her restaurant wasn't in the best condition at the moment. The beautiful old wooden floors were covered in unopened boxes. Half-constructed chairs and tables were scattered about in no particular order, and all her dishware was stacked on the bar waiting to be put away.

The place was a mess, but it wasn't a tavern. A tavern was something Americans said to class up sports bars. Even among the clutter she saw the incredible opportunity the building offered. The wooden beams lining the ceiling and the brick fireplace in the corner connected the building to the rich history of the area. Sturdy wooden columns held the structure up, and someone had carved boats and waves curling up their body in a beautiful piece of art. It had everything needed for the classy, homey look she was going for. Once she added the antique furnishings she'd purchased in the city and finished assembling, it would be the place of her dreams. She wanted her restaurant to be the middle ground between rowdy pub and classy restaurant. A place where anyone could get first-class seafood.

"You live here?" he asked, looking at the stack of boxes.

"I live upstairs," Claire explained with a sigh, "and next week this part will be open for business if all goes well." She glanced to see him staring at the place with an impressed look on his face. Pride warmed her at the sight; seeing his awe made her feel reassured in her work.

"So, you'll cook here?"

"Yes." She brightened. The prospect of talking about cooking always made her chipper.

"But where is the man that you serve? The owner of this tavern. Is he here?" Argos looked around eagerly. "I would like to speak to him."

Her mood curdled. "*I am* the owner."

He turned to her, face slack in a humorless expression. "You cannot be the owner," he said simply, at her raised brow he explained, "You are a nymph. You have no husband. How can you run a tavern by yourself?"

Claire frowned at him. She hadn't missed how the man talked like he was stuck in some bizarre period film. But *nymph*? She didn't know if she should take it as a compliment or an insult. The slight tip of his mouth made it seem like a term of endearment, but men often thought of their pet names as endearing.

She'd dealt with enough of that at her old job. Politicians in upscale suits demanding she recook their meals, their words trailing behind her: *the kitchen is hot, but the chef is hotter.* She'd sought to open her own place to escape that. Not to be demeaned in her own building.

"I am not a nymph. I am a normal human woman. And I own this building and this restaurant." She poked a finger against his firm chest to emphasize her words. "And I was going to feed you before I changed into some warm clothes, but you know what? You can wait. Hope you're not too hungry."

She took the stairs up to the apartment two at a time. Behind her, Argos called out but she ignored it. The hinges of her bedroom door squeaked when she wrenched it open; another reminder of one more thing to fix before the place opened.

She spared one last look behind her to see the man staring up like a lost soul. His loincloth was soaked, as was the blanket she had wrapped around him. The small droplets of water that trailed down his tanned skin were just begging to distract her from the tasks at hand. A genuine look of confusion crossed his features, forcing a sigh out of her lungs. She always did have a bleeding heart. "Don't look so sad—I'll come right back. I'll... try to find something for you to wear. In the meantime, don't touch anything."

The door closed with an audible slam behind her, closing her off in her small nothing-of-an-apartment. It was a depressing sight and did little to improve her mood. A mattress with no bed frame sat on the floor against the wall, and a decorative rug was placed in the middle of the room to give it a little more cheer. Her thick suitcase, packed to the brim with clothes, was open, spilling its contents onto the floor. The mess made her cringe, but there had been no time to organize her belongings.

In the future, when she had more money and more

time, this apartment would be an extra room to seat guests. Maybe even a party room. It wasn't supposed to be an apartment. There was no kitchen, but who needed one when there was a large kitchen just downstairs? No washing machine or dryer—the laundromat down the street had been working out just fine.

For now, this was her home.

Despite the mess, she was already overly fond of it. The wood flooring and thick beams that hung over head gave the place character. Sure, there were a few spots that dripped in the rain, were dripping right at this moment, but it was hers. It had been her father's before, his dream. When he had died both of those things had fallen into her care.

Her mother had encouraged her to wait until she had a husband before tackling the place. No single woman just went and got themselves thousands of dollars in debt—that kind of loan did not attract future husbands—but Claire couldn't care less.

Her mother looked at men as means of getting her dreams accomplished. The current husband—number three and hopefully the last—was rich enough that Darleen Winters could stay in her ritzy D.C. apartment and gossip with all her friends at black-tie parties.

Claire had once been a source of pride for her mother, who couldn't stop talking about the politicians who requested her daughter's plates specifically. Or when she'd taught a cooking lesson at the White House.

Darleen couldn't see past her own glowing pride that Claire had been miserable. Living in the city and cooking for people who carelessly threw away her food or barely touched it because of unreasonable diets.

So far, her mother had only come by once in the

months it had taken to spruce up the place, and then only to see how her loaned money had been used. She'd taken two steps into the building and promptly walked out. The homely state of the restaurant reminded her mother of a past and a man she would rather not remember.

Claire didn't mind. She'd grown used to her mother's dramatic behavior, and the location of the restaurant was just far enough away from the city that she always had time to prepare for one of Darleen's visits. Not that she visited much—driving out of D.C. was a challenge that her mother was not often up to.

Throwing on a pair of dry sweatpants and a loose shirt from her old college rowing team, Claire felt a million times better. Her hair was quickly drying into soft waves that hung loose around her face.

She grabbed a spare blanket from the closet. A cheap pink thing she'd bought on sale, but it was the best she could do for Argos, since the last time she'd had a man over was well beyond a year ago. It had been hard to date in D.C. All the men her mother suggested wanted nothing but a trophy wife, and the men at work were too focused on their own careers to spare time for her.

Her stomach made a rumbling noise that tore her away from those thoughts. With all the excitement of the day, she'd given her lunch to her starved guest. It was probably time to feed him again, she supposed, opening the door and descending the stairs back to her homey restaurant.

She found Argos sitting at the bar playing with the coin around his neck. As her foot hit the last stair, he perked up and turned around. "Claire," he said quickly, so fast the *r* barely sounded off with his accent. There was a look of apology in his gaze that made her smile as she offered him the blanket.

"Here, I don't have any clothes that will fit you, but this should keep you warm until we figure this whole thing out," she explained. He shivered under her touch, causing her to pause. "Geez, I'm sorry. You must be so cold; I was just a little upset." Her fingers quickly went to rubbing the blanket over his cold muscles.

Argos shrugged off her touch. "I did not mean to upset you," he said, not even acknowledging her earlier statement as he wrapped the blanket around his shoulders. "I should not have questioned your capabilities. I have seen you navigate and anchor a boat soundly by yourself. This century is strange for me and I am having a hard time adjusting to the years I've missed."

If Claire had to name one highlight of the evening, seeing a bare-chested grown man huddled in a pink wool blanket was probably it. But his apology was a close second.

She tried to hide her smile behind her fallen hair. "Seriously, don't mention it. I mean... how long did you say this Circe woman kept you?" Sarcasm was, as her mother would say, a one-sided joke—and Claire's worst habit, which honestly wasn't that bad. But from the considering look on Argos's face, she'd have to learn not to use it so much around him.

"Well, when I went to her island it was 1507."

It was a little unnerving how he could keep such a straight face. A trip to the hospital was needed as soon as the storm passed. The area tended to flood during hard rain. Luckily her place was located on top of a hill, but the old, beat-up Honda Civic she owned wouldn't be able to make it if the lower streets were flooded.

"Well…" She forced a laugh, resigning herself to the fact that she would be stuck with the man for a few more hours. At least he wasn't half-bad to look at, and his company was a nice change of pace from her usual lonely nights. "Welcome to the twenty-first century."

✍

THE TWENTY-FIRST CENTURY.

He had missed so much. Talking with Claire as she prepared a meal allowed him to pick her brain. He discovered that women could not only run a business by themselves and own a ship but vote as well. They'd stepped up, moving into jobs such as doctors and politicians. There was new technology, like the contraption Claire was constantly checking. It glowed in her hand like a bright spirit and reacted to her touch. Then there was the television, hung up across the bar for his personal viewing pleasure. It was fascinating, showing him glimpses of the new world. He could not wait to find out what else had changed and wondered how the others had adapted in such times.

While she concentrated on their meals, he was left to appreciate Claire's beauty. She had covered her body in loose clothing: pants that draped over her legs and made them look as thick as tree stumps, and a loose top with a rowing oar on it with the words *Catch me if you can.* The idea of chasing her down and catching her was highly appealing. His body was used to constant sexual activity; the lack of it these past days had his skin tingling. Claire was not even trying to seduce him, yet the sight of her strange clothes was enough to arouse the curse.

He pushed those thoughts away, focusing instead on how she deftly prepared their food. Her eyes shifting between the pots and spices with ease, answering all his questions calmly, sometimes with a strange look on her face and a laugh in her voice.

He could not remember the last time he'd seen food prepared. The chore had never appealed to him before, but her movements flowed like a dance to which she knew all the steps. Watching her was mesmerizing.

She was fascinating…

No, he could not think about that. Those feelings were his body trying to give in to the curse. His lust had gotten him nothing but trouble and he would be damned if it did so again so soon. He asked more questions instead.

"So your tavern—"

"Restaurant," she corrected from the stove where she hovered. He could see her through a small window cooking their meal, the smell wafting back at him along with her voice. Claire said it added to the restaurant's charm. If people saw and smelled the food that was being prepared, then they were more likely to enjoy it.

Argos could easily see that logic; his stomach was clenching hungrily. "Restaurant," he amended. "Surely it has a name."

"Oh, it does." An excited smile appeared on her face, a reaction that he noticed happened whenever she talked about the building or her love of cooking. "I'm calling it The Saucy Leg."

"I do not understand," he admitted.

Claire turned away from the food to give him her full attention. He liked that. Those eyes focused on him, allowing him to fully appreciate the excited motions of her hands. "It's a joke. Because we serve crab legs here, get it?"

"No," he said, despite smiling, "your jokes are not funny."

She snorted, turning back to the steaming meal. "Well, I am talking to a guy who claims to have been on an island for five hundred years."

"I was," Argos argued. "Has your generation forgotten the gods and monsters that plague this land and the heroes who protect it?"

"Gods? Monsters?" Claire laughed. "Sounds like something out of a book." She shuffled about the small area, collecting dishes and silverware before plating the food and bringing it out.

Argos meant to snipe back with another retort, but the sight of the meal coming his way made his mouth water. She placed his plate in front of him and curled up on the barstool to his right. He stared down at the food. "What is it?"

"Soft-shelled crab"—she smiled—"with steamed vegetables, rice, and some sauce, of course."

"It looks delicious."

"Thank you." The compliment made her preen before they both dug into their meals.

A wave of pleasure washed over him as the crab melted on his tongue. Whatever Claire had done to it made the food taste unlike anything he'd ever had before. Even the vegetables fell apart easily in his mouth, revealing flavors he had never imagined carrots holding.

Argos did not hold himself back; the plate was clean in a matter of minutes. His stomach graciously thanked him for filling it, but a different hunger still piqued his senses as he watched his companion eat.

The sauce and juices from the crab dribbled innocently down Claire's chin as she moaned in her own delicate way. "This really hits the spot."

I could hit a spot, a good one down in her nether region that would elicit another moan from her lips. He shook his head of that thought quickly.

Claire noticed the movement and pushed a glass of water closer to him. "Do you have a headache? You're probably still dehydrated. Seriously, drink more water."

She was too sweet. An innocent, really, on her own for her first time, with no tribe or man to keep her safe. Claire was resourceful, but she did not know the dangers that were embedded in the earth. In his current state it would be difficult to protect her.

He rubbed the coin furiously, praying for strength, but there was no inkling of the magic Zeus himself had bestowed upon the coin. Magic that had been reserved for only the greatest of their heroes.

The coin was the thing that tied them to one another, the promise of brotherhood. If one called, others would respond and lend their skills to his aid. It was a deep union. Without it, Argos truly felt lost. But no matter how much he rubbed the coin, he felt no spark of familiar warmth.

If they would respond, he would not have to worry about controlling his curse for very long. With their help he would be able to pursue Circe, get his vengeance and set sail on a new quest. One that would lift the curse and regain his immortality. Like in the old days.

He might not have been around to see women vote or ships without sails be invented, but he had sailed with

Norse warriors, he had seen the rise of Britannia, and he had trekked across continents at the dawn of their discovery. The years of quests and battles were long in the past. By the time he was imprisoned on Circe's island the monsters had been pushed into hiding, allowing mankind to progress and expand. Eventually people had forgotten about the gods, and Hestia had grown needy for his attention.

Then he had betrayed her, and Hestia had punished him because of it.

That was the reason he could not summon his fellow heroes. The realization struck like one of Zeus's bolts.

He was not one of them anymore. Being mortal again meant being ripped away from the men he would give his life for.

The thought made his stomach churn.

Claire made a soft noise beside him. "Are you not feeling well? Maybe you ate the crab too quickly." A soft groan trailed after the suggestion. "Please don't tell me the food made you sick."

"No, Claire." He shook his head. "It has simply been a long day."

"I'm sure." The look of understanding in her eye told him it had been a long day for them both.

Without his men, his brothers… he would need to rethink how he would get his vengeance.

"I think I would like to rest." The alone time would allow him to think of a plan, one that would take his mind off the fascinating nymph next to him.

Claire's eyes widened. "Oh right… I, um… didn't really think about sleeping arrangements," she admitted, looking apologetic. "Why don't you take the mattress upstairs? It's more comfortable, anyways. I can snuggle up in one of the booths."

Her eyes trailed over to one of the booths and Argos's gaze followed it. When he realized where she would be sleeping, he frowned. "You are not sleeping on that table."

"It's fine. I'll just put some blankets and pillows on the bench." Her eyes narrowed dangerously, daring him to tell her again what she could and could not do. "It will be cozy."

He loved the challenge, maybe a little too much as a heat flared down his body. He gritted his teeth, biting his tongue to keep himself in check.

The mattress might not be so bad if he got her out of his sights immediately. He sighed. "Fine, I graciously accept your offer."

"Great!" She beamed. "Let me just go upstairs and grab some blankets and then the bedroom is all yours."

She scampered up the stairs before Argos could get another word in, but at least she was gone. He took another deep breath; this was harder than he thought. His curse was a living thing, wiggling under his skin now that he had recovered from his escape. Threatening to take over every time his gaze lingered. If he stayed with Claire, he honestly did not know how long he would be able to last.

Eventually he would break.

V

THE NIGHT SHOWED him no relief.

His heart hammered in his chest as the fire of desire licked across his skin. Crawling across his insides as it reminded him of the subtle touch a woman could bring. The flame called out to him, cooing Circe's name in the steady rhythm of the rain outside.

Circe wanted him, she would take him back and help him soothe the ache. Except...

No.

He refused to consider those lies. The only pleasure he had received on that island was by his own hand. Circe knew only how to take pleasure, never how to give it. She cared not if he received relief, though she took a wicked pleasure when he begged. If he went back she would not welcome him with pleasure, but with pain.

Still, his body ached and he cursed it between gritted teeth.

His fingers clenched the sheets around him, feeling a sheen of sweat drip down his forehead, as he fought the urge. Even in freedom, the curse still lingered and made him its slave. His strength was of no use; this was a test of willpower.

He was free of Circe, and he intended to keep it that way. He would not think of her, not for this. Instead his mind clung to the only other woman he had seen in nearly five hundred years.

Claire.

The beautiful nymph who had saved his life. His mind clung to the image of her when he'd first laid eyes on her. The view of her breasts above his head, her legs straddling his hips. He bit back a groan at the memory. He pictured her in his mind's eye. The clothes she had worn earlier that day melted away to nothing, revealing soft curves of bare flesh.

He inhaled sharply and found her scent floating around him. The fragrance of the sea salt and flowers mixed together with a soapy undertone. It lingered on the pillow under his head and gave life to his mind's images of her.

A perverse need had come over him since the moment he'd laid eyes on her. Despite his vow against taking another woman, his body wanted her.

Dread filled him even as the fantasy played out. There was no point in stopping it; he needed release now and Claire was the right woman to erase all memories of Circe.

Her breasts, which he had seen so easily in her drenched clothing, would fit perfectly in the palm of his hand. He imagined the noise of encouragement she would make if he played with her nipple.

He had forgotten what it felt to have a woman melt in his hands. Circe had always been in charge of their bed play, but his fantasy was to make a woman moan under his touch.

The need to touch himself became unbearable. Desperately his hand grabbed his cock, nearly tearing the only scrap of cloth he had away from his body. He groped, feeling the swollen hardness of his member. Painful and crying for a release. With a shaky breath he began to stroke. He turned his head to inhale the sweet scent of Claire from his pillow and allowed his fantasies to go further.

In one swift movement, he rolled fantasy Claire over. Pinning her small body under his own and trapping it there. She squirmed, naked and ready for the taking. But her intelligent eyes sparked in understanding of the game. If he felt her, she would be wet in anticipation. Then with the same authority she used to boss him around on the ship, she commanded him, "*Take me.*"

Her words were delicious.

A strong shiver took over his entire body at the words, both in fantasy and reality. He wanted nothing more than to take her. Over and over, until true satisfaction numbed both of their bodies.

He imagined her eyes rolling up in pleasure when he sank his fingers into her entrance. The tightness between a woman's thighs was something every man dreamed about, and he was no exception.

"Yes!" He hissed the words into the empty room as the woman of his dreams screamed out in pleasure.

Imagining her in such bliss made his balls clench. His aching cock pressed into her entrance. The rolling thunder of climax began to build at the base of his cock, but he had only just gotten started.

Lost to the pleasure, he drove into her, causing her

entire body to jerk with surprise. He needed to taste her, licking her neck like a cat, trailing his tongue upward until it found her mouth and filled it.

Her body melted against his, giving full control to him. It was the moment he had been waiting centuries for. The trust of a woman who needed satisfaction. The freedom to set the pace of their lovemaking. Two things that had been absent in his nights with Circe.

On the bed he swallowed hard, his cock nearly bursting at her consent.

Her imaginary moans echoed in him, urging his cock as he pumped his fist faster. Matching the rhythm with that of his fantasy. Harder, faster. Not because the curse demanded it, but because he was lost to his own pleasure. His and that of Claire.

The idea of being inside of a woman, any woman besides Circe, pushed him over the edge. His entire body seized as an orgasm overtook him. The force of it shook him to his core, making his muscles tighten almost to the point of pain. Never before had he come so hard. He nearly bit through his lip to keep a low groan from escaping. It would not do to have Claire hear him.

Slowly, he came back to himself. His labored breathing echoed in the empty room. Sticky liquid dribbled between his fingers and onto his stomach, reminding him that he was indeed alone. No Circe, but no Claire either.

It is for the best, he told himself, wiping his release off where he could. Claire would not appreciate that he had stained her blankets, but if that was the least of her worries, it would have to do.

Against the rough cloth that lay against his loins, he could feel his cock stirring again. Just like in his fantasies, it would not be calm for long. He sighed deeply and closed his eyes, knowing full well this was just the beginning.

Even so, a sense of peace seeped into his muscles for the first time in years. He closed his eyes and felt Hynos's influence threaten to overtake him. Behind the darkness of his eyelids, his image of Claire burned bright, refusing to be forgotten.

The real thing would not be nearly as submissive, he thought in amusement.

His cock stirred again, agreeing with the sentiment, and Argos cursed against the pillow.

⁓

Generally, rainy days were her favorite. The way the droplets looked falling on the water, making the sea dance under its steadily beating rhythm. The soft pitter-patter against the window was perfect noise to read to, and on rainy days Claire had a special chili she always made that warmed her entire soul.

Unfortunately, the chili would have to wait, and so would curling up with a nice book. There were a ton of things that still needed to get done in the restaurant, and she refused to postpone the grand opening because of rain.

Even when her back ached, unhappy with the night spent curled up on the hard booth, she would not falter. There was a *list* and it wasn't even close to done.

The storm outside wasn't the usual quiet rain. The wind howled against the walls, stirring the trees to look like restless monsters. From the window, she could see *Sebastian* remained secured in place.

She'd awakened early to the storm's disturbing sounds and flipped on the television above the bar to catch the weather report. These were near hurricane conditions. Strong winds and high levels of rainfall had come out of thin air. The weatherman stumbled over an explanation and settled on urging people to stay in their homes.

Which was fine, she had plenty to catch up on anyway. It was Argos she was worried about. She wasn't a doctor, that was for sure, and she wasn't equipped to help the man if he had any serious injuries. Claire's own motto had always been *wrap it up and get back to work*. But in this case, that wouldn't work; she didn't know how to wrap up someone who'd been at sea for days.

She tried to search the internet for any missing person reports matching his description and found nothing. With a huff, she sighed, slid the offending laptop away and bit into her piece of toast.

The only option was waiting for the storm to pass. She liked her setup in Edgewater. The small town lived up to its name, placed conveniently on the water with its own local pier. It was just a bridge away from the tourist hub of Annapolis, with slightly cheaper real estate. But that meant the closest hospital was a bridge away, and during a storm, most of the roads were likely flooded. Tomorrow, then, she could pass him off to the proper authorities and the whole issue would be resolved. At least for her.

She shivered at the thought of just dumping Argos off at the hospital. Alone, without the assurance that anyone would come to help him. That was something her mother would do without batting a lash, but her father... he would help the man. Even at his own inconvenience.

It was a trait her mother complained about constantly. Instead of taking an extra shift at the restaurant where he worked, her father would use his time off to help the people around him. Lending his boat out to friends looking to fish, assisting with a home renovation project. He was always quick to offer assistance, even when it meant not working towards his dream.

He wouldn't want her to put the restaurant before someone in need. With a sigh, she resigned herself to help Argos. As best she reasonably could.

She turned the thought over while watching the local news, hoping for some mention of a lost sailor, when the stairs squeaked.

"Good morning, Claire," his sensual voice rumbled behind her, and if he *must* have that accent could he go back to spouting off nonsense about islands and immortality? A simple good morning was almost too normal for her mind to process. The fact that he was possibly deranged was the only reason she was fighting any attraction towards him. If he went about acting normal and smiling at her with his perfect grin, she didn't stand a chance.

Claire turned and found Argos standing on the stairs staring at her. She stared back.

"Are those my bedsheets?" Her voice hitched in shock as she took in the sight before her.

Argos smiled, looking proud as he smoothed his hands down the lavender-colored Egyptian cotton of her sheets. "It is a chiton. Do you like it?"

The man was wearing a makeshift toga. And… it didn't look half bad. A little long, hanging below the kneecaps with extra fabric thrown over one shoulder.

God, she needed to get the man some clothes. He was a complete and utter distraction without them and even the newly applied bedsheets did nothing to hide the tent sprouting underneath.

She quickly turned back to the television. Heat licked at her face as the image refused to part ways with her mind. In all her years, Claire had never seen anything that even hinted at being so large.

Eyes firmly set on the television, she pushed the plate of fruit and toast towards the open seat next to her. Just for good measure, she inched it over one more spot, so his body wouldn't be in her personal bubble.

He got the message and gave her space. The food seemed to work as a good distraction as he cleaned the plate of the apple slices and grapes. A man his size was probably used to an eight-ounce steak for breakfast with a side of eggs. While that thought made Claire's stomach hum in agreement and she mentally added "think up a brunch menu for The Saucy Leg" to her list, she was not up to making him a full breakfast.

"It's still raining," she told him, trying not to watch as he licked the fruit juices from his fingers.

Argos looked out the window with a slight frown. His eyes stared at the glass for a full heartbeat before he sighed, "She's really stirring up trouble looking for me." When his gaze fell back towards her, the air was knocked out of her chest. "I should leave before I get you in trouble."

"Yes, well…" Claire licked her lips, helpless as she tried to find the words she wanted. "The roads are flooded. I can't take you anywhere until the storm passes."

"Then I will walk." He stood up as if ready to walk out in an instant.

She copied his movement. "Are you serious? I saved you from being lost at sea and now you want to walk out into a hurricane? Do you have a death wish?"

His brows narrowed at the question. "I do not."

"Then you're staying here until I can take you to the hospital. It's their job to keep people alive. You'll fit in great there."

"Is there not a temple nearby that I can visit? I must get in contact with the gods as soon as possible." His voice didn't leave any room for argument. Claire could only stare at him.

"If you really did live in the sixteenth century, you'd know temples have gone out of style."

A cheerful grin cut across his mouth and made his eyes crinkle. "Maybe as far as you're aware, mortal."

She snorted. "You're a mortal, too, and that's exactly why I can't—in good conscience—let you leave."

"And what do I do in the meantime?" He scowled, giving the window another long look.

Claire sighed. "Well, you said you would repay me, right?" She waved a hand towards the restaurant. "I still have a lot of work and I could use the help."

"Ah, cleaning the hearth?"

She wagged a finger at him. "You better not mention anything about a woman cleaning. I have actual work to do."

The smile didn't fall away; instead, it grew. "I will help however you ask. The hearth is a sacred place, not just for women, and it just so happens I know exactly what Hestia likes best."

"Hestia?" That was the first time he'd mentioned a woman to her. Maybe he was married. It wouldn't be a surprise, but still her heart gave a little squeeze of displeasure. The same way it did when someone had given her food a bad review or she doubted the success of the restaurant.

Just like those times, she forcibly pushed the feeling aside and tried for a neutral tone. "Who's that?"

"The goddess of the hearth," he said. "If you follow my instructions, I'm sure she'll bless this place. Even if it is a tavern, it's still your home."

He hummed merrily, taking in the restaurant with eager eyes, and continued. "She likes the windows to be open, with nothing in front of them. And flowers, she encourages the hearth to always have flowers on it."

"What is she, some interior decorator?" Claire said irritably as she followed his gaze to the tables next to the windows. "Because it sounds like she doesn't know anything about restaurants. People want to look out the window when they eat, and this isn't a wedding. I am not buying flowers just to replace them every week."

He laughed. "Just as well. Hestia probably would not look at this place if she knew I lay here."

The word *lay* caused Claire's mouth to go dry. It took every ounce of willpower in her not to look down at the loincloth again. She had to fix this. Quick, or risk throwing herself at the man and offering to help him with his wood problem before he helped with hers.

Thinking quickly, she grabbed one of the many spare aprons she'd stashed under the bar. They were plain black; a little simple, but for now they would do. Clearing her throat seemed to bring his attention back at her and the piece of cloth she was unceremoniously shoving towards him. "Here, put this on."

"What is it?"

"It's... something to cover you up a little more," she said, voice cracking just slightly.

He gave her a solid stare. "Claire, you would not be

intimidated by my manhood, would you?" There was a purr to his voice that had not been there before. It sent a chill down her arm as she realized he wasn't asking it as a question.

"N-no." She forced a laugh and tossed her hair over her shoulder, turning to look at him just to prove the point wrong. "I just don't want you... your body to get dirty."

"And that's all?"

"Yes." She stared at him with all the confidence she could muster. *That's all*, she reminded herself, *there is no time for distractions.*

Argos snorted, breaking their stare-down first as he took a deliberate step back. "Then I will wear it," he said firmly, more so to himself than to her.

She gave him an appreciative nod. "Alright, then, let me show you the tables we'll be putting together."

☙

He needed a distraction if he wanted to keep himself under control. For a moment, he had lost himself to the call of Claire's sweet body, and she to him. He could feel it, could see the attraction in her eyes. But when she pinned him with a look, defiant and so sure of herself, he could not bring himself to taunt her anymore. Doing so would only fray what little control he had. And *that* was not a good idea.

That was a downward slope neither of them would be able to recover from.

He was grateful when she gave him labor to busy himself for the rest of the day. There were crates full of wooden pieces that needed to become chairs and tables. Claire watched him assemble one of the tables quickly enough. The crinkled piece of paper she called directions was hardly needed. He knew how to put a table together, though the tools that sat in a pile next to him were a mystery.

All he needed was a hammer and nails. That got the job done just as good as any.

Still, Claire hovered over him. "You're not going to use the screwdriver?" she asked, pushing a metal rod his way.

He shrugged carelessly. "I know how to build a table."

"But I think it will be more stable if you used the screwdriver."

"Nymph…" he warned carefully, but when he turned to her she was slack-faced and innocent. His warning died with a soft sigh. "My hands have built many things in the past. A table will be simple."

"Fine, have it your way." She rolled her eyes once before they continued to stare at his work. One down, six more to go.

Eventually Claire diverted her attention to her own project. She took on the pile of wood that was meant to be chairs. She worked slower than he did, constantly flipping back and forth between that damned paper and the stack of work in front of her, but eventually a chair was formed.

Argos had to admit to being impressed. Not only did the woman own her own business and sail, she was not useless with tools. She was resourceful, in a way he'd seen in few women over the centuries.

He could have used a woman like her on his crew. She would have fit in splendidly. If her meals did not win over the hearts of his men, then her sailing skills would have. Barcus would have loved her food; he had always had a soft spot for new flavors and meals. Xanthus would have loved her spirit; as a Spartan he was used to women who spoke their mind and trained alongside men. Without a doubt, no one would have been able to deny her anything when she smiled.

She was the type of woman who would have made a perfect wife for a hero such as himself. A woman with the need for adventure, the need to be her own person. It was a need he could relate to well.

He would love to see what the future had in store for her. To see the tables he was building filled with people and her business become successful. But he had his own dream to realize. Vengeance that could not be forgotten and a life he needed to return to.

Small noises of frustration came from her as she worked on the next chair. Noises that went straight to his groin. He could not stand to hear them along with the thoughts of what could have been. Moving the wood and tools together became a quick blur as he concentrated fully on the task at hand and not the woman nearby.

Maybe when his immortality was secured again, when Circe was dead, he would return to the tavern by the ocean and fulfill a new quest.

But that was far in the future from now.

⚜

Something was different with Argos. The man hadn't said one strange thing since she'd put him to work. It was almost like he was ignoring her, but that couldn't be right. Claire tried to make small talk with him as they worked, tried to be appreciative of how he'd finished building all six tables before moving to help with the rest of her chairs. They finished before dinnertime, and when she'd expressed her joy at having one less chore to worry about, he'd merely grunted and asked for another task.

She asked him to start hanging pictures while she cooked dinner. Maybe the apron had been a bit too much for him; maybe he was angry at her. The thought made her stomach clench as she stirred the chili on the stove. A rainy day always called for something warm. The news blared behind her; it sounded like the rain would not be letting up anytime soon. Her skin began to itch, the stress settling back in her bones. If the rain didn't let up, she might have to push the staff interviews to next week, which would push the opening. And who knew how long it would take to find Argos's family? With an irritated flick of her wrist, she turned off the television. Enough bad news; she needed to calm down.

As the chili simmered, she unlocked her phone and brought up a music app. A soft acoustic pop song filled the kitchen, bringing a smile to her face. She knew the words. The song had become popular over the summer, playing every hour on the radio. As she tended to the pot, her body swayed to the rhythm.

A sprinkle of pepper flakes. Add some ground cumin. She tasted and licked her lips. *Mmm, needs more spice.*

Her eyes flickered up, peering past the high bar top that separated the kitchen from the main seating area. The sound of Argos's hammer had paused, and when she glanced up she knew why. He was watching her.

A slow smile was on his face, but the moment their eyes met it disappeared. He turned back to the wall.

Somehow his makeshift toga managed to stay on as he worked. Its presence was a godsend. She tried to imagine the man helping her in the loincloth she found him in and smiled. Not even one of her aprons would have been enough to cover his manly bits. Her sheets did a fine job of covering him for the most part. They still revealed his muscular arms for admiration, and if the cloth tightened just right she could catch a glimpse of his cock straining against the material.

Stop ogling him, she told herself firmly. The guy was a virtual stranger, could be married or have a girlfriend for all she knew.

Hestia. She remembered him speaking of her, or maybe it was that Circe woman. A man like him probably had lots of women he knew intimately, and she refused to get caught up in the fuss.

Still, Argos wrapped in bedsheets was a sight to behold. Her mind went down a sinful rabbit hole as she noticed how the purple color stood out against his tanned skin. Really, what female didn't fantasize about having an incredibly gorgeous man in her home wearing nothing but bedsheets?

The opportunity would never show itself again. Married or not, she still snuck her phone out and took a picture when he wasn't looking. Something to remind her of their shared time together once he was gone.

A loud click sound interrupted the music. Claire froze, horrified when she realized the camera hadn't been muted. Argos turned around and caught her holding the thin piece of technology red-handed.

Oh God. Blushing, she scrambled to pocket her phone and pretended to concentrate on the soup she was cooking, but it was too late. Argos's interest had been piqued. He walked across the restaurant's wooden floors and leaned against the small opening that peeked into the kitchen.

"What is that thing?" He didn't look amused or annoyed, merely interested as he eyed the phone.

Claire's face burned; she couldn't help but glare at him.

"I know you've been through a lot, but you must know what a phone is."

He hummed. "I do not. Did I misspeak when I told you I'd been trapped with Circe for hundreds of years?"

She scoffed. "Hundreds of years. Yeah, right, you didn't seem so clueless when I turned on the lights. Or at the indoor plumbing." Her eyes watched for a reaction. He could pretend to be some ancient castaway as much as he liked, spouting nonsense about taverns and monsters, but there was a modern man under those intelligent eyes.

Argos didn't seem at all shaken by her accusation. He shrugged. "I have seen many amazing things in my lifetime, Claire. I once witnessed Zeus smite a man in front of my very eyes. The brightness of his bolt made the sky as white as a pearl for hours afterwards and the earth cracked so deep I swear the islands shifted around us."

"So… you really aren't impressed with electricity?"

"Oh, it's impressive. Mortals have found a way to command light. You've created boats without crews. The world is always changing. Thoughts, ideas, inventions, and countries all eventually bend. But you know what does not change?" He pointed towards her chili. "Food. Drink. Sex. Our basic needs are always the same, and if that is a constant, then I have nothing to fear." Leaning over the bar, he gave her a devilish smirk. "You have managed just fine unknowingly in a world full of gods and monsters; I will fare the same in a world of new inventions."

She turned her head and laughed. "I don't think I know anyone who adapts to change as quickly as you do. That must be how you speak modern English so well."

There, now she had him. But Argos's smile did not disappear. Instead, it tilted into a knowing smirk. "I told you, I was immortal. I have lived through the development of several languages and can speak most fluently."

Damn if the guy wasn't committed to the role. "You must be pretty smart."

"Well, they used to say one needed to be clever to be a hero."

"And so modest too." Claire shook her head, biting back another giggle. "But at least I got you to smile."

Something dark flashed in his eyes and he stepped closer. "Do you like my smile that much?"

"N-no. I-I just meant you seemed a little distracted this morning. I thought you were mad, about …" Claire took in their proximity. *About me drooling over you* was what she had been about to say. But admitting the words aloud was too mortifying, and now she was doing it again.

God, she'd made a mistake. She had unknowingly flirted with the handsome stranger. Her mind worked quickly to change the direction of the conversation. "Or maybe you were upset that I drafted you into helping me with chores. I can understand that. You need to find your family and here I am forcing you into chores and—"

"Claire…"

Crap. She was babbling now. It wasn't uncommon when she found herself backed into a corner, with little sleep and a deadline looming over her head. The babbling problem happened more often when she talked to her mother, not men. Her mouth clamped shut before any more words could spill out.

The spell that had lightened the mood between them was gone. The handsome smirk was gone; his expression was unreadable. Great, now she was making him feel uncomfortable.

He croaked, "I am not angry with you."

"You have a right to be. That picture of you is pretty embarrassing."

"I am not," he repeated. "I enjoyed helping you. It made me feel… useful."

"Oh, good." His words seeped into her with lingering relief. Relief she didn't dare let herself dwell on. She'd enjoyed having him help her too. *No time. There is absolutely no time for that.*

He was a distraction, one that would soon be gone. She straightened her shoulders and refused to look at him. "Thanks for everything today."

The man didn't say anything for a long moment. Claire ached to see the expressions that were no doubt dancing across his face, but she held her ground. For the restaurant and for her own sanity.

She served the food and they ate in an awkward silence. As she scraped the bottom of her bowl, she tried to bring back the flow of conversation. "The news said this storm should pass in a day."

Ugh, the weather? How awkward. But strangers talked about the weather, and that was what they were. Right? Strangers.

Silence followed her words for a long time. Argos looked thoughtfully down at his empty bowl before nodding. "I will leave as soon as possible so you can concentrate on your tavern."

"Oh…" She hadn't meant to kick him out, but this was a good thing. There was a lot for her to do, and taking care of Argos was just one more item on the list. Still, unease twisted her stomach.

He nodded in agreement, then stood suddenly, his chair

scraping the hard wood. "I think I'll sleep early tonight. Good night, Claire."

"Good night." More words tingled against her tongue, but she held them back. This was for the best. She didn't need romance, not now.

VI

T FIRST, SHE thought it was the rain that woke her up. Overnight the storm had become a fierce pounding against windows. She could hear the wind howling louder than usual as a strong breeze tickled her bare skin.

Claire shivered and groaned as she woke up, already cursing the new leak. The air around her smelled damp; water had gotten in somehow. Over the rain she could hear something else, a deep guttural noise that almost sounded like snoring. She blinked into the dark room and looked around, half expecting Argos to be nearby.

Instead she found a shadow crouched at the end of the bench where she had made her bed. A long slender figure whose glowing yellow eyes took her aback.

Her breath caught at the sight of white teeth as the jungle cat growled in her face.

The sight was so jarring, Claire's brain did the only sensible thing. It shut down. Completely and utterly failed as it zoomed in on the giant cat gazing hungrily at her.

Across the room, the door to the restaurant swung back and forth in the storm's wind. It banged against the wall. The same sound that had startled her awake now broke her out of a stupor.

Stalking through the doorway, a lion appeared, along with a cheetah and a panther prowling out of the rain. Each looking disgruntled and leaving wet paw prints as they wove between the tables.

Then before her eyes, the jaguar shifted. With another low growl, its face slowly became longer, its haunches curved in on themselves, and the small patterned fur dissolved into pale flesh. A man stood where the cat once had, and he smiled at her, thin lips pulling up as he sniffed and pawed at his long nose. "Do not worry, sweet, we are not here to harm you."

If this was a nightmare, she needed to wake up.

It was then that her mind had had enough. Sensibility kicked down the door to the rest of her body and she screamed.

The jaguar man was quick. His bony hand circled around her throat, effectively cutting off the scream before it could hit full pitch.

Claire choked on the rest of the noise as long fingers squeezed painfully around her throat and she was pushed down into her nest of blankets. Above her the stranger growled, "That was a very stupid thing you did there."

A rumble of agreement came from the other animals. She couldn't see them, couldn't hear their movements as they stalked through her house. For all she knew, one of them could be near her feet, ready to tear into her at any moment.

She closed her eyes at the thought, toes curling

subconsciously, and the stranger barked out orders. "He must be here. Go look for him."

Over the pounding of her heart, she heard the familiar creak of the upstairs door, and then the hard thump of a body hitting the wooden floor. The fingers released her neck as the man spun around. "What the hell?"

He was distracted. Claire acted before hesitation could stop her, kicking out and twisting her body. It was enough to surprise him and throw him off-balance. She scrambled over the table, desperate to put a barrier between herself and the intruder.

From there she could see what was going on in the rest of her restaurant.

The cheetah was lying at the bottom of the stairs, wounded from its fall with Argos towering over it, as naked as the day she had found him. Seeing him was a relief that nearly made her entire body tremble.

"Argos!" Claire cried out.

His eyes snapped up and locked on to her. Completely ignoring the monstrous lion that was prowling less than a foot away from him, ready to avenge its fallen comrade.

She scrambled to move towards him, instinct driving her to a safer place than wedged behind the wooden bench. And there was no safer place than next to a man who had thrown a cheetah to the ground.

A hand suddenly seized her wrists as the jaguar recovered. His nails dug into her and held her arm in place with impossible strength. "Good to see you again, hero," her captor snarled in Argos's direction.

Argos's eyes narrowed, unkind recognition sparking across his features. "Do you wish for me to kill you again,

Etros? The island's magic will not bring you back to life out here."

Etros sneered and yanked Claire's body in front of his own. "I was not fully myself then," he hissed, "but this time *we* are prepared to handle you." The other cats in the room let out a low rumble, and Claire frowned. He had to bring three giant cats to handle one man?

Argos didn't look at all impressed. "Let go of my woman." The usual throaty voice became a dangerous command.

A shiver traveled up Claire's spine. *What did he just say?*

Etros laughed and jerked his chin towards him. "The island no longer protects you either, mortal. I doubt you will come out unarmed this time." A wicked smile punctuated the word in a way that made Claire's stomach churn.

What did that mean?

Argos's attention was carefully divided between Etros and the lion snarling circles around him. With his back to the bar, he couldn't see the panther, who had climbed on top of the wooden beams. Its black body was a shadow against the ceiling, nearly invisible, but Claire saw it. She jerked as it prepared to launch itself. "Behind you!"

A blur of black jumped towards him, but Argos was just as quick, spinning around and catching the animal by the throat. His long limbs and broad muscles held the giant cat in the air as if it was nothing but a stuffed animal. Claire's eyes rounded at the sight.

No way. Her mind had been doing a good job keeping up with everything, but this was too much. She almost missed it when he yelled at her, "Claire, move!"

Seeing his arm pull back as if about to throw a baseball

was all the warning she needed. Etros saw it too and dropped his hold on her as he tried to move out of the way.

He was too slow. A ball of snarling, angry black fur flew as easily as a sack of flour and landed right on Etros. Claire fell to her hands and knees against the hard wood floor. Her head snapped up in time to see the human and cat trying to untangle themselves. Claire scrambled to her feet and hugged the wall as she distanced herself.

The lion decided it was his turn. He swiped angrily at Argos. The man scowled back at the cat, looking just as fierce.

God, Argos was facing down a lion.

It quickly became apparent that the lion was just biding time until the cheetah shook off its shock. Etros and the panther righted themselves and moved in as well. Argos might be strong, but he wouldn't be able to hold off all of them.

Claire bit her bottom lip and looked around for something to help. Her eyes quickly found the spare fire extinguisher lying by the corner of the bar. There wasn't a raging fire, but it would work nicely as kitty repellent.

Out of the corner of her eye she saw the circle close in on Argos. The cheetah lashed out quickly and managed to nick the back of his thighs.

Argos hissed, his teeth clenched in pain. "I'd rather die than return to that gods-forsaken island."

Etros shrugged. "Unfortunately, we were ordered to bring you back alive. But do not worry, we will only bring you close to death." A wicked smile pulled at his lips, showing sharp teeth. "Once you are back where you belong, it will hardly matter."

Argos let out a roar of defiance, loud enough that even the cats took an unsure step back.

At that moment Claire grabbed the fire extinguisher and pulled the pin. There was no time for a warning, not with the threatening look in Etros's eye and the way the cats kept licking their lips. She let out a frantic battle cry.

All eyes fixed on her, both man and feline, as she fired the contents of the extinguisher. A yowl came from the panther as it jumped away, giving her enough room for her to take up a position next to Argos. She fired on their attackers, randomly at first and then more focused, pushing them back into the kitchen.

It was almost too easy.

The jungle cats cowered at the white foam. Etros looked equal parts appalled, scared, and confused when she shot a chunk at his chest that knocked him to the ground. She let out a burst of laughter. "That's for using me as a human shield, you asshole."

Suddenly a hand wrapped around her elbow. She spun around to see the gleaming look on Argos's face.

He was... proud of her. There was no denying the amused smile that played across his lips even as he said, "Move quickly, Claire." The hand pushed her forward but she still held the extinguisher up, ready to fire another round.

Together they sprinted out the front door, broken glass crunching under their bare feet. Stepping out into the rain and the chilled wind was a shock. Soft ground slipped under her feet; she would have fallen on her ass if Argos's grip did not hold her up.

"We must make it to your boat," he urged.

"My boat? Where are we going?" Her voice barely carried over the storm as she followed him down the hill.

"Away from here," Argos answered simply, turning to look over his shoulder.

Claire did the same and froze when she saw the shadows of four giant cats quickly approaching them. The jaguar was back in full form among his brethren. Her head nodded in agreement. "Right, the boat. Probably our best bet. Cats hate water, right? Even big cats?"

"I will hold them off." His hold released her with a firm push forward. "Get the boat ready for our retreat."

She opened her mouth to argue but quickly closed it when he turned to face the oncoming threat. He wouldn't last long against four wild animals. Time was of the essence and she could not waste it trying to think of another plan.

Quickly she sprinted the rest of the way down the hill. The cry of an angry lion resounded behind her, but she dared not look back. She clutched her extinguisher close to her chest and ran.

If Argos went down, it would be the only thing between her and being torn apart. She was not going down without a fight.

⤙

He had known Circe would eventually find him; he just hadn't expected it to happen so soon. No doubt the boat he had stolen had been a beacon for her minions.

He would die a hero's death before allowing the filthy scavengers to drag him back to the island. If the gods had truly turned their backs on him, he would ask Hades why, face-to-face in the underworld.

But before that, it would be a pleasure to break Etros's neck once again.

The animals moved forward in an organized attack,

the lion flanking his left and the cheetah coming up on the right. Etros's jaguar form stayed back, ready to land the killing blow when the chance presented itself. Argos counted his enemies again: the panther was missing. It could be anywhere in the underbrush, waiting for its chance to attack.

Best not to wait. Already, adrenaline pulsed through his veins. Argos hungered for the fight. It was the perfect way to blow off the building tension in his body, distracting him from the other needs his body demanded.

If he could not fuck away his problems, he could always fight. And when he had seen Etros holding on to Claire—daring to touch her, to use her against him—the sleeping hero within him had awakened.

He had stormed temples, raided ships, and hunted down monsters. In all the battles he had been in, he had never waited for the enemy to come to him. That would not change. He charged towards the lion. The movement caught the beast off guard. It barely knew what was coming before he tackled it.

In his arms the lion squirmed, making it difficult to get a good grip, but his hands eventually twined themselves into the mane and skin before jerking the head to the side in a clean snap. Its neck broke with ease as if it were a chicken. He twirled to meet the panther running out of the darkness towards him. He threw the carcass, already beginning to change back into human form, just as the panther lunged.

He did not see the cheetah, though.

The creature yowled as it jumped on his back, digging its claws into his skin. Pain electrified throughout his body, sending bursts of white light in front of his eyes. They were not holding back. Circe's men would bring him to the brink of death to do their mistress's bidding. He threw himself to the ground, pinning the creature under his weight. It hissed, hot breath leaking into his ear. Rolling left, he heard its fragile rib cage crack and the animal howled. Argos struggled to his feet. If there was blood running down his back, the rain quickly washed it away. It would take several minutes of agony for the cheetah to die, but that was still better than it deserved.

All that remained was the panther and…

Etros streaked past him towards the dock, his powerful claws cutting into the ground.

"Argos!" His name barely resounded over the storm but he did not miss it.

Claire.

A chill ran through his body that was not caused by the rain. Without a second thought, he started for the boat, aware that there was still one cat left and it was hot on his heels. He could not spare the energy to look back.

The boat hummed to life in the distance. Claire's small form was hugging the wheel as *Sebastian* slowly pushed away from the dock. He could tell Claire was purposefully trying to keep the boat within reach for him, but that only made it easier for the jaguar to climb on.

His feet slammed on the wood of the dock. The boat was within reach. So close, his gaze slid away from the boat and concentrated on the woman steering it. Suddenly her body jerked, letting go of the wheel and falling backwards.

An angry tail lashed back and forth behind the railing as the boat pitched sharply and turned away from the dock. Argos sprinted harder, hurtled himself over the dock's edge, and caught the railing of the small boat. Saltwater splashed up around him, stinging his wounds as he hauled himself up the side of the boat.

Behind him, the panther roared but did not attempt to join them.

Once he was on the deck, he fought to move forward as the boat jerked and pitched in every direction. Claire climbed to her feet by the steering wheel, clutching the strange metal cylinder she had used in the restaurant.

She was pale and soaked to the bone as her chest heaved with each inhale. A bloody tear across her shirt nearly stopped him cold, but when her frantic blue eyes fell on him, an exhausted smile pulled at her lips. "You made it."

Seeing her unharmed eased the tightness in his chest. Suddenly, it was easier to breathe. "Where is Etros?"

Her eyes darted to the boat's small covering, and his followed. There, Argos saw the jaguar snarling from a corner. Blood dripped from its mouth. When his eyes moved back to Claire, he noticed the teeth marks and numerous dents on her weapon.

She forced out a laugh. "He snuck up on me."

"You did well," he said, already thinking of the most painful way he could kill the animal.

His thirst for revenge would have to wait; an interrogation was in order first. One step forward and he could see realization flicker across the animal's wide green eyes. A spark of human intelligence that told it death was staring him down.

Sebastian lurched to the side, tipping ominously as a strong wave hit, throwing them all to the deck. Argos scrambled to his feet looking for his prey, but Etros, the man, had climbed out to the bow of the boat. Wiping the blood from his mouth, Etros looked smug as he got to his feet. "Looks like neither of us is winning today, hero."

Carefully maneuvering his body in front of Claire,

Argos yelled over the wind, "Go and tell your mistress that her minions failed her, because next time you see me I will be immortal."

Behind him, Claire gasped, and Etros laughed. "The gods have forsaken you. The next time I see you, chains will be binding you for another five hundred years of torture under my teeth."

With that hollow warning, the coward threw himself over the boat's railing and allowed the water to swallow him whole.

VII

"**D**O YOU BELIEVE me now?"

She expected him to gloat, to see the dimpled smile and flash of white teeth. Instead Argos just looked exhausted. It had taken hours for the storm to pass, and in that time he had managed to keep the boat upright and away from the narrow shoreline of the Chesapeake. Claire would have been more impressed if she weren't so sure that she was going into acute shock.

They anchored just as the morning sun was coming up above the trees. The water was peaceful, as if no hurricane had just disturbed the entire ecosystem.

They were the only ones on the water. In the distance, birds were singing their morning songs. It would have been romantic if the terror from last night didn't tingle in her nerves.

If she was completely honest with herself, the whole thing felt like a dream. Overnight she had gone from having just one strange problem to so many she couldn't even wrap her head around them. But Argos graciously gave her a good place to start.

"Yeah... I believe you. I did see a jaguar turn into a man right in front of me." She watched as he peeled himself away from the railing and collapsed next to her. They both reeked of exhaustion. Claire's mind could barely pick which question to ask first. She quickly decided it didn't matter. "What... were those things?"

"Circe's *Pets*. Other men who had been trapped on the island. She turned them into animals when she was done with them, but their loyalty will always remain with her."

A shiver tore through Claire's body. "Did she do the same thing to you?"

"No, she tortured me in other ways." His lips thinned at the memory.

"What if they find us again?"

"We should be safe for now. I cut all ties to her island when I cut the rowboat free. It will be harder for them to track us now."

"The boat?" Her brows frowned at the memory of the beautiful little rowboat she had found him in. "Are you sure?"

Argos nodded. "Circe's magic is unpredictable, and that boat was cut from the wood of her isle. I'm positive she was able to track me with it."

Her stomach twisted in guilt. All this time he'd been telling her the truth and she had shrugged it off as delusions. It was still hard to make sense of everything, but now was the perfect time to start. With a soft sigh, she gave him a gentle nudge. "I'm sorry I didn't believe you. How did... how did you wind up with Circe?"

"Hestia sent me there as punishment." Argos's green

eyes closed at the memory while Claire's mind whirled to remember the name.

"Your...girlfriend?"

"Yes, we were lovers, but she is also a goddess."

Eventually Claire would have to get used to the matter-of-fact way he said things, but it was still too strange. "A goddess?" She shook her head, blinked at him and tried again. "Like a real goddess? And you were romantically involved with her?"

"Well, not in the sense that you think." A smile tugged on his lips, bringing back the Argos she'd known in her restaurant. "The goddess of the hearth is a virgin in all things. I have never tasted her lips, and the only time I have seen her figure has been in the portraits done by the great artists. We were lovers of each other's souls. I was her favored hero for hundreds of years."

Claire visibly winced. "That's... a long time to be with someone." And not be able to kiss them. The thought made her shudder. Maybe the Greeks did it differently, or maybe the word *love* was a loose term in the many years Argos had lived, but she couldn't imagine loving someone and not touching him intimately.

"So, what happened?" She tried not to pry, but it was clear that if a woman who he claimed to have once loved had doomed him to years of torture, something must have happened. She didn't even realize she was holding her breath until the man answered.

"I loved Hestia dearly, did nearly anything for her. But after so long I had my own needs, so I slept with another woman." He shrugged his shoulders easily. "I was foolish then, thought I was good enough to keep a secret from the gods."

Arrogant is more like it. Claire frowned, giving him a sideways look. "Wait a second, you loved her and yet you cheated on her?" Argos mimicked her look, brows scrunched in confusion. It was the only answer she needed. "Who was the other woman? Did you love her or something?"

"The woman? She was just a stranger I met in Rome. I do not even remember her name."

Claire gave him a firm punch on his arm; he barely blinked. "Seriously? What's wrong with you? Can I be frank? I'm going to be frank."

"Frank?" Argos asked, but she pushed forward.

"You might have loved Hestia once, but you definitely weren't *in* love. You don't cheat on someone you love. They should be enough to fill your every need. Even their shortcomings are enough for you." His eyes crinkled in an unreadable look, causing Claire to take a deep breath. Maybe she'd been out of line to say it, but after living for so many centuries, you'd think the man would know a thing or two about women.

Then again, some people could go their entire lifetimes not knowing true love. Her mother had known it once and was resigned that it would never happen again. And Claire… well, she'd never been in love with anyone but was certain this was how it worked.

"I'd be willing to bet," she continued, "that Hestia didn't really love you either. If she did, she wouldn't have punished you so harshly. Five hundred years, probably longer if you hadn't escaped. You don't doom someone you love like that."

Argos still wore his unreadable expression, staring at her like she was a three-eyed fish. Slowly she leaned away, trying to break his stare. With a shake of his brown mane, he tore his eyes away from her and laughed. "You must really wish for the goddess's wrath to rain down upon you, Claire. Denying her flowers in your tavern and talking about her love thusly. You are very brave."

Claire couldn't help but straighten her spine at his words. She wasn't sure if she was being brave or not. A small part of her still didn't believe that a goddess like Hestia or Zeus or any of them could really exist. This part was currently in a heated debate with the side of her that had readily accepted last night's events.

She tried not to let her indecision show. "She just doesn't seem like a very benevolent goddess."

"She's not all bad," Argos said, with an old look of fondness.

He couldn't possibly still have feelings for her? Not after all she'd done to him. But then again, she imagined it would be hard not to think fondly if you had loved their soul for hundreds of years.

Being immortal must be its own hardship on a relationship. Claire couldn't even keep the passion alive for a few weeks, let alone half a century.

"So, what do we do now? Should we head back to The Saucy Leg and—"

Argos interrupted her with a shake of his head. "We cannot return there. Circe will have men stationed, watching for our return. We'll have to stay away, at least for a couple days."

The news felt like another storm had hit her full force. "Are you serious? I can't go back for a couple of days?" The grim look on his face told her he was dead serious. "What are we going to do in the meantime? Huh?"

"I have a plan," he answered, voice as hard as steel. And just as unbreakable.

Claire rolled her eyes, remembering what he had said the other day. "To become immortal again? How does a person go about doing that?"

Argos tried to match her movements, sitting up straighter to meet her sarcastic look with his own humorless one, but it failed and he winced at the movement. With a long exhale, he gingerly tried to settle back down. Where he had been leaning against the cabinets, there was now a streak of red.

Claire hissed at the sight. "Jesus, you're hurt!"

"I've had worse," he murmured softly, protesting only slightly as she started to pull him down for a better view. There were three gashes along his arm and back.

She let out a watery breath. "Worse? A lion practically mauled your back."

"It was the cheetah," he muttered as she pawed open a nearby cabinet. The contents inside rattled; loose maps, tools that had been carelessly tossed inside right next to a plastic first aid kit. She put the first aid kit in her lap and examined the largest wound on his back. It was still slowly oozing blood, the skin red and inflamed. Luckily it didn't appear to need stitches.

She talked to distract him. "Yes, you seemed to have no problem taking out the cheetah trying to maul you." A burden-filled sigh escaped her as she recanted how ridiculous those words sounded. "I guess this all really means that you're some ancient solider?"

"Hero," he corrected, then hissed as she poured the peroxide on the wound. His next words growled out of him between clenched teeth. "I worked hard for that title. I am of the same class as Achilles himself."

"Sorry, I spark-noted most of English class." The years of her high school education where they'd read Homer and talked about Greek mythology were a blur. Generic schooling was all a blur for her. Reading, writing papers, doing math wasn't at all what she wanted to do. She'd been much better at the classes that required hands-on activities. Gym, wood shop, and home economics. That was where she excelled.

The only reason she'd managed to pass with decent grades was because math and reading played an essential part in her real love, cooking.

She did retain some information, though. "Achilles," Claire repeated, "he's the one with the heel problem."

"The one with the—" He sputtered for a moment, looking at her as if Claire had defiled the most sacred of topics. "Achilles was considered the greatest among the heroes. His legend should be known to all living mortals."

"Was? I thought you heroes were supposed to be immortal."

"We are now." Argos's hand absently came up to rub at the coin that hung around his neck again. The close proximity allowed Claire a good look at the coin. She stared at the metal's uneven edges and worn engravings. It certainly looked old. "You must have heard of the great battle for Troy."

"Heard of it, yes."

Argos didn't bother to ask how much she had heard and barreled on. "That battle was why our Order was founded. It was there that the greatest heroes of Greece were gathered in one place for the first time, where they became real heroes." His eyes closed as if recalling a memory, but instead he began to recite something.

"Generations of men are like the leaves.
In winter, winds blow them down to earth,
but then, when spring season comes again,
the budding wood grows more. And so with men:
one generation grows, another dies away."

Claire didn't move an inch while he spoke. Her hand still hovered over his bandaged back, her mouth slightly ajar. "That was... really nice. Did you fight at Troy?"

"Me? No, it was years before my time."

"You sound as if you know it well."

"All heroes know the old stories well." Argos shrugged as Claire snipped the end of the bandage and tied it in place. "They were told at nearly every feast, and I had the good fortune of meeting a few of the living heroes myself."

"But not Achilles?"

The smile on his face diminished. "No, not Achilles. Many of our heroes died at Troy. It was a massacre as much as it was a glorious battle. In the end, the gods cried over the loss of such great men and struck a bargain with the living victors. It was Zeus who offered the trade, a god's task for immortal glory, and thus my Order was born."

She hadn't realized it before, but there was something poetic about the way he talked. Where it had once sounded like the ramblings of a madman, it was easy now to understand what he meant when he explained things to her. No, explain was the wrong word. He painted a vivid picture with his words. Claire found herself doing the unthinkable.

She wanted to hear more. "And what task did the gods give you?"

"My quest came from Hestia, whose temple I had visited nearly every day since I was a boy. She gave me a torch of fire and asked me to light the altar in one of her temples." His gaze slid to her. "The flame was part of Hestia's hearth, you see. She keeps Olympus warm with it, and it was a part of that fire that she bestowed on me. A flame she wished to keep eternal in her temple."

"Well, that doesn't sound very hard."

Argos gave a slanted smirk that warned her against saying things so casually. "The temple was two months away by boat plus an additional six weeks of traveling by foot. When I got there, it was buried under rubble after a chimera attack."

Claire's mouth went dry. "And you managed to deliver it in one piece?"

"Aye." He leaned his head back against the cabinets and let his eyes drift away from her. He stared at nothing, lost again to the past. "For me, her quest proved to be one of the most difficult things I've ever faced. Ask me to slay a monster or beat a man in combat and I found no challenge. But ask me to care for something as fragile as a flame for months? That took skills I had never exercised, and she knew it. Her flame was both a blessing and a curse; it kept me warm at night and proved to be a valuable weapon as well as a way to cook food. I grew to love it. Last I heard, the temple caretakers kept that flame going for many years after I lit it."

He closed his eyes then and moved his arm away from her touch. She felt a chill at the loss of contact. "But I suppose," he finished, "the flame had to burn out eventually."

She finished dressing his wounds in silence. The second she declared the job done, Argos shifted in place, testing the bandages. He barely moved his arm when he let out a low, guttural noise. For a split second, Claire worried his injuries were the cause of his discomfort, but then she saw it. A squeaky wail of indignation escaped her at the sight of his very large, very erect penis. "Come on! Seriously?"

Argos's brows frowned at her. "I'm sorry. Did I do something wrong?"

"You…you…" She tried to think of something, but all she could do was stare. He really was adorable—the genuine look of confusion, dark brows scrunched together, like he didn't know. "You seriously still have an erection?" she all but shouted at him helplessly. And, in case there was any more confusion, she waved her hand at the offending, but soooo impressive, erection that was peeking out of his tattered cloth.

Hello, Claire, it said, *I'm here just for you.*

And here she was thinking they were having a moment. "You're an absolute pervert," she said weakly, looking at him.

To her surprise, he did look ashamed. His nostrils flared, and his jaw was clenched tight. "I'm sorry, Claire. I cannot help it. 'Tis my curse."

A laugh bubbled up her throat. "Curse, yeah, that's what all the guys say."

Pain tightened the skin of his face. When he spoke, it was through clenched teeth. "As I have been doing for the past few days, I am telling you the truth. I could not get rid of it even if I tried, and believe me, I have tried. But I have been cursed to forever crave a woman's touch."

The laughter died in Claire's throat as she stared at him. "I thought… being trapped on that island was your curse."

"No, that was simply my punishment. The gods are not merciful when they are crossed, and Hestia was no different. She left me on that gods-forsaken island, but she also cursed me. I was trapped there because I could not leave Circe's side. Even a minute without her touch was enough to drive me mad."

Oh God. Claire's head reeled with the realization.

"At first I enjoyed it. I did not even realize I had been tricked. I thought Hestia was letting me be my own man. But then the first decade passed, and I wished to return to my men. It was then I realized I was not a visitor to the island but its prisoner. Circe lusted after me, and against my will my body responded." He shook his head at the memory.

Claire was still struggling to understand. "But you didn't seem that way when I first found you."

"My body needed time to recover. After we returned to your tavern, believe me, my thirst was already moving on to something else." He gave her a knowing look and she blushed at the memory. Seeing his body react for the first time. How he had tried to avoid her touch. It all made sense now.

"I have been fighting the urge for the past two days, Claire."

Her fingers curled. "You... can't take care of it yourself?" she asked.

"I tried"—there was no shame in the confession—"but it does not last long. My body will only be satisfied with one thing."

Suddenly his insistence on finding Circe and killing her made sense. Even Claire wanted to punch the woman in the face, along with a certain goddess. She couldn't believe a woman who had once sworn to love Argos would hurt him so thoroughly.

When she'd first allowed Argos into her home, if he had wanted to take advantage of her, there was nothing she could have done. The man was made of one hundred percent raw power, even as a mortal. He'd kept her safe from more than just Circe's Pets and a storm. Argos had protected her from even himself.

Her heart clenched at the thought.

"I don't expect it of you." Argos's voice was soft, but the words broke Claire out of her own thoughts.

She blinked. "Expect what of me?"

"I don't expect you to help me, Claire." The words carried an invisible weight to them. Argos looked more exhausted then he had a few moments ago. "I am a man who has lost his honor, but I will never ask you to do something that would make you lose yours as well…"

"Excuse me?" Was he saying what she thought he was saying? He was cursed with a constant hard-on and he wasn't going to ask for her help because he thought she was… an innocent?

If he asked, would you say yes? She swallowed hard against that question. A lot of answers ran had through her mind, each one carrying a new promise. It was better to hang on to her anger that he, for some reason, thought she was a delicate virgin to protect. She wished he'd called her a nymph instead.

"Argos, you're making a lot of assumptions there and I…" She stopped quickly. He wasn't looking at her with his usual amused smile. Wasn't looking at her at all really.

Somehow, he'd fallen asleep, propped up against the cabinets.

Claire stared at him in disbelief, and continued to stare when a loud grumbling snore escaped his mouth. Then she could only laugh and allowed the man to sleep. He had killed a lion after all. He deserved a rest. And she needed to figure out what the hell they were going to do next.

VIII

S HE LET HIM rest while she busied herself with trying to navigate somewhere familiar. They needed somewhere safe, somewhere they could regroup. Her mind got to work quickly, taking in their surroundings. She knew the Bay like the back of her hand, and it just so happened there was one place close by that would offer them shelter. But did she dare risk it?

Her hesitation only lasted for a moment before she shook it off. Argos had said they were safe now. Not trusting him the last time had meant staring down a jaguar. With a destination in mind, she steered *Sebastian* across the calm waters.

The quiet around her did little to help her nerves. Argos's story repeated in the back of her head.

Can't go back. Too Dangerous. Gods. Witches.
Curses.

It was all still hard to swallow, but she couldn't deny what she'd seen. One thing was for sure, they were in this together now. Wordlessly she peeked at the sleeping figure.

Leaning against the ship's hard cabinets couldn't be the most comfortable position, but he seemed dead to the world. Not even *Sebastian*'s rumbling engine woke him up.

It was the perfect time for Claire to view him in with a new light.

He'd called himself a hero, and last night he'd certainly acted as hers. There were worse people to be stuck in a life-or-death situation with, and she supposed she was just grateful he wasn't the delusional castaway she'd originally thought.

The story of his curse stood out the most to her. There had been undeniable shame in his voice when he talked about it. As if being betrayed by Hestia wasn't enough, then Circe…

Claire shook her head, forcing the pity away. *Empathy is all well and good, Claire*, she told herself, *don't just pity the man.* Help *him.*

But how?

That question kept her occupied for the rest of the trip. Slowly, more and more boats came into view. A few people stared at her tuckered little antique fishing boat, but she just smiled and waved, hoping the distance was enough that they wouldn't notice the claw marks that streaked down the front of the boat.

The Bay was filled with little creeks and salty outlets with homes propped along the water. She navigated down a familiar narrow passage. Homemade docks and the boats that lined them filled her view.

Some of the homes had remained in the same family for generations. In recent years, a more expensive crowd had moved onto the canal, buying the run-down homes and transforming them into elegant getaway lodges.

One home caught her eye. A bright yellow house that was well hidden under the thick leaves of the nearby trees. She could just barely see the backyard and the stairs that led up from the dock towards the house. A sign on the dock read "Kings' Place," and she knew they had arrived.

Argos didn't stir from his sleep as she slowed the boat down and parked it at the dock. The poor man deserved more than just two hours of sleep.

Besides, her mind reasoned, *Laura is going to have a heart attack when she lays eyes on him.*

Claire mashed her lips together at the thought. Laura was going to have a heart attack just looking at *her*—barefoot, scratched up, torn pajamas. She was slightly less damp, thanks to the breeze on the Bay, but it would be easy to tell she'd spent the night out in the storm. How was she going to explain all this?

Without a word, she jumped off the deck and got to work securing a rope to the dock cleat. On the opposite side of the dock rested a small yacht with elegant purple-and-yellow lettering named *Queenie*. She was a beautiful boat, small but homey, and a longtime friend of *Sebastian*, just like her owners were longtime friends of Claire. After tying the last knot, she didn't hesitate to step onto *Queenie* and steal a warm-looking blanket from a bench. Laura wouldn't mind.

Argos shifted as soon as the blanket touched his skin but remained asleep. Only his impressive assets, even in an exhausted fit of sleep, were awake and demanding her attention.

Claire yanked the blanket stubbornly over that part.

The curse, she reminded herself. *He can't help it.* Claire bit down on the attraction that riled up inside her. *Being on the run with the guy does not mean you can sleep with him.* She knew when the whole thing was over, she would be days behind in her grand opening. If the restaurant was to open at all.

That thought made the attraction die quickly. She had to keep it together.

A mantra of "keep it together" carried her all the way up the quaint wooden staircase and towards the back door of the house. Laura and Kevin knew her better than anyone else, and they wouldn't settle for just any lie. She'd have to approach them with a story both solid and realistic. Pulling the screen door back, she knocked once and waited. Noisy grumbling came from behind the door before it was pushed open, revealing Laura King. Her silvering hair was in a messy ponytail; she wore loose slacks and a shirt that proudly proclaimed ANNAPOLIS.

She hadn't changed at all in the few months since Claire's last visit. There used to be a time when she'd visited the King residence weekly, summers when she and her father had practically lived in the old yellow house. Those were some of her fondest memories, learning to tie knots on *Queenie* and eating fresh-caught crab.

Laura's eyes widened at the sight of her and then at the *sight* of her. "Claire," she breathed, already preparing herself for the worst. "The storm, you're…"

"Everything is fine," Claire blurted out quickly, eager to wipe the worry from the woman's face.

"Jesus, get in here." The older woman didn't wait for a response before she was pulling Claire into the house. Without pause, she grabbed one of the spare jackets hanging near the door and threw it over Claire's shoulders. "What are you doing here? Like this? Your restaurant is opening in a week."

Claire winced. "It's just… something came up."

"Something?" Laura repeated slowly. For a moment her face was blank, the shock fading as she worked her brain for a reliable translation. It didn't take long for her to shake her head dismissively. "We'll talk over food. Do you need a drink?"

"It's early…"

Laura huffed. "Oh, forget whatever nonsense your mother burned into you. Do you need a drink?"

It never took long for Claire to adjust to Laura's way of life. Her shoulders slumped and something gave way in her muscles. All politeness and pretense melted away with two words: "God, yes."

The back room led directly into the kitchen, where the smell of baked goods was practically burned into the walls. Claire sniffed, and the mouth-watering aroma of blueberry scones assaulted her senses. As usual, the kitchen was a mess; its small size emphasized the stacks of dishes on every available countertop. It wasn't that Laura didn't clean her dishes; they were just constantly being used.

At their arrival, Kevin King looked up for a second and then back down to his book. "Claire, what a pleasant surprise." His hair had thinned to almost nothing, and a pair of thick-rimmed glasses sat on his nose as he read a fat book.

"Pleasant?" Laura huffed. "Did you even look at her?"

Kevin made a slightly annoyed noise and marked his place with a spare napkin. He looked up again as Laura pushed Claire into a nearby seat. "Does it matter how she looks? It's always nice to see her."

The tight knot in her stomach loosened at those words. Claire smiled, and from across the table, Kevin smiled back.

Laura shook her head. "I'm going to go find you some dry clothes. Kevin, get this girl some food."

"Aye-aye, Captain."

Kevin quietly cleared her a space, then went to the stove to fill a plate. The house shook around them as Laura's footsteps stomped upstairs.

"Next time, it might be nice to call us first. Spontaneous visits aren't like you, and that has her worried," Kevin said, placing two hot scones in front of her. He returned to his seat, where Claire expected him to open his book again, but he didn't continue reading. Instead he was giving her a look over the brim of his glasses. "Seems you got caught in the rain.... in your pajamas?"

"There's more to the story than that."

"I'm eager to hear it."

"I'm not in trouble if that's what you're thinking."

"That's too bad, because trouble is something I can handle."

Not this kind of trouble. Claire grabbed the closest jar of homemade jam and scooped a liberal amount onto the plate. Her mouth watered at the sight, anticipation building in the back of her throat. She took a bite of the thick dough and closed her eyes in pure bliss as the sweet blueberry jam licked against her taste buds. She moaned and filled her mouth again, using the extra time to concoct a logical explanation about her appearance and the man sleeping on her boat.

She was making little progress when the back door slammed open. The blueberries threatened to leap back up her throat as fear seized her. A hard cough shook her core even as she tried to spin around and see who—*or what*—came through the door.

Argos stalked into the kitchen, the blanket snuggly wrapped around his waist in a slim show of modesty.

His eyes darted about the room until they found her and then landed on Kevin. Uh-oh. "You," he said to Kevin, "dared to take Claire away from my side."

"I was not taken. I am perfectly safe," she managed to protest, giving the hero a firm look before turning to Kevin. The look of shock on the man's face was a first for her. *You still think you can handle trouble?*

She held Kevin's gaze as she gestured at the hulking man beside her. "Kevin, I can explain..." She glanced back to Argos, her eyes sweeping over the blanket that he clutched over his groin. No explanation came out.

Kevin's eyes followed her gaze. "Is that my blanket?"

"I found some old clothes you left here, Claire," Laura said from the other side of the room as she walked in. Her arms full of folded cloth, she stopped abruptly to take in the new arrival in the room.

"Oh," Laura said softly, clearly in a state of shock, before she thinned her lips and said, "Claire, why is there a naked man in my kitchen?"

"He's... er... well, you see..."

Guilt lodged itself in Claire's throat. The thought of them being involved in her suddenly confusing and dangerous life was too much.

Neither of the two spoke. She risked a glance in their direction and saw exactly what she had been afraid of. Kevin, fiddling with his glasses. Laura, not smiling. "He's not exactly your type...," the older woman said.

It was hard not to be dismissive of those words. No one knew exactly what her type was, not even Claire. She hadn't dated much, and even when she did, the number of boyfriends who'd managed to meet the Kings was a grand total of zero. And since starting work on The Saucy Leg, there had been no time to meet any men, except of course…

"Argos is a contractor," she lied. "I hired him to help me with the restaurant when it looked like we wouldn't be able to make the deadline. He's very good with his hands and…um, building things."

"He's not wearing any clothes," Kevin pointed out, nose buried back in his book. His face had turned the exact same shade of red as a homegrown tomato.

Claire took a deep breath. The things she would do to protect those that she cared about. "Alright, you caught me… us. The reason we were out in the middle of the storm was because Argos and I have been more than a little stressed and we wanted to relieve some tension. The storm caught us by surprise."

"I see," Laura finally said. The Not Smile was still in place. Claire couldn't recall a time when the woman had stared at her so sternly. "Well, I'll have to fetch more clothes, then. Argos, was it? You must be hungry."

Claire snatched at his hand quickly, squeezing it in warning. She saw the question easily for what it was. A trap. Her touch should have alerted Argos to keep his mouth shut, to let her do all the talking. Unfortunately, it was too late. "I am."

"Lovely. Why don't I make you something to eat, and in the meantime I want to hear all about you and how you two survived the storm last night."

❧

This would not do. Argos took in the two strangers closely. They were in their elder years, which would do nothing to aid them. The woman, Laura, bustled around the kitchen with an energy that could rival Claire's own. The man, on the other hand, barely moved from his place at the table, a book open in his hand.

This definitely would not do.

Claire had promised a place of shelter. Somewhere safe. Yet the small house had no more fortification then her own tavern. Even worse, it appeared that he faced threats even inside the hideaway based on how Laura kept eying him as if he were some sort of blight.

When Laura's back was turned and her husband's head lowered to read, Claire leaned close to him. Her warm breath tingled against his ear as she whispered, "*Please* try to fit in. Don't say anything too out of place, and make sure they don't see your injuries." She tugged the blanket higher to cover the wounds on his back.

"Do you really think these are the right people to help us?"

Her eyes darted around the room quickly. "No, this is only temporary. Very, very temporary."

There was no time to respond. Laura came back to the table, setting a plate of food before him.

She stuck her body between the two of them, prying them apart. "Soooo, how long have you been working with Claire?"

Berries and jam ran over the dish. It smelled delicious, and he was fighting a losing battle against two different types of hunger. He picked up a fork and took a bite. "Only two days."

Laura's brows shot up. "Two days."

"I was being spontaneous," Claire grumbled.

"You're not spontaneous." Kevin's voice echoed from behind his book.

"No, but I am stressed. Stress causes people to do crazy things."

"So do hormones, dear," Laura muttered.

Silence punctuated the end of the conversation. Only the metallic clatter of silver against plates rang in the small kitchen as Claire busied herself with the food in front of her. This was not going the way he would have hoped.

"I have some questions of my own," Argos said, giving the couple a withering look. If he was going to defend Claire and get his immortality back, he needed to know who these new allies were. Claire groaned, cupping her face in her hands.

The man blinked. "Yes?"

"Who are you?"

"Who are we?" The woman turned abruptly, sending Claire a wide-eyed look. "You didn't even tell him who we are?"

Claire sputtered for an explanation, but the older man shut his book with a hard thump and set it aside. He looked at Argos, blinking slowly. Argos had dismissed his presence as a passive one at best. He had barely looked up at the guests in his home and let his woman do most of the talking. But in that instant, the man's shoulders straightened.

Argos recognized the type of man who commanded others with a quiet personality. There was more to this man than met the eye. He was not a hero, no. He was something else. "I'm Kevin and this is my wife, Laura. You are in our home and with a girl that we care for very deeply. Claire's father was a good friend of ours, a very good friend."

Ah, her father. He wondered where the men in her life

had been. The husband. The sons. The father. But Kevin had said something that gave him pause. *Claire's father* was *a good friend.* A figure of the past.

The three of them had at least one thing in common: they all cared about Claire. And Kevin had proven that he had a spine after all. Argos reconsidered everything he thought he knew.

They would do nicely.

Beside him, Claire let out a loud yawn.

"We'll sort this whole thing out after you two have rested," Kevin suggested. "Claire, you and your friend can have the guest room upstairs."

Claire nodded in response, unable to hide her relief. When she stood, Argos noticed her movements had a slow, dreamlike quality to them. She would fall asleep standing up if they allowed it. He placed his hand on her shoulder to steady the small body.

"Tell me where we need to go," he asked Kevin.

"Upstairs," Claire murmured back. Despite her exhaustion, she led the way up the stairs, leaving the hero to hover behind her in case she asked for assistance. To allow such a thing went against his nature. He did not spare attention to the building around them, eyes only on Claire as they moved down the hall to the open door at the end.

Then she froze, sleep quickly disappearing from her body.

It only took Argos a moment to see what caused the sudden alarm. He stared at the big bed in the center of the room with an overwhelming sense of dread. His loins caught on fire at the sight, knowing the devilish things that happened on large beds and knowing he was expected to share it... with Claire.

IX

SHE WAS FULLY awake now. There was no way she couldn't be. She was sharing the bedroom with Argos.

It was difficult not to be hyperaware of the things in the room—the bed, the man, herself. She was already drained from their exciting adventure; it was harder and harder to keep her usual conviction. If she let her guard down for one second, that was it. She'd be through.

What was Kevin thinking? Was this some kind of test? A way to see if she would chicken out and tell them the truth of her misadventures?

Argos must have been wondering the same thing. His entire body tensed at the sight of the room. When she dared to glance down, there was his cock, alert as always. An invisible ripple of electricity sparked between their bodies. It stirred something in her, a warm glow of pleasure that pried at her again. *Why not?*

He needed relief from the curse, and she needed relief from the stress building from this mess. If he left her alone, she'd be a mess. Her mind would focus on how far behind she was on the restaurant. How long it would take for Argos to get his revenge. How long before she could even return home.

She didn't know. And not knowing would drive her insane.

It was Argos who spoke up first. "There has been a mistake. I will go ask for another room."

She reached out and grasped his hand before he could reach the door. His body stilled like an animal caught in a trap. Claire cleared her throat; she should have thought this out better. But for once, she was acting without a fully coherent plan.

Her voice hurried to catch up with the rest of her body. "Don't go." She closed her eyes, wincing at how pathetic the words sounded out loud. "I mean, I can help you, right?"

Argos sucked in a sharp breath. "You do not know what you're saying."

"I do," Claire stated, giving his hand a stubborn squeeze. "We've both been through hell the past couple hours, and I want to work off some of this stress." Then, gathering her courage, she moved forward and grabbed him. "We should help each other…"

We should help each other…

Gods, more precious words had never been spoken. Argos cradled them, cherished them, just like he did the small leaf of a woman who offered them up to him. She did not need to emphasize what she meant; the hand that firmly grabbed at his front made everything very clear.

His body could not help but react. What it had been

starving for was finally offering itself to him. Eager and ready. He did not even realize his hand had grabbed hers in a solid grip, pulling it away from his aching cock. Claire blinked her owlish eyes at him, her lips parted in surprise.

A groan worked its way up his throat as he forced himself to stay in control. "You are already helping me, Claire."

"You're right," she said stubbornly, "I am." She trailed her free hand up his arm and across his collarbone. Her lips followed, pressing a trail of kisses against his heated skin. Argos watched in fascination as each kiss sent a jolt of lightning threw him. He wanted those lips against his own. He needed her to look at him.

Finally, she did, her eyes beseeching. Her lips parted, silently begging for him to claim her.

Defiant little nymph. She was not an innocent. How could he ever think that? The Claire in front of him matched the confident seductress who infiltrated his fantasies. The woman commanded attention and refused to let it go.

Argos could not help it. His body leaned forward, aching for her touch. He sucked in a sharp breath, feeling his control slip.

Of course, it was at this moment that Claire pulled back, startled by the noise that escaped him. "I want this to be good for you as well," she amended softly, looking torn. "Tell me what you need."

"I need you not to tease me," he nearly growled, swooping down to capture her lips. It was a proper kiss. The thing he had been wanting since first laying eyes on her lush lips. As he had dreamed, they parted easily for him, allowing his tongue entrance. An delightful noise arose from Claire and his curse ached for more. "I need you. All I need is you."

Claire gasped as he picked her up. Her body hardly

weighed more than his old shield. He easily tossed on onto the bed, her nightshirt hitched up, revealing unmarked white skin.

Looking down on her turned his entire body into a burning flame. He worried it would burn them both alive. It felt like a century since the last time he'd touched a woman, though it had been only a few days. He wanted to ravage her, but that would not do.

She was helping him. The least he could do was make the experience one she would never forget.

"What are you doing?" Claire propped herself up on her elbows, looking at him with excited eyes. Her hair was disheveled from their escape, but it only made her more beautiful to him. In a few moments, it would be even worse. He wanted her to fall apart under the pleasure he gave.

"I fear that once I start, I will not be able to stop," he breathed, giving her one last chance to quit while they could.

Her lips parted, but the words refused to come out. Slowly she pulled herself into a sitting position and reached for her top. The air left Argos's lungs as she pulled it over her head, showing two perfect, pale breasts. They were the most beautiful things he had ever seen. Small and soft, barely holding on to the same tone of color as the rest of her body.

"I don't want you to stop." Her hands, little deviants that they were, slid down to her pants. Argos snapped back to himself at the sight and quickly reached forward to stop the movement. She had already stolen the pleasure of peeling off her top. He would not let the same slight happen again.

The bed dipped under his weight, bringing Claire's body closer to his own. She froze at his sudden movement, looking down to where his hand covered her own in a firm grip. A smile creeped along the edge of her lips when she looked up. She must have seen something she liked, because she leaned forward—a determined look glittering in her eyes.

∽

Kevin had been right. Argos was not her type. At least, as much as a gorgeous immortal warrior could not be anyone's type—which boiled down to all the practical reasons. Sure, he was strong and had a way of talking that made her toes curl, but if Claire had met the man under normal circumstances, she could never picture the two of them going on dates, meeting each other's families, or more importantly, running a restaurant together.

Considering that their situation was the farthest thing away from normal one could get, Claire would let all that slide away for a moment. She promptly turned off all logic in favor of withering under Argos's large body as he licked the junction of her collarbone. The heat of his mouth against her skin made her squirm in delight. God, it felt so good.

His erection pressed against her; the thing was as demanding as its owner. And now she could finally give it the proper attention. Her hand brushed under his blanket and barely managed to wrap around the large shaft. Argos's entire body went rigid on top of her.

"Claire." His voice came out like broken glass. "If you do that, I will not be able to last very long."

"Don't you want to get off?" she asked breathlessly, stroking the soft skin. The erection was at full hardness, responding to her every touch.

He shook his head, bucking his hips forward in an

attempt to get her to stop, but all it managed to do was rub his cock against her mound. They both groaned at the contact. "You deserve your fill first," Argos said.

His body slipped down; the presence of his groin disappeared. Claire wiggled in disappointment, peeking her head up to see what he was doing. The next thing she felt was the hard yank of her pajama pants coming off. A squeak of surprise escaped her lips as her midnight-colored panties were revealed to the room. Argos gazed at them with the same starved look she'd seen the first day they'd met.

That look made Claire forget about her own self-consciousness. All the sharp edges of her body, how her legs had an uneven tan from the days she lay out in the sun. He kissed her hip bone, and then along the line of her panties.

Her breath hitched as she watched him, waiting for the moment when his mouth dipped lower. Soon he would be kissing a much more sensitive part of her body. He glanced up and smiled at the sight of her watching, and then he put his mouth against her mound.

The heat was delightful. Claire nearly cried out as he switched between gentle kisses and mouthing her through the fabric of her panties. "You're wet," he observed, voice heavy with pleasure.

She couldn't help but giggle in response. "Well, yeah. All of me got wet."

A finger trailed between her folds, causing her laughter to stop. Argos looked smug. "You know what I mean. I can taste you."

Oh. A shiver raced through her. She had never really been one for dirty talk in the past, but this was nice. She liked the way his voice dipped into a gruffer accent, how it rolled over her body.

His tongue went back to where lace met skin. a small sound of disappointment creaked up Claire's throat before she felt a gentle tugging. Argos drew the band of the panties into his mouth and pulled it down. She heard him panting. His eyes were glued on the V between her legs, and never once did he look up. It was a shame; she wanted his beautiful eyes pointed at her.

But this was the awfulness of the curse afflicting him. Even she could feel it; the need to have him inside her was overwhelming. Was this what he felt like all the time? Claire studied him as he hurriedly reached down and pulled out his erection.

And then she froze, reality crashing into the lustful fantasy. "Wait…"

He stopped immediately and pulled back. Disappointment cut through Claire as she took in the look of pain on his face. "Did I hurt you?"

"No, it's just… I don't have any protection."

"Protection?" he repeated with a huff of frustration. "Am I not enough protection for you?"

Laughter bubbled out of her at his confusion. "You are, but I don't think even you can protect me from getting pregnant if you put that thing in me."

He didn't seem to understand what she was saying, and now was not the time to get into the practicality of safe sex. She wanted him inside her, fucking her until the memories of the Pets and her looming deadline felt like a bad dream. But that would have to wait for another time. Now, she just needed that mouth back on her.

She reached up, stroking her fingers along his jaw in reassurance as a plan began to form. "Let's try something else."

Confusion flashed across his face. Claire offered what she hoped was a sexy smile and guided him down on the bed as she crawled on top of him. It had been a long time since she'd had done anything besides basic missionary sex. But tonight she felt adventurous. Living in the presence of a man like Argos was having an effect on her.

She just prayed to Argos's gods that she'd be able to pull something like this off.

Argos watched her as she positioned her pussy over his face. Without another word she bent down and took his erect cock in her mouth. Her name broke off into a groan as Argos arched up into her mouth. The length of him pushing into her nearly made Claire gag before she found a tempo.

She'd never had anyone as large as Argos before. He smelled of pure, musky sex, and the more she sucked, the more she wanted it.

Hands fell on her hips, guiding them down before Argos's tongue returned to her folds. She groaned against the cock in her mouth and sucked harder, taking more and more of him in with every passing moment.

Argos was thrusting into her mouth, the rhythm becoming more frantic. He was close. They'd barely even started, but he was near bursting. "Claire," he whispered, "I need—"

"Just relax," she said, licking him from base to tip, "let go." Her hand came up and stroked his balls lightly as she gave one last hard suck.

A cry echoed in the dark room as his cock twitched. Hot sperm soaked her hand and dribbled down Argos's stomach. All at once, the hard body under her relaxed for the first time in days.

Well, if there was any doubt from Laura and Kevin,

that would assure them of the lie. There was no way they hadn't heard that. Old houses were notoriously bad at keeping sounds muffled.

Despite the thought, Claire smiled and gave the cock one last lingering kiss. Then something brushed against her thigh. The pleasant tingle of Argos's beard followed by his soft lips. "Now it's your turn," he murmured.

"You don't have to—" Her words broke off in a moan as he returned to her pussy. God, his tongue was huge, just like the rest of him. On instinct, she leaned back into his touch and began to fuck herself on his mouth.

Her breasts bounced from the momentum. Argos's hands moved, caressed her skin and began to play with her nipples, twisting them and stroking them. They were beyond sensitive after months of stress and no sexual outlet.

It was too much. "I'm almost there," she panted. "Oh God."

He nipped at her sensitive pussy. The touch almost brought her to climax, but then his mouth was gone. "Which god do you cry out to, Claire? There are many."

"Is there a god for good sex?" She squirmed as he squeezed her breasts.

His answer was a long, vibrating hum as his mouth returned to her pussy and it was all she needed before orgasm took her. She trembled as the wave of pleasure flowed over her with the force of a storm.

She turned her head against her arm, trying to smother any noise, but it was too late. A cry spilled from her lips as her body clenched around him. Her vision went white from the pleasure. For one glorious moment, she did forget everything, all the worry, all the stress. The relief was so overwhelming her muscles turned to noodles underneath her.

When the aftershocks passed, they were entangled in each other's arms, shivering and panting like two survivors of a storm.

❧

Later, soft with pleasure and drawing shapes across the broad chest beside her, Claire asked, "So where do we go from here?"

Argos blinked. "Go?" he repeated. His eyes drifted away from her, towards the ceiling, where they stared at nothing in particular. "Next, I find a way to get my revenge. I will make my way to Circe's island and kill her."

The sleep that had been pressing down on her evaporated. Claire's finger stilled in the middle of a circle as she sat up on her elbows. "You're kidding," she said, finding the words more as a statement then a question.

Argos's face didn't change and his eyes couldn't help but glance down at her exposed bosom as he kept talking. "Of course, first I'll need to find my brothers and a weapon."

The man had a one-track mind, and it had fallen on her to snap him out of it. "The woman has giant jungle cats," she pointed out.

Argos's lips twitched as if he were amused. "I disposed of them easily before, did I not?"

"Oh, don't be arrogant. You didn't leave that fight completely unscathed, remember?" She wanted to reach out and poke the wound left across his back, but instead her fingers fell gently against the bandage and stroked down. "You're only human," she said quietly.

Of course he was, she had yet to meet someone who wasn't, but after everything they had been though, the words came with a new meaning. Argos had fought like a man who believed nothing could kill him. He was fearless and powerful, but that didn't change the fact that if one of those cats had sunk their teeth into him, he would have died.

The room fell quiet as Argos seemed to process the words as much as she. "I know that," he breathed, "I have a plan. I will find a god to grant my immortality again."

"Ah." She nodded. "And how does that work?"

He smiled. "Our immortality is a favor given from the gods once we prove ourselves. They give us a quest, someone to kill or something to steal, and when it is completed we are granted the status of hero. With that comes immortality and brotherhood with the other heroes."

"How many of you are there?" she asked. The idea of other men like Argos had never struck her before.

He considered her question for a long moment before answering. "A least two hundred, maybe more these years."

"Two hundred!?"

"Back in the old days we were few. Men with great skills were hard to come by. There was maybe one man out of a dozen armies who deserved the status of hero. But as the years went on, our numbers grew. The gods did not run out of errands to hand out to mortal men willing to prove themselves."

Claire struggled to imagine it. "But there aren't any more monsters to slay. The world is a very different place. What do men like that do?"

The body next to her shook with laughter as Argos's arm reached around and drew their naked skin close. "No more monsters? Did you forget who is chasing me?"

She frowned. "Point taken."

"Times have changed, but there is always a need for

heroes." Argos's voice grew soft, almost as if he were drifting to sleep, but his eyes were still open, alert. "Monsters have not disappeared. They have simply gone into hiding. The gods still war between each other. Lost treasure still needs to be discovered."

"Do you really think you have time to take on a quest when you're trying to escape Circe?" She didn't want to poke holes in Argos's plan, but the man was impulsive. He didn't appear to think things through completely.

A heavy sigh from Argos managed to move both of their bodies up and down, like one being taking in a single breath. "I do not know, but it is the only chance I have."

She bit her lip, considering everything he had told her. There was still one thing she didn't understand. "Why are you so intent on getting revenge on Circe? Why don't you want to hurt Hestia as well? She's the one who cursed you."

Argos stared at her for a moment, as if the question didn't make sense. His voice was utterly calm when he answered, "I am not a fool; Hestia is a goddess. I could not kill her even if I wanted to. No man, mortal or immortal, could. But Circe is a demigoddess. Even the son of Zeus died when his body was drenched in poison. It won't be easy, but I intend to kill Circe."

"I guess I'll be coming with you," Claire mused, already doing a mental tally in her head of the repercussions.

Out of everything they had discussed, that was the thing that seemed to get a reaction out of Argos. He shifted, turning onto his side before Claire could even gather up her mental checklist of things to do. He pinned her down with a firm stare. "You will not."

"What?" She gawked, startled by the low growl of dominance that had been present in the three words. "Of course I'm going with you. What else am I supposed to do? I can't really go back to my home."

"You can stay here," Argos stated simply, waving a hand around the guest room.

"While you what? Go off on a quest for God knows how long?"

"Yes."

Finality filled the word and anger burned the pit of Claire's stomach. This was Argos, a man from a different time, a man who couldn't believe a woman could captain her own ship, or run her own business, or even help him.

Her lips flattened in annoyance and she tugged the blanket towards her, dragging the edges off his thighs and covering up her own skin. "And how exactly do you plan on finding a god without a ship? Without clothes?" Claire raised a knowing brow as she watched Argos open and close his mouth.

"Well, I…"

"Where my ship goes, I go." Claire gave the words the same finality Argos had given her seconds earlier. "I will not sit by and wait. I'm putting my restaurant, my dream, on hold because of this mess. I would like to see it through as fast as possible, and if you think I'm going to just sit by and wait for you to finish your business, then you are very wrong, buddy."

Despite the bite she tried to put in her words, Argos smiled. "It sounds to me like you have a plan of your own, Claire."

There was no argument, no rebuttal. Just a look that said he trusted her. She brushed off the pleasure that sizzled down her throat. Maybe he wasn't as barbaric as she'd thought. "I don't have much to offer, but we can use my boat and I'll buy some equipment. Then, together, we go find a god who'll give you a quick and easy quest."

He seemed to consider this, jaw squared and eyes intense as he stared at her, as if trying to determine the pros and cons. Claire worked to school her features. She was just as set as he was. It was either her plan or nothing.

"Poseidon would probably be our best chance. He is the easiest god to reach considering our location," Argos finally answered.

Claire nodded, remembering the name vaguely. "Right, and he is…"

"The god of the sea, also Hestia's brother."

"Oh." That piece of information caused her to pause. "Are you sure that's a good idea?"

"No," Argos answered with a sigh, "but it's the only one I have."

Claire's fingers continued to move nervously along his injuries as she pondered. Her knowledge about the Greeks was limited to the blur that was her high school years. She felt vulnerable, unable to make an educated guess about their next plan when she didn't know whom she was up against.

A finger touched under her chin, lifting it up. The touch was so gentle she was surprised to remember it was Argos doing it. "My promise to you has not changed, Claire. You do not need to accompany me on this journey to ensure that I pay you your reward."

"Pay me?" Claire nearly recoiled in offense before she remembered the claim Argos had made when they'd first met. Treasure. He'd said he would repay her in treasure. At the time, she hadn't believed him, but now…

Argos smiled at her. "Yes. I kept a hoard of treasure

from my adventures. Once I reunite with my brothers, I will be able to retrieve it. By now it should be enough for two restaurants, if you would like."

Now she didn't know what to think. Her mind raced in excitement at the thought. Two restaurants? How loaded was this guy?

She saw his offer for what it truly was—one last chance to back out. Argos was reassuring her that in the end she would get a reward that would be well worth putting her restaurant on hiatus. Because if she went with him, that was what would happen. There was no way to know for sure how long it would take for Argos to get his immortality back.

"I know," she breathed. "That means a lot, but I'm still going with you. I can't sit by and wait for you, Argos. I just can't. If I'm going to accept your treasure, I'm going to help you."

"Stubborn nymph," he mumbled to the ceiling, but there was no mistaking the quiet quirk of his lips.

X

SUNRISE WAS HER alarm clock. She was used to getting up with a fresh list of chores on her mind and her body already in motion to work. That was not the case the next morning, though. Claire blinked as sunlight assaulted her eyes. She'd slept an entire day away. That hadn't happened since... since... she didn't even know when. Maybe she had been working herself too hard the past couple days, and maybe the fear of Circe's Pets had left her more exhausted then she was willing to admit.

Getting out of bed turned out to be a chore in itself. The soft mattress and the warm comfort of another body made it a sanctuary Claire hadn't realized she'd been missing. A place where she could collapse after a day of hard work, next to someone who would listen to her worries.

Speaking of which, she took in the slumbering giant next to her, his hair tussled and mouth slightly ajar, making a picture only a model could emulate. She melted a little at the sight. It would be easy to just lie in bed until he woke up, see if he needed her help again and...

No, no, no. Don't think like that, Claire. There was no point in getting close to Argos. They were just two souls who were stuck together for the time being. After he regained his immortality, he was going to leave her. It would be best if she learned how to leave him first, starting with the bed.

As quietly as possible she crawled out from the covers, then, remembering the mayhem Argos had caused the last time she'd left him alone, she scribbled a quick note. Hopefully he could read her modern-day chicken scratch.

The clothes Laura had provided her turned out to be vacation clothes she'd left at the house summers ago. A pair of baggy sweats and a couple of tank tops. She clumsily stepped into them, then moved out of the room. The hallway lights were on and the smell of breakfast wafted up. Her stomach tightened at the thought of food.

The stairs creaked as she descended, alerting the house that someone was awake. Her chest squeezed knowing she would have to talk to Laura now. She was out of excuses, and after their conversation yesterday, something had felt off between them.

Laura was disappointed in her. Laura had never been disappointed in her. Ever.

She passed the open double doors of Kevin's library. A lamp gave a dull glow to the room, illuminating the man propped in his leather armchair, book in hand. He glanced up and smiled at her as she walked by. The fact that he wasn't seated at the table spoke volumes about what was coming.

Finally, Claire came to the kitchen. The space was still a hazard area, dishes cluttered on the counters and small mementos decorating every inch of available wall space. Kevin's books had been moved to the floor, replaced by plates of steaming breakfast. Her mouth watered at the sight.

Sitting at the head of the table, arms crossed and looking expectant, was Laura. She was still in her pajamas, a tank top that exposed a variety of old tattoos across her arms and her hair frizzed in a feminine impersonation of Albert Einstein. Laura gave her a small smile. "Claire, take a seat, sweetheart. We have a bit to talk about."

Claire winced at the tone. Laura had always treated her in a way even her own mother refused to. Like an adult. But now she was being lectured like a teenager who had been out past curfew. She had nothing to be ashamed of. She had saved a man's life, was still trying to save it. If Laura knew the truth...

She didn't, wouldn't. Claire refused to drag them into her mess.

Laura pushed a plate full of eggs and toast towards her seat. "This isn't like you."

"Which part?" Claire poked at her eggs. Nothing that had happened in the past couple days was like her. Putting herself in danger's path, ignoring her responsibilities, sleeping the day away, sleeping with a man she barely knew.

"Don't play cute with me," Laura huffed. "I mean, being with a man like that when you're so close to the opening date of the restaurant."

"I told you. I got carried away."

"You barely know each other."

That was one thing they couldn't hide. But Claire did know Laura, and because of that she let her frustration leak into her words. "Are you sure you should be lecturing me about this?"

Laura sighed, expecting the rebuttal. "Claire, I do know what it's like to find a man and fall for him deeply.

I know how tempting it is to fall into everything. It's fun. It's exhilarating."

Claire forced herself to tear her eyes away from the food and look at Laura. "And regrettable?"

That put a pause to the talk. Laura sighed, cupped her chin in her hands. "Not always. Sometimes it turns out for the best. But I needed someone to help me back then. I wouldn't listen to a darn thing anyone said unless they had big brown eyes." She touched a small ink spot on her wrist. Another tattoo, one of a mermaid.

"I didn't know what I wanted and Kevin did. He helped me navigate until I could make my own way. The difference is, you already know your path. You've been dead set on that restaurant since you were fifteen."

She was right, of course. Claire would never give up her dream for a man she'd just had a fling with. It wasn't logical, it wasn't her. But wasn't that what she was doing? The date was being pushed back so she could help Argos. She'd insisted on helping him. "I still am. Argos... he's going to help me."

It was the truth, and that made her feel marginally better.

Laura shook her head. "If you say so. I just don't want to see you make a decision you'll come to regret. If your father was here he'd give you the same talk. I feel it is my duty as his best friend to do so in his place."

Emotion stole the breath out of her lungs. "Thank you, Laura."

"You've made enough sacrifices, Claire."

Laura never pushed issues with her. She was more like a best friend than a mother figure. Which reminded her...

"Please, don't tell my mother about this. She won't take it nearly as well as you did."

The older woman tossed her head, indignant. "You act as if I know that woman's number."

She did, of course. In case of emergencies, which this might count as, but Claire didn't point that out.

❧

He woke up alone, again. Once it had been a fantasy of his, not to be disturbed or to have another's body pressed against his own for just one day. The reality of that dream now left him feeling cold and anxious. Claire was gone, run off to do something on her own again. He had promised to keep her safe, dammit, and he could not do that if he continued to sleep while she ventured off.

This thought alone propelled him out of bed. He nearly ran out of the room looking for her again, naked as the day he was born, but she had not appreciated that last time. A pair of soft pants and a shirt lay on a nearby chair, and he pulled them on before leaving the room.

The Kings' home was a strange building to him. The walls were covered in colorful ornaments and paintings. He glanced at them, noticing the mixture of subjects: ships, crustaceans, food, and men in uniform. A cluster of paintings hung at the end of the hall, uniformed men and women in dirty work clothes.

He recognized Kevin's face, which remained the same, his body in its prime dressed in a dark uniform. The young woman cheering next to him, curly hair flying in a gust of wind, could only be Laura. Argos stared at the realism of the artwork, unable to find a single brushstroke.

A moment captured in time. The wonders of the new world would never cease to amaze him.

Greedy eyes took in the other portraits, quickly finding the largest in the bunch. In it, the Kings were younger, posed easily near their boat. Next to them was a man and his young daughter. Her large eyes and impish smile told him instantly he was looking at Claire.

He smiled back at the picture, committing it to memory before descending the stairs.

A spring found itself in his steps on the bottom floor. He felt good—no, he felt great. The heat of the curse was absent and his body well rested. Like this, he could take on Circe's hunters and maybe the Sea Witch herself. The smell of food led him to the kitchen and he followed it, the soft sound of women's talk apparent the closer he got.

These were things that did not change, no matter what century he found himself in.

He did not hear the call of his name at first, but a fierce tug on his arm brought him to a stop. Argos whirled and found Kevin grasping his wrist. The older man gave a smile of apology and shrugged his shoulders. "Give the girls some privacy. I think they need to talk a few things out."

Argos could only nod as he stared at the hand that gripped his own. It was a firm grasp. He recognized immediately there was hidden strength behind it.

Kevin released him without another word and motioned for the hero to follow. They stepped into a nearby room, one covered wall to wall in thick books. The smell of paper and bound leather hung like perfume.

Without a word, Kevin sank into a worn chair, where he picked up a tome but did not read. "Argos, right? That's a strange name you got there."

"I'm from Greece," Argos explained. He'd heard the same thing from Claire. Maybe his name was strange, but he had been named after the mighty city of Argos, home to the hero, Perseus.

"A contractor from Greece, living here? Strange." Kevin shook his head before turning it down, dismissing him.

Strange. That word formed a lump of worry in Argos's throat. Claire had used it plenty of times to describe him. Which meant he had messed up again in this new world. It was true what he'd told Claire, that the advancements of men did not bother him much. Instead it was the little things that took much longer to understand. Cultural things. Like women who lived on their own or the sound of his name.

Being strange attracted attention. He needed to be more careful.

"What are you doing?" Argos could not keep the question locked away. He never met a man who enjoyed scripture so much.

"Researching. And if you don't mind, I'm at a particularly interesting page."

"Is there a reason?" he pried. "You've been researching something since the moment we met."

Kevin's eyes glanced at him over the edge of his glasses. "A reason? Well, I'm a professor. It is my job to constantly be learning and teaching those things to my students." He wiggled deeper into the chair, as if he had no intention of leaving it.

The chair looked comfortable, as did its twin sitting just a few feet away. Hesitantly Argos moved towards the furniture. The luxurious leather that covered it reminded him of the grand seats in his old prison. He sat down slowly.

It was difficult to squeeze his large form into the armchair, even more so to appear normal as he tried to get comfortable in the seat. After a few minutes of adjusting, he found a less awkward position.

"This is a good chair."

"They both are," Kevin agreed.

Argos turned to the man, surprised when their eyes met. He wanted to study the stranger, to puzzle out the type of man he was, and apparently Kevin had wanted to do the same. Another thing they had in common.

He started first. "I saw those portraits of you upstairs. You wore a uniform."

"Served twenty years in the Marines." Kevin shrugged. "Fought in Desert Storm and all that."

"Fought?" He tried searching for a modern term that would not put him out of place. "You're a soldier?" It must have worked, by the smile on Kevin's face.

Argos noticed the coin around his neck, held by a silver chain. It was larger than his own, different. Not blessed by the gods, but he recognized the similarities. Even without the blessing, there was no doubt Kevin was a man like himself.

"I do not mean to offend, but you do not look like it."

Kevin huffed in laughter. "You'd be surprised how much I get that. I don't have the soldier's body I did in my youth, and I've always been a bit of a bookworm. Not your typical jarhead."

"And now you teach?"

"Literature." Kevin thumped his book against his thigh. "Gotta make sure our boys get a well-rounded education. People scoff at the idea of a military man with a degree in literature, but these books tell stories about all types of heroes. It isn't always the bravest or strongest man who wins in the end. Sometimes it's the smartest."

Argos found himself smiling. He knew that better than anyone. The great heroes of Greece often excelled at out-thinking their opponents. "Like Perseus fighting Medusa or Odysseus against the Cyclopes."

Kevin beamed at him. "Exactly. Quick minds find the small holes in logic that others missed."

He found himself leaning forward. "Tell me more about these soldiers you teach."

Kevin smiled. "Oh, don't get me started. Laura says once I start, there's no stopping me."

That was hard to believe. Kevin had struck him as a quiet man, but now there was a fire lighting his eyes. Argos found he did not much care if his ears turned hot from a lecture. "I will not stop you."

❦

Argos was impressed. Kevin could indeed talk at length about numerous books. Even more impressive, Argos found he was not lost in the conversation. He had been alive during the rise of the Roman Empire, the invasions of the Northern Isles, and the exploration of the world. He knew the state of mankind during those times, the stories people held dear. When Kevin mentioned reading the work of Plato and Aristophanes, Argos felt as if he had found a sliver of solid ground for the first time. No longer were his thoughts considered strange; they were what Kevin deemed "insightful."

"Well, I'm glad to see the two of you getting along."

Argos lifted his head to the sight of Claire hugging the door frame, her face open with curiosity. Who knew how long she had been standing there staring at them, and he had not even noticed. How could he not notice, with her hair still ruffled from bed and an obscene amount of skin showing from her outfit? He knew he should not stare long, lest he encourage the curse to roar through him once more, but he dared not look away.

"Claire," Kevin greeted her with a smile, "you failed to mention yesterday that Argos is a history buff."

"Did I?" If Claire was surprised by her friend's new-found enthusiasm, she did not show it. "Well, breakfast is ready if you two want some."

"Of course. Kevin and I were just finishing up our talk about Homer's epic poetry. You remember, Claire, we talked briefly about it on the boat." Argos smiled at her innocently. Since talking to Kevin, an idea had formed in his mind, one he intended to unleash it upon his lovely companion.

Claire hesitated. "We did?"

"Yes, Achilles and Odysseus. I was explaining to you the stories behind those two." His smile broadened, he could not help it, and Kevin played an easy accomplice to the plan.

"You know, I teach those stories to my students. Every good sailor should read the story of Odysseus and I find it has just the right dose of adventure to keep young minds occupied. Plus, it's fascinating, simply fascinating, the history that we can find in those tales." Kevin adjusted his glasses in a way Argos identified as an excited tic.

"Ah, well. Argos mentioned them briefly to me, but I do not know them very well," she admitted, and he could tell it pained her to do so.

Kevin stopped fidgeting. "What? You don't? Well, that's

a shame. Luckily, I have several copies. Here's *The Odyssey*. You can use this one."

"Oh, Kevin, I don't know. I really don't have a lot of time to read and—"

"Claire," Argos interrupted, "I think reading that will help you more than you think."

He watched his words sink in. She had told him to try to fit in with her modern world, and he could, but she would need to educate herself on his. She had insisted on helping, after all.

Kevin placed the book into Claire's limp hands. She considered it, her mind working out Argos's meaning. When she did, her fingers curled around the thick pages in a death grip. Argos smiled at the sight.

XI

SHE COULD FEEL Argos's eyes roaming over the area. When Kevin had driven them downtown, he'd been remarkably quiet. Only she had noticed the rounding of his eyes when the car roared to life or how he pressed his face a little too close to the glass as the scenery zoomed by. Now, he seemed to acclimate to the robust world around him.

Their first stop was a clothing store. Cargo pants and a couple of tops for her, jeans and polos for him, plus shoes and a few other items had been acquired using Laura's credit card. Claire would have to dig into her savings to pay her back, but it was worth it.

Summers were a delightful time in Annapolis. People sat outside the many restaurants, digging into their fresh seafood. Excited parents of Naval Academy students proudly wore their newly bought T-shirts, and some of the most expensive boats on the East Coast created lines of pearly-white bows poking against the docks.

The main street was a hub for tourists, where there was

a small opening strictly for pedestrians to walk around. Strangers could get a close look at the boats anchored at the dock and stare out into the distance to see who floated by in the bay's waters.

On either side, old boathouses had been converted into hip pubs and cozy shops to appease sightseers. It had been a couple of years since her last visit to the town. A few stores had been swapped out since then. There was an ice cream shop that was new, and across the street there was a small comic bookstore she knew hadn't been there a few years ago.

They strolled around it all, heading towards Laura's restaurant for lunch. Claire was excited to see Argos's face when he walked into Laura's pride and joy, The King Crab. It was exactly what her own restaurant would look like once everything came together.

She studied Argos as he took in the area around them, head swiveling one way and then the other, eyes intense. He adapted quickly to the world around him, the people, the clothes, and the noise. In all respects, he appeared to be just another tourist in the crowd, but Claire would be lying if she said there wasn't something that made him stand apart from others. It wasn't his looks either; there was a confidence in the way he moved that she'd only seen a few men have.

Argos sucked in a deep intake of breath and breathed out. "It does not smell like the ocean," he commented, looking intently at the boats lined up in front of them.

"Technically, it's not." Claire shrugged. "We're pretty far from where the Chesapeake turns into the Atlantic. But we have some of the best seafood on the East Coast here. You'll see when Laura cooks for you."

"Kevin and Laura are not your family." It wasn't a

question. She'd forgotten to explain her exact connection to the Kings, but it seemed he had figured it out.

"*Like family.*" The words were emphasized with an unspoken amount of love. "Kevin was good friends with my dad. I would come and stay with them for a couple of weeks every summer. Laura taught me how to cook while Kevin and my dad taught me to sail."

The memories of those summer days warmed her in ways the summer heat couldn't. Mornings spent out on the water catching fish and learning the ways of the Bay. The evenings spent inside the Kings' restaurant, where Claire taste-tested everything and watched Laura manage her cooks with keen eyes.

Claire loved her mother dearly, but there was a disconnect between them that no amount of mother-daughter bonding time would ever mend. They disagreed on money, on success, on the number of times a person could fall in love.

For Darleen Winters, men and money made her entire life. Once she hadn't cared about those two things, back when her father had been alive. But his death had been a blow to both of them.

The chemo had sucked all the money they had. It had taken years for her mother to pick up the pieces of her life, and Claire had spent all that time with the Kings. Pawned off to them while her mother had tried to figure out what would fill the void. Darleen had tried to go back to school, moved into a new home, taken a self-enrichment trip to Europe where she'd met husband number two, Francis—and all that time Claire had been just as broken.

But for a thirteen-year-old girl, there were no trips abroad, no shopping to ease the pain. The only thing that worked was making tray after endless tray of cookies. Grieving cookies. Together, she, Laura, and Kevin had eaten them all that summer.

She looked towards Argos, taking in the solemn set of his mouth and the deep crease in his brows. It took a moment for her brain to figure out the expression on his face.

Understanding.

"I do not remember my family," he told her kindly. "My brothers are my family."

Brothers, he had called them, but not by blood. Of course he understood. A man who was immortal would have to cling to those who were like him, living eternally while watching his loved ones disappear with the passing of time.

Argos was trying to reach them, to rejoin his brothers before his body gave into mortality.

She couldn't imagine what he had been through. Watching his entire family die so long ago he had forgotten their faces, then spending centuries separated from the only people he cared for.

She leaned against him, offering comfort with the touch, and was rewarded when he echoed the movement. Where there had once been the constant presence of his bare skin, new cloth stood between them. A quiet longing for his touch burned in her lungs.

"I promise you, I'll help you find them." Argos stared at her, his mouth opened to whisper something in response, but Claire was already moving. Her lips grazed against his in a chaste kiss. She didn't know where the courage came from; maybe it was from finally feeling like she understood Argos a little better. And for the first time since finding him, the man who had held her so gently last night looked utterly and completely lost.

She didn't expect him to kiss her back. His response was virile as he groaned against her. A hand cupped her cheek, bringing their mouths closer together. Claire opened to the kiss in response, deepening as a spark rippled through her body. Memories of the night before flashed across her mind and, dear God, she was turned on!

She broke the kiss with that thought, fully aware of the way his body moved closer to her own. *His curse*, she reminded herself. She wasn't helping him. She was hurting him. "I'm sorry."

"Why are you sorry?"

"I shouldn't have… your…" She glanced down between them. Not that she was trying to sneak a peek. Argos's new pants did a better job of hiding his obvious problem, but it was still obvious.

The muscles of his face tightened as if he had just noticed the problem. "Right."

She touched his arm, drawing his attention. "Are you… er, feeling alright?"

He stepped back, just out of her reach. "I am fine."

No strings attached. She had told herself that the other day, and it had been fun—hell, it had been a lot of fun—but that wasn't what this was about. She'd grown to care for the man, enough that if he needed her help she'd be ready. And if he didn't, she'd respect that.

Really, it wouldn't hurt her pride at all.

"Claire…" He said her name in that same breathless tone he had used in their bed. The sound went straight to her core.

She knew exactly what he was asking her. Looking

around, she grabbed his hand and pulled him away from the tourist-littered area. Just two streets over, she found a quiet alley. She pulled them both out of the way and pressed his body against the wall. She could feel the swell of his cock press against her abdomen. His mouth sucked in a sharp intake that muffled into her hair. Time to throw caution to the wind.

"I've never done this before," she whispered.

"What do you wish to do, Claire?" His hot breath tickled her ear with the question.

She stepped closer, feeing bold. "Have sex in public." There, she'd said it. "And I think you do too."

His lips pulled into a smirk. "So, you are not as much as an innocent as I thought."

"Hey—" Her retort was cut off as he pressed his lips against hers. She melted into the touch, allowing him to turn them so her back was against the wall.

Electricity sparked through her as he tangled his fingers into her hair. It felt as if he didn't just need her; he *wanted* her. Claire opened her mouth and welcomed him into her space. Her hands wandered down, cupping the bulge there. Argos groaned.

"What were you saying about being fine?"

A few incoherent words fell from his lips and Claire smiled. Feeling his reaction made her lower region slick with want. She remembered the other night, the things he had done to her, things no man had done for months, and it made her chest tight from how much she liked it. But she shouldn't like it this much, right? This wasn't Argos's attraction to her; this was his curse.

That thought was a buzzkill. She pushed it away for now and concentrated on the task at hand.

Her fingers undid the button of his pants and pulled the zipper down. Argos thrust his hips forward, eagerly reintroducing her to his throbbing cock. Claire grabbed its velvety head and began to stroke.

A groan of pleasure tore from the man in front of her. She stroked again, cutting the next outcry with a kiss. "You'll have to be quiet; we don't want to get too much attention."

He replied by turning his head and letting his lips find hers again. Together their mouths muffled any noise. A hand hooked under her leg and lifted her off the ground with ease. Claire let out a squeak of surprise before Argos's lips returned hungrily to hers. He balanced her weight against the wall and nestled his cock between her thighs. Even fully clothed, the friction between their two bodies sent ripples of pleasure through her.

With a sigh she wrapped her legs around his torso and let him set the pace. It was brutal, and quick, but damn if she wasn't turned on by it all. She could come just from this.

Claire knew he was close. The cock in her hand was hot and Argos's thrusts were becoming more and more wild. Then he jerked, and a jet of warm liquid fell against her hand. Their lips separated, and Argos leaned his head against her shoulder. Slowly his grip eased her to the ground, where she stood on shaky legs.

"I do not know if I can ever thank you enough for everything."

Claire swallowed hard. "Don't mention it." Seriously, she wished he wouldn't. It was a stark reminder that there were conditions to their coupling.

She reached into the shopping bag where their borrowed clothes sat and used her sweatpants to clean them both up. It turned out spontaneous sex had its drawbacks;

who would have thought? But at least nothing had gotten on their newly purchased clothes.

Argos didn't take her cleaning in silence. He planted kisses along her collarbone, the scruff on his chin scratching delightfully against her skin. Then his hand moved down along the curve of her body, cupping her ass before his fingers worked on her pants. A gasp escaped Claire as she realized his intentions.

"Quiet" he mimicked, hot breath tickling her ear.

Argos turned his head, planting kisses on her other side while simultaneously checking to make sure they were still undiscovered. The thrill of it sent a jolt to the lips of her pussy. Then Argos stilled and suddenly it wasn't thrilling anymore. It was dangerous and stupid and obscene and—

"Is someone there?" Claire asked, pushing his hand away.

Argos didn't answer as he stepped back. She could see his face clearly now, awe forming against his mouth. He wasn't looking at the mouth of the alley, though. He was looking at the wall behind them.

There, painted along the wall of the building was a mural. Its paint had faded over the years, leaving parts nearly unrecognizable. She squinted, taking in the figure that took up the entire center of the wall. A man, nearly naked except for a thick cluster of grapes placed strategically to make the painting PG-13. Beside the figure were more grapes, fields of wheat, and bottles pouring red liquid.

Claire blinked before stepping back. She looked towards the building that shared the wall. A winery.

She hugged the wall again; Argos was still staring at the painting. "It's... um, nice. Isn't it?"

"It's the best thing I've seen since leaving the island," he admitted breathlessly.

Ouch. It wasn't like she was expecting the water or food she'd handed to him to be the best thing he'd ever seen. Or even her body, for that matter.

"The wall?" Disbelief hitched her voice high as she turned to give the painting another look. It looked like a normal mural. They weren't an everyday sight in Annapolis, but she'd seen tons of streets and shops with artwork decorating their exteriors in D.C. This was nothing different.

"It's not a wall," Argos said. "It's a temple."

❧

There was no mistaking it. He would recognize the symbols for the god of wine anywhere. Dionysus's face might have faded with time, but he knew the familiar curl of blond hair and the ever-present grape vine wrapped around his wrists. The building was marked by him.

Claire was not silent for long. Her voice was a hushed whisper. "How could this be a temple? It's just a wine store."

"Dionysus is the god of the wine. The people who own the store are probably his followers."

"He still has followers?" Claire could not keep the disbelief out of her voice.

Argos smirked. "The followers have always existed. As the years went on, new religions came about and pushed the old ways to the background. We were forced to turn our tributes into mundane things an Atheos would not look twice at but others of our cult would know." The painting was marked by the small white building drawn in the background, almost unnoticeable among all the colors that drew the eye.

Claire hesitantly touched the wall, her face slack.

"Okay, so there is a temple here. How do we get in? Is there a secret passageway or something?"

Argos smiled at her willingness to believe him. Her newfound trust was a precious gift he had finally won. "No, we'll use the front door."

"The what?" Claire's voice called after him as he twirled her towards the front entrance.

"A follower of the gods will know exactly how to help."

"Wait! We can't just barge in here and ask—"

He pulled her into the small winery. Argos grinned at their surroundings, taking in every charming aesthetic of Dionysus that decorated the tiny space. The walls were covered from ceiling to floor with wine bottles, grape vines, and olives dangled across the shelves, and a few small statues of various gods were laid out on display. It felt like home.

A few of the patrons looked up at their entrance. Claire pressed close to his side. The softness of her new blouse was silk against his skin and his hunger for her flared, making it difficult to focus on the mission at hand.

He stepped back, out of reach of Claire's touch, but she did not seem to notice. She was too busy inspecting the shop. "It doesn't look like a temple," she whispered.

"We're not in the temple yet. We need one of Diony-sus's followers to take us there." He remembered the first time he had visited the small temple in his home village. Iolcus had many temples for the gods, but one of the most sacred and important belonged to Poseidon. There had been a large stone statue in the middle, made by the best sculptor in the village. Being so close to the water, they had been reliant on the sea's ability to give them food and bring their men home from war. His mother and the other women had prayed hard and brought offerings when they could.

Of course, as the years had gone on, the world had changed and so had the temples.

Devoted servants had moved them to their households, hiding them from the new religions who wished to snuff out the old ways. In the end those people had won; the great temples of old were nothing more than ruins. Their statues and icons whisked away in war, the ground turned into nothing more than a place where people could visit and imagine history.

It had been years since he'd last stepped foot in a god's home. His gut clenched in anticipation of what was about to come.

Dionysus was, at least, one of the more level-headed gods. He probably would not even recognize Argos. Time was a drunken fog for the god of wine, which would work in their favor. Becoming immortal again might be an easier task than he had originally anticipated if he could convince the god of his virtue.

He spotted a woman standing near the far corner of the room, situated behind a counter as she bagged up a purchase and carried on polite conversation with a client. There was no mistaking her heritage from her dark hair and eyes, the elegant curve of her nose, and the long swan neck. In her youth, she must have been a true beauty; now she was a woman who had no time to worry about looks.

The way she cradled the bottle of wine in her hands, gently placing it in the bag with her fingers lingering on the label, exposed her as a follower of the wine god.

"We need to talk to her," he whispered to Claire, keeping his voice soft as if the woman were a horse, easy to startle.

Claire's head snapped away from the shelves of wine to look at him. "Her? Are you sure?"

"She will take us to the temple." There was not a doubt in his mind, but Claire did not seem to agree.

She glanced over at the woman, pulling her bottom lip between her teeth. Uncertainty clouded her eyes. "Argos," she started slowly, picking the words with special care. His name from her lips fully caught his attention. For once it was not being said as an exasperated sigh.

Her fingers clutched at the cloth of his new shirt; he could feel her thumb stroking the fabric nervously. "I don't want to crush your hopes or anything, but this is all happening really quickly. What if... what if this is a trap?"

His muscles stiffened at the word, as if they had realized their own careless mistake. She had a point. What were the odds of finding a temple in the middle of their hiding place? Circe would easily be able to predict his plan—it was the only one they had—but would she have found them so quickly?

His heart drummed with indecision. Only one thing he knew for sure. "I'll protect you. No matter what happens."

Claire turned her head up, blinking at him with wide eyes. Her face relaxed the slightest bit. "You don't even have a weapon."

"I do not need one," he promised.

The grip on his shirt slipped down to his hand and gave an eager squeeze. "You can do all the talking this time."

Argos took his cue, moving forward at a pace that betrayed his eagerness. The woman smiled politely at their approach, appreciation lighting her dark eyes. "Hello, do you two need help finding anything?"

"Indeed." With his free hand, Argos reached towards

the neckline of his shirt and fished out the coin. He leaned forward, close enough for the woman could get a good look. The gold was warm between his fingers as he flashed both sides. "We're looking for the temple of Dionysus."

Her face paled at the sight, body recoiling from the counter as if he had just shown her a weapon. Unmistakable fear sparked in her eyes before it disappeared, quickly replaced with narrow-eyed fury. "*You.*" She breathed the word in a quiet hiss.

Argos's confidence faltered as he watched the woman holler to another girl across the shop. "Helen, come manage the counter for me. You"—she pointed at Argos with an unwavering finger—"come with me." Then, loud enough so the rest of the shop could hear it, "I'll show you where the restrooms are, sir."

A young woman stepped up to the counter, sporting some of the same facial features as her mother. She had a small glistening jewel peeking out of the side of her Roman nose, and numerous jewels in her ears. Dark bangs hung over her kohl-framed eyes, eyes that were currently staring at him as if he had grown horns.

Her mother was quick to shoo her behind the register. "Don't look at him like that."

Argos could feel Claire's trepidation grow, and his own rose up to meet it. He had never been greeted so coldly before, not by a fellow worshiper of the gods and certainly not by a woman. He moved to follow her into the back room when the salesclerk's voice snapped at them, "She can stay here."

Argos frowned at her. She was working hard not to disrupt the atmosphere of normality for her other customers, but he would ruin it if Claire would not be allowed to follow. If this was a trap, he would rather have her close than in another room unprotected.

Claire seemed to agree. In a loud voice she announced, "I need to use the restroom as well." Her apologetic smile was flawlessly real, but her thumb began to rub nervous patterns along his wrist.

The store clerk stared at them for a moment, considering her options. "Fine, follow me."

Claire sighed in relief before flashing him a reassuring smile. They followed her into another room. It was well lit and full of stacked crates of wine. The harpy led them away from the door, into the back, before she reeled around and let her anger hit with full force. "How dare you come into my store? I was promised none of your kind would ever step foot in here again."

"You are confused, woman—" Argos started, sure that a mistake had been made.

She cut him off with words that were swift and fierce. "Thalia. My name is Thalia, and I am not confused. If you think I will let you come in here and boss me around again, you have another think coming, brother of Achilles."

"Again?" Claire repeated. "Do you know him?"

Thalia snorted. "Not him, but I know your brothers very well. We had an agreement. So you can be on your way."

"We are here to speak to Dionysus," Argos answered, feeling his patience dissolving, "that is all."

Thalia's arms crossed over her broad chest, emphasizing her message as she declared, "We are no longer a temple for Dionysus. You can thank your brothers for that."

The words rolled over him like water, hitting with a cold splash that iced his very core. Argos glared at her, no longer amused. "You're lying."

"I wish," Thalia seethed, her anger suddenly justified. She no longer looked at him. Instead, her attention was drawn to Claire, a mere bystander in their angry face-off. "Happened nearly twenty years ago. Men came in here flashing their coins, seeking a place to stay for the night. We've always welcomed the Order of Olympus into our home with wine, food, comfortable beds. Ever since my great-grandparents set up this shop. There were at least fifteen of them. I was just a girl back then. I assumed they were on a grand quest."

Her words grew heavy with grief at the memory. "But that night, with wine and food in their stomachs, they changed, started acting up, talking blasphemy. Their strength and the wine made them arrogant. They destroyed the temple."

Argos felt his mouth go dry; his tongue felt like stone. His brothers were the most virtuous men in the world; they would never speak ill of the gods. Not unless they'd been wronged, but even then, destroying a god's temple was sacrilege. An act meant for barbarians and invaders. Doubt weakened his protest. "They would not..."

"They did," Thalia shot back. "I know your kind, hero. You won't believe me unless you see it for yourself." Her head tilted up. The fear that had been present earlier was gone, replaced with an air of defiance. "I will show you what's left of Dionysus's temple, but know that no matter how much you beg for them, no gods will come here."

XII

CLAIRE HAD IMAGINED something grand, a hidden passageway or even a staircase under a floorboard, but no. In the back of the shop was a plain door tucked behind crates of wine.

A single piece of aged wood was nailed into the edges of the door. Argos easily dismantled it and Thalia led the way down the stairs. Descending into the darkness was like stepping back in time. Their feet hit slabs of stone that looked ancient and out of place. There were no lights. The only sound around them was the echo of their footsteps. Squinting against the darkness, she steadied her hand against Argos's back to steer their direction.

It still wasn't clear if they could trust Thalia. The woman clearly had a dislike for Argos and motivation to work with Circe. Claire tensed at the thought, preparing herself for any sudden movement in the dark.

The stairs led deeper than expected, deeper than a normal basement. A dampness clung to the air along with a sudden chill that threatened to make Claire shiver. When she felt a shift in Argos's height, she knew they had arrived. A light flicked on. Her eyes blinked quickly, taking in the dingy room they had walked into.

Stone covered the floors, and two long tables were pushed out of the way against the cement walls. One was broken, messily split down the middle with debris scattered by its wooden legs. Thalia frowned at the mess. "This is where the heroes stayed. There used to be beds set along the walls but we… threw them out."

There was a slight pause in her words that caught Claire's attention. She looked over to Thalia. A woman who had worn her emotions like a black cape now let the shadows fall across her face. Her arms wrapped around her chest, mouth set in a grim line.

"It's been a while since anyone has been down here. Wouldn't be surprised if the lighting cuts out on us. Follow me." Thalia walked under an arched doorway into the next room.

A monstrous cave opened before them and Claire gaped in awe. The ceiling arched up, reminding her of the inside of a church. More foreboding stone, but where the archway met the wall, a trim line of elegant shapes were cut into the hard surface. When she finally tore her gaze away from the vaulted rooftop, the other items of the temple caught her attention. Ceramic vases lay in pieces on the floor, next to the broken remains of their marble stands.

Claire bent down to touch the broken bits. Their edges were jagged and sharp as glass. It was impossible to make out the black-painted figures on the pieces.

"My ancestors collected those over hundreds of years before bringing them here."

"Did the heroes do this?" A mixture of both surprise and horror clung to her words.

Dark eyes narrowed on her as Thalia bristled. "Most of the damage, yes."

"Who did the rest?" Argos's gaze settled on her with accusation, but the store owner lifted her narrow chin and scoffed.

"My father took it very hard when the gods decided to abandon us."

"Why didn't you clean up this place after they left?" Claire asked, looking up to where Thalia stood in front of a statue that had met the same fate as everything else in the room. The finely carved man was now mutilated, missing an arm and its head.

Thalia frowned. "We tried. It did nothing. Dionysus never graced this temple after the heroes left. His absence left our shop in ruin; we lost all of our money, all of our customers. We prayed and prayed but he never returned. My father added to the damage in his grief."

An echo of rumbling rocks pierced the stone temple. Claire turned to the noise to see Argos picking up the head from a fallen statue. The nose and mouth had caved in from the fall.

"I do not understand," Argos said, speaking up for the first time since they had walked into the room. "Why would they do this?" He stood near another statue of the wine god, this one miraculously intact.

Thalia's face crumpled with anger again. "I was wondering if you could tell me that."

Even with the distance between them, Claire could see Argos's jaw clench. He'd been so quiet, she hadn't noticed how his own anger slowly filled the space. It rolled over his body and seeped into his muscles. His silence suddenly felt heavier than the stones they were surrounded by.

His voice was nearly a growl when he demanded, "Names. Tell me the names of the men who did this. I will see to it myself that they will pay for not respecting the gods."

Claire felt the breath leave her lungs at his words. "Argos." She stepped towards him, no longer caring about the shards that crunched under her shoes. "You don't have time to hunt these guys down. We need to get your immortality back, remember?"

She didn't want to mention Circe or the creatures chasing after them, not in front of Thalia. The woman already seemed to have enough reason to hate them, and if they brought more trouble to her door, that wouldn't change.

But Argos didn't waver. "I know the names of every man who wears this coin. If you tell me who did this, I will see them punished."

The hardness that had settled across Thalia's face since the moment they had spoken to her eased. "It was a long time ago, but I remember one name."

"Tell me."

"Xanthus."

❦

Argos felt himself recoil. It could not be. "What did he look like?"

He held on to the hope that it was not the same man. It could easily be someone using Xanthus's good name to stir up trouble. But Thalia did not even hesitate before giving her description. "About your height, bald. He wore the same coin around his neck as the rest of you, right next to a jagged scar."

They all had their scars, markings from their mortal years before joining the Order. Xanthus's had been one of the most gruesome Argos had seen in his lifetime. A token of his quest from Ares, the god of war. Go to the underworld and steal a feather from one of the Erinyes. It had been a grisly task, one that Argos and Barcus had insisted accompanying him on.

The Erinyes were known to have their own sense of judgment when it came to unjust crimes and war. They were tormentors of those criminals in the afterlife.

Few men had ever stepped foot in the underworld; fewer men had seen one of the Erinyes and lived to tell the tale. Xanthus had barely survived. The Erinyes's whip had nearly cut his body in half; instead, it had left a scar of torn flesh from cheek to naval. Ares had not healed the scar and had forced Xanthus to carry it for the rest of immortality.

Argos brushed away the memory. There was no mistaking the man whom Thalia spoke about.

Thalia took in his silence with pursed lips. "You know him, don't you?"

It was not a question, more an accusation. Argos closed his eyes. "I do."

"Of course. He is your precious *brother*. Will you still make him pay for what he has done? Will you hunt him down?" Her words were mocking.

When he'd agreed to receive his coin, he had agreed to protect the people. He remembered the past well—when armies would raid lands, burn crops, take women, slaughter children. When monsters would eat entire villages, flaying the villagers alive for their own amusement, torturing warriors returning from war.

The world had been a much different place back then. It had been in desperate need of men who could stand up and fight. As the years had worn on, though, he had watched it change before his very eyes. Everything around him became less chaotic. Centuries later, the chaos had become stability; at least that was the world Claire had described. Argos could only assume that without something to fight, his brothers had turned to prey on the very people they had sworn to protect.

Thalia was still waiting for his answer, her shoulders taut in his silence.

"Once I regain my immortality and join my brothers, I will find Xanthus."

Thalia's dark brows pulled together. Surprise flashed across her face. "Regain … what do you mean? You are a hero, are you not?" A slender finger pointed at his coin.

Argos reached up and twirled the coin back and forth. The metal was still cold under his touch, unresponsive. "I was," he told her. "Like this temple, I lost favor with the gods five centuries ago. I came here hoping Dionysus would help me."

He remembered fondly the look of utter disbelief that Claire had worn when he'd first told her his story. How adamant she had been about lying to the Kings, knowing they would never believe the truth.

When the woman in front of him barely blinked at the tale, a wave of relief crashed against his chest. Thalia was not like Claire. She was a daughter of the devoted, and she had grown up knowing the gods' power and temperament. She took the news with a respectable amount of surprise. Even for her, a hero losing favor with the gods was unheard of.

"Which deity took away your favor?" she asked, her tone lacking its earlier hostility.

"Hestia." The admission hurt as he remembered his own arrogance all over.

Thalia snorted. "Sometimes the goddesses are crueler than their brothers. Men often overlook the power of women; you wouldn't be the first to be cursed by their love."

Circe's face appeared in his mind before Claire spoke up, chasing it back to the shadows. "Maybe this will sound a little naïve, but why didn't the gods do the same to Xanthus... you know, take away his favor?"

Argos paused. Why indeed? His slight against Hestia was nothing compared to a man wrecking a god's temple. "Maybe after that incident they did."

Thalia's lips thinned into a straight line. "If they did, it hasn't made a difference. Two years ago, a family devoted to Apollo was slaughtered in their homes. Their temple was left in shambles. Since then more people have abandoned the old ways."

Argos's attention sharpened at this. "And the gods have done nothing?"

"The gods always do nothing," she snapped. "In all the years of my father's devotion, I never saw their miracles. He said they helped our business, yet here I am succeeding where he failed. I separated myself from that life long ago and never looked back."

Dread crept up his throat. The situation suddenly grew much more complicated. He could not imagine the gods taking such an insult so lightly. Usually the Order would clean up such a mess for them, but if his brothers had betrayed the deities, then Argos could not rely on them for help.

One sliver of hope still remained. "When Xanthus was here, did you meet or hear of anyone named Barcus?"

Thalia considered the question; her head gave a faint nod. "I remember hearing that name. I don't know who he is to you, but Xanthus had nothing kind to say about him."

That was good news at least. If Xanthus had turned his back on his brothers, then at least it sounded like Barcus had not joined him. Perhaps the other heroes were still out there after all.

"You think he'll be able to help?" Claire asked, her voice edged in caution.

"Perhaps, but I will not be able to do anything until we find a god who is willing. This may work in our favor," Argos realized. "If they are desperate to stop Xanthus, then they might give me a menial quest. Something that can be completed in a day."

"Is there another temple close by?" Claire sounded hopeful, even adding an edge of a plea to the question.

The older woman rolled her eyes. "Like I said, the number of temples has drastically declined. There used to be some, but I think they've all been abandoned. Your best bet is the sea—go and ask Poseidon to help you."

Argos felt himself deflate. "I did," he said, remembering the heat of the sun and the hollow starvation he had felt after escaping Circe's island. "He did not help me when I called upon him at sea. I was left for dead."

One of Thalia's dark brows rose in interest. "You don't say? Did your offering offend him?"

Argos blinked, repeating. "Offering?"

Thalia snorted, actually snorted. Her attention turned

to Claire. "Men. It's always the ones who are favored by the goddesses that rarely have to give any true offering. They forget that dealing with the gods means sacrifice."

He gave her a hard look. "Hestia never required me to give her an offering."

Thalia laughed. "Not that you realized. I'm sure you showered her in gifts to show your devotion. I'm suryou shifted time from family and friends for her. Gave her your heart, maybe?"

The words were like a sword to the gut. He was guilty of it all, had given them freely to the goddess, thinking of them as acts of love, not an offering. That word insinuated that he gave her those things in an exchange. A flash of heat raced down his belly, stirring his sleeping curse. Everything he had done for Hestia had been given freely, but now bitterness seeped into his veins.

It had all been for nothing.

"This is good news, I think," Claire said, dragging him out of his downward spiral. She gave him a look of encouragement and stepped up to squeeze his wrists. "You didn't know why Poseidon wouldn't help you, and now we know the answer. We just have to give him something." She turned to Thalia. "What kind of things does one offer to a god?"

"In the old days, our ancestors would have held banquets. They'd cut the throat of a goat or chicken and offer wine," Thalia answered.

Claire hummed under her breath; a gleam lit in her bright eyes. "We don't really have any farm animals to slaughter, but I think I can manage a banquet."

XIII

"I WOULD LIKE TO talk to the girl alone."

Claire's head snapped up at the words. They were back in the storeroom, which was a relief from the dreary underground temple. Thalia stared at her expectantly, arms crossed but face soft.

Argos paused, suspicion visible in his clenched jaw. "For what reason?"

"I just want to talk to her," Thalia said sternly. She was a woman who had learned not to bend over backwards for any man. Claire respected that; she knew no harm would come from a conversation. Gently she pressed her hand on Argos's broad shoulder and pushed him towards the door.

She smiled. "It's just a talk, and you'll be right outside the door. Don't worry. If Thalia meant to harm us, she had plenty of chances to do so." She didn't need to separate Claire from Argos to strike.

Argos reached the same conclusion, but his voice was low with threat as he told Thalia, "I'll be right outside."

"We'll see you soon." Thalia wiggled her fingers at him, waving the hero off.

It was strange when he was gone. Since the moment she had pulled him from the rowboat, Claire had only spent a few moments without him by her side. God, that was only a few days ago. Her body fidgeted, fingers clenching nervously at her sides as she turned to Thalia.

The woman was still staring at the door where Argos disappeared, even as she started speaking. "Feeling nervous without your man by your side?"

"He's not exactly my man."

Thalia's head tilted. "Then what are you to him, girl?"

She shrugged her shoulders. "I'm all he has right now, until he can regain his immortality."

"Foolish," Thalia said. Her next words came out slow, each one meant to hit a mark and send a message. "Do not let yourself be a victim to his quests. Men like him have tasted power and they are sick with it. They are not gods but believe their abilities make them equal to one. They are strong, immortal. They've seen things we can only dream about, and they consider women like us nothing more than pawns. He will break you."

If the words had been a knife, they would have slid in past the ribs just close enough to graze her heart. She could see the dark place in Thalia's eyes where the words were coming from, felt the knife twist at the sight.

Claire had thought no harm could come from a simple conversation. She had been wrong.

"I'm sorry if that's what happened to you."

She expected a flash of anger or another dismissive grunt, but instead Thalia closed her eyes. Lush lips parted for a quiet breath that had difficulty leaving her body. The moment hung between them for what felt like an eternity before she finally opened her eyes again and shook it off.

Without her anger, Thalia looked tired. "Claire, was it?" she asked. Claire nodded, watching carefully as Thalia looked around the vast storage room. "You were an Atheos?"

"A what?" Claire frowned; she'd heard Argos use the same word before but had never questioned it.

"It means 'without gods.' The word evolved into the modern-day atheist, but to us who know the existence of the gods, you are all the same."

She'd never really thought about her beliefs in the great unknown. She had thought there was a God, a heaven. Believed and prayed hard when she was young that her father had gone somewhere nice. But meeting Argos had changed everything.

Thalia hadn't said she was an Atheos, though. She'd said *were*. Past tense. It was hard to plead innocence when she'd just promised to make an entire meal for a god. Even after this whole thing was over, when Argos left, she wouldn't be able to go back to her normal life. She'd seen things that skewed her entire worldview.

Nodding, she answered, "I guess I was."

"This world is not kind to weak women, Claire. You will need to be strong if you want to be by his side." Before Claire could reply, Thalia moved towards the back of the room, where boxes had piled high. She bent low, her movements deliberate as she moved one box and then another before pulling out a long object, encased in a brown leather sheath. In one tug, metal peeked out from the leather, its gleam caught in the storage light.

"Oh my God. Is that a sword?" Claire's surprise overrode any sense of panic. It wasn't a reaction she was proud of, but then again, she'd seen things the past couple days. Maybe she was becoming desensitized to it all.

Thalia watched her reaction closely. In a graceful movement the sword twirled in the shop owner's hand, until the blunt handle was extended out in offering. "Take it. You never know when you'll need it."

It was a touching gesture, leaving Claire nearly breathless. "Thank you, but I'll have to pass. I-I don't know how to use a sword, and I have my own weapon." She reached into her new pants and pulled out the same pocketknife that had once never left *Sebastian's* hull.

After the incident with the Pets, she had decided never to be caught without a weapon again. It probably wasn't as practical as Thalia's intimidating sword that could easily cut off a few fingers and toes, but the pocketknife fit her personality. It didn't look threatening, but it would do the proper job of harming any enemy that threatened her.

She flicked it open to show at least some skill with the weapon and watched as a genuine smile crossed Thalia's lips. "Well, it looks like my warning wasn't needed."

It wasn't, but that didn't make the warning any less meaningful. Claire returned the smile, feeling the thin existence of a bond forming between them. They were both survivors, both humans in a world that was much larger than them.

A sudden cry from the store interrupted the moment. Claire jumped, realizing it was Argos.

Thalia was already moving towards the door, her movements quick and deliberate. The sword was still gripped in her hand as she called out, "Helen!"

Claire followed behind, her pocketknife out and ready

to strike whatever they might find on the other side of the door.

The shop was completely empty, door left ajar. Claire's eyes took in the red that stained the countertop. *Blood!* But none of Circe's Pets were in sight.

Argos stood, pushed up against the wall by Thalia's young daughter. A broken piece of a wine bottle jabbed dangerously close to his thick neck. And with that, Claire realized what the red stain really was, and that the threat was not as immediate as they had thought.

Beside her, Thalia clicked her tongue and demanded, "Helen, move away from that man."

The warrior seemed unfazed by the situation, keen eyes taking in the girl with respect. Helen, however, looked mortified at her mother's return. "He came back alone. I thought—"

"I'm fine," Thalia said curtly.

Helen's eyes rolled with the exaggeration only a teenager could muster. "Clearly, but a heads-up would have been nice. I chased out two customers just so I could jump this guy."

"And how did you do that?" Amusement tinged the mother's voice.

Pink lips pursed into a pout as Helen stepped away, putting space between herself and Argos. She waved the broken bottle in the air as if it explained the entire story. "I improvised."

"You'll clean all this up after they leave," Thalia said.

Helen deflated. "That's the thanks I get for protecting your honor?"

"I am very capable of protecting my own honor, thank you."

Featherlight touches danced up Claire's arm. She turned to find Argos looking her over with narrowed eyes. "You're okay?"

She gave him a pointed look. "Are you? I thought those creatures had found us."

His lips twitched up. "And were you going to scare them away with your little knife?"

"It's a pocketknife!" Her outcry didn't make it sound any better. "How am I supposed to feel safe when a teenager got the best of you?"

"She's fast," Argos answered, the amusement leaving his voice for a moment as he spared Helen a look. She was leaning against the counter, sizing them up while Thalia scolded her.

It took a special kind of girl to beat Argos in speed. Claire had seen the man take on three large cats with his bare hands and live. Then again, considering who her mother was, it wasn't surprising the amount of fight Helen had in her, and her father...

Claire froze over that word. She took in the girl's appearance once again. Before she had mistaken the girl as a teenager, but she carried herself with a confidence that only came with age.

Thalia did say Xanthus had visited nearly twenty years ago.

"You're lucky he lost his immortal strength," Thalia continued to chide. "That man was one of the gods' chosen. You need to think before you act next time."

Helen's eyes widened. The broken piece of glass in her hand slipped a fraction before her quick reflexes caught it. "A hero?" She turned to Argos. "You're a hero? Like a real *live* hero."

"Helen," her mother growled, cutting off the young girl's gabbing.

Helen gave a low wolf whistle. "If all heroes look like him, then I'm in trouble."

Thalia moved forward, her actions just as fast and purposeful as her daughter's. Before Claire knew what was happening, she hit the girl upside the back of the head so hard the noise had an echo. Even Argos winced in sympathy. But Helen was quick to recover, giving her mother a stern death glare as she whined, "What was that for?"

"I raised you better than to ogle our customers."

"Customers?" Claire asked.

Thalia snorted as she turned to the wine on display behind the counter. Bottles that had collected the faintest trace of dust from years of waiting. "These are the drinks favored by the gods. At least that is what my father told me. We left them out every time we made an offering. You may have one."

"Oh no, we couldn't accept anything else. You've been too kind."

"This isn't kindness," Thalia snapped. "This is an investment. I'm counting on you two to fulfill your end of the bargain. I can't guarantee it will work as an offering, but it will help in appeasing them." A ghost of a smile appeared briefly. "Fail and you'll have to pay me back."

Claire nodded respectfully. With the wine in hand, her mind was already compiling lists of food that she could whip up. The bottle was a beautiful red, with the logo of a woman draped across a couch, wrapped in silken finery. A decorative grape vine rested on her head like a crown. Now they had a place to begin. They could finally get to work at getting Argos's immortality back. She turned, expecting to see his usual bright grin.

But Argos wasn't staring at the bottle. Instead his gaze was occupied by the sword in Thalia's hand.

———

"That sword..." Argos could not finish the sentence. His throat constricted at the sight of the old metal. It was a basic short sword with a handle shaped like a temple column. A xiphos sword, unmistakably Greek. But more than that, it was Xanthus's sword.

A stab of pain slipped past his heart, as if Thalia had pushed the blade into him. He could not help but remember his own weapon. A blade with a golden grip and his name carved into it. He could picture it gleaming in the sun, splattered with his own blood as he desperately tried to hold on to the weapon before Circe's men managed to pry it away. The sound it had made when it had hit the ocean's surface before it had sunk to the bottom still echoed in his ears.

"How do you have that?" His mind could not wrap itself around the sight of the sword without its master.

Helen's attention snapped to the weapon in her mother's hand. Surprise hitched in her voice as she exclaimed, "Mom! How dare you have such a cool sword and not even tell your only daughter?"

Helen reached out for the weapon, but Thalia held it out of reach, ignoring her daughter's plea. "This isn't for you. It's for him."

"What?" Helen yelped at the same time Argos breathed the word.

Thalia looked at her daughter, her gaze open and honest. "The man who destroyed my home left it here, and when he left, he looked … satisfied. As if nothing could stop him. He didn't need it to bring my father to his knees. He threw this on the ground along with his coin. His final defiant act against your Order. I never wanted to forget the helplessness and anger I felt that day, but those are not memories I wish to pass down to my daughter." The joking smile on Helen's lips disappeared at her mother's words.

Defiant. The word rang out in his mind, trying to remind him that Xanthus was not the man he had once known. He reached out, palm open and expectant. Thalia stared at him, apprehension in her eyes. She might have accepted his bargain, she might even help them, but she still hated what he represented.

He was a hero, a dangerous man, and with a sword in his hand he would become more so, but his promise still hung between them.

Finally, she handed it over.

The moment his fingers curled around the handle, something eased inside of him. He had always loved the feel of a sword in his hand more than the spear. Like himself, the sword had adapted well to the changes of war as the centuries carried on.

The weight of the sword came as a small surprise. It threw off his balance, but only slightly. He could learn to use it again. He gave it an experimental swing, testing the weight with a few old forgotten moves. With each stroke it became easier and easier to hold. A laugh exploded from him as he slashed through the air, feeling like a young man again. Feeling immortal.

"Careful, hero, you break anything in here you buy it." Thalia frowned.

"We'll have to wrap that up. You can't go walking

around this town with a sword in your hand," Claire said, but she was smiling at him in a way that nearly made Argos drop his new weapon.

Thalia turned to him, her eyes returning to their hard and cautious stare. "What is it?"

"I have one last question."

Her face broke as she shook her head and laughed. "Of course you do. You seem to be full of them."

"You are the only one I've met who's had any answers," he said. "I'd like to know why you kept his sword. You could have just left it in the temple. Let time and dust overcome it, but instead you held on. But this blade has been cared for. I thought you hated Xanthus."

Her eyes flared at the name. Even Helen looked away at the mention of the old hero. The name was a curse that would hang over the family for generations, it seemed.

Thalia tossed her head defiantly. "I hate that man, I always will. After he desecrated our temple, I took that sword—his sword—and I was prepared to get my revenge. I wanted to hurt him the way he hurt my family, I wanted to kill him with the things he discarded so easily. But... circumstances kept me from accomplishing that dream. It's been years now. I've grown older—I have a family now..." Her voice trailed off before she realized she had said too much. With a shake of her head she regained the same determination that had made her hold on to the sword for two decades.

"You promised me you'd kill him," she said finally. "I want you to kill him with that."

XIV

THE ISLAND ALWAYS called them home. Its pull was as sweet as a siren's song, and the moment his feet hit the soft sands, Etros had always felt a sense of relief.

This time he felt no comfort coming home. Dread seeped to the bottom of his stomach, a heavy anchor dragging across the ocean floor. Circe found failure unattractive, and their latest failure would place him and his men at the mercy of her power. It had been a long time since he'd faced his mistress's ire. The favoritism had been evaporating for years, but he feared this might be the final straw.

What would she do to them when he reported? The very thought brought a shudder to his lean body.

The only flicker of light came from the end of the hall, the lounge room, where Circe was waiting. An odor of cooked meat filtered back towards them, causing the shifter to frown. The dread grew to outright terror as he realized Circe was holding a feast. A feast for an immortal who never needed to sleep nor eat.

He looked back to his companions. Their bruises had healed the moment they'd stepped back onto their goddess' island. Still, their solemn faces told the story of their defeat. Etros squared his thin shoulders and pressed on, stepping into the grand room far too quick for his liking.

A long banquet table filled the length of the hall. Fruits of every color under the sun covered the golden surface. Silver chalices were filled to the brim with fragrant wine, and perfectly baked bread was cut into thin slices. It was beautiful, reminding Etros of days when he had visited festivals with similar spreads. The memories were dull but there; the constant prattle of talking women and laughing children, prayers murmured to the gods, and a touch of soft hands that warmed his skin.

But that was long ago. Before he'd dedicated his life to Circe. His goddess.

She sat at the head of the table, draped on a plush pillow as if she herself were a part of the feast. Etros's mouth watered at the sight of her.

Her black hair glistened like water over her bare shoulders. She wore no cloth, for the island was her domain. Etros could perfectly see her large breasts and their pert brown nipples.

Despite his fear of whatever news she might unleash on them, his cock stirred. He wanted to take her, lay her out and lick at her skin. It was the only hunger he ever felt anymore. The olive skin that shimmered as if it had been bathed in oil, and the glistening eyes that were half-lidded in a way that made his groin ache. It was a look similar to the one she always gave her bedmates. One that said she would do the devouring.

"Welcome back, Pets." Circe's voice rang with false cheer.

"Circe." Etros spoke, trying not to let his fear seep into the word. His eyes did not move from cooked pig on the table.

Circe's eyes followed his and she smiled. One delicate hand reached out, pulled a chunk of meat off and popped it in her mouth. "Argos is not with you?" Just like that the purr lost its warmth. Her eyes were no longer sexy, but cold and dismissive as she chewed.

"He escaped, my lady. A woman aided him." The second bit of information was added in to distract her from his own failure. It worked. He saw the subtle shift in her body, the way she repositioned herself as if the mere mention of another woman brought on competition.

"A woman," she said coldly. "A mortal woman and my Pets could not kill her?"

"The warrior protected her," Etros continued, knowing it would only anger his mistress more. His only hope was that the anger would be focused on something besides himself. Quickly, he glanced at the cooked pig on the table. "I think he cares about her."

A quiet noise filled the room that took him a moment to place. It reminded Etros of his cat claws tapping against the stone floor. He realized Circe's nails were drumming against the table, leaving deep indents with every click. On her face a surprised "oh" formed around her lips and she raised a glass of wine. "I think I would like to meet this woman. When you get Argos, bring her as well."

Relief flooded through him like a drug. "Of course. We'll go out and continue our search at once."

"Please do so. Take all the Pets you require. I'm sure

they will be eager for the hunt. But maybe you need more assistance, Etros..." Her voice trailed off as if bored. Even from across the room, Etros could see the light of magic flickering across her eyes. His body reacted, breaking out into a cold sweat of fear when he realized she was staring at him.

And then her eyes slid to the two men standing at his left. He only heard a sharp intake of breath from Aratos before the man transformed into a panther. The large cat's hackles stood up and its face contorted in an aggressive hiss. Across the hall Circe's amusement trickled out with an airy laugh. It struck Etros then that his comrade had not transformed into his beast form of his free will, but by the power Circe commanded, and then the panther began to shrink, its fur falling off in chunks as it changed into a sniffling pig. The animal's squeal of fear was sharp glass against his eardrums.

A moment later, the second man transformed, but what stood next to Etros was not the usual sleek cheetah. Next to him was a monster. The noises coming from it sounded pained, and the eyes—*were those eyes?*—seemed to be wide in horror. He stepped back, wary to give the new creature space as it thrashed. A feeling of horror that he had not felt in years sank into his stomach.

⁂

Walking into The King Crab felt like coming home.

Located right off the bay, The King was packed with old locals, young academy cadets, and tourists stopping by for the best crab in the area. *Everything has a soul*—that's what her father had believed. Chefs poured theirs into food, and the food filled the building with it. The historical restaurants in Annapolis, the seafood and crab shacks off the Bay, they had soul. Years and years of soul—and that was what Claire loved about them.

The building was alive with the hum of conversation and the occasional shouts of those watching a summer baseball game. Every time she saw the large sign of a crab wearing a lopsided crown, a smile crept across her face.

They'd managed to beat the lunch rush, Claire noted as she watched a line form around the hostess. Relief sank into her limbs. Laura would have found them a seat somewhere if the place was full, but their table was perfect for the task at hand.

"Alright," she sighed, pointing at the wooden wall where an oar hung on display next to a map of the Chesapeake. "This is where we're at. It's a full day's travel by boat before we reach the mouth where the Bay meets the Atlantic."

Argos nodded, stuffing a piece of bread in his mouth. His face softened in delight at he chewed and swallowed. "And *Sebastian* can get us there?"

"Of course he can." Claire hoped she looked unmoved by the question, but worry nudged at her mind. *Sebastian* was an old boat, and maintenance was expensive. She'd been lax in an effort to save money, and she only took him on short trips when she had a few hours off, but after battling a storm and being clawed she had to wonder if the boat was up for the trip. Getting out to sea, contacting a god, doing a quest, finding a sea witch, and getting back home would take… a lot of time and money.

Her heart sank as she realized the grand opening of The Saucy Leg was farther away than she thought. Already her mind was trying to calculate how much time she could afford to lose before she hit financial rock bottom. The promise of Argos's reward sizzled at the back of her mind, but she wouldn't see any of that reward if Argos didn't become immortal again.

A sudden cheer rang out from the men gathered around the bar. She looked up to see the Orioles' pitcher featured on the screen. Some of the men wore jerseys for the local team. Others wore Navy Football shirts that strained against their middle-aged builds. Kevin sat among them, smiling as he sipped a beer.

She buried her nose in the menu, muttering, "I need a beer."

Argos smiled. "Ale sounds delicious. What do you suggest?"

Luckily the waitress came around faster than normal, her blond hair suddenly let down and her lips bright pink with gloss. Claire ordered their drinks and sent the waitress away as quickly as possible.

"Back to business," she said for both her benefit and Argos's. "*Sebastian* can get us there, but what do you know about this Poseidon guy? Will he try to spear me with his trident if I serve him fish? Would that be like offering him a relative?"

Argos raised an eyebrow. "I'm not the best person to ask about offerings to gods."

"Crap, sorry."

"But I do not see anything wrong with offering him something from the sea."

"Guess I'll have to add that to the list." Claire nodded. Immediately her mind raced to the recipes that would go well with the wine Thalia had provided.

❧

"Well, if it isn't the most attractive couple in this city." Laura's loud exclamation jolted them both. Laura smiled at the sight of Argos's new clothes, a faint blush touching her sunburnt cheeks. "Well, you sure do clean up nicely. Did some shopping, I see." She gave a pointed look to the packaged sword, bags of clothes, and the single wine bottle. "Do you two know what you want to eat?"

Argos turned back to the thick booklet in his hand. Only a few of the items listed out were familiar to him, but the rest was in a foreign language for all he knew.

Laura waved off the concern. "Don't worry about it. I think I know just the thing to fill your stomach. On the house, of course. Be back in a sec."

Claire watched the older woman leave, her eyes glued to the swinging doors that led to a bustling kitchen. Again, the dreamy look was back on her face and Argos felt his heart sink.

The life she wanted, the one she dreamed about, seemed utterly boring to him.

In his day, men either answered the call of the sea or became a farmer. But to him, there was no glory in digging up dirt, no spirit in planting seed. He was meant to roam, and after years locked on Circe's island, he was impatient to explore all the world had to offer.

The storytellers were wrong about the sirens being great temptresses. It was the sea who lured all to fall in love with her. Though they might fight the feeling, there was no escaping the ocean's gentle touch or her temper.

Claire respected the waters, yet she did not look at them the same way she did the large tavern they sat in.

Even he recognized the look in her eye.

At Thalia's, he had shown her a glimpse of the world

he remembered, and she had not shied away. She seemed excited about their upcoming adventure. She was brave, his Claire, but it was clear now that when given the choice between a world filled with adventure and putting down roots, she would pick the more peaceful choice.

In his long life, he had said goodbye often. His family. His men. The old and familiar gave way to the new. Each one was hard in its own way, but he was a man that looked toward the future. Always ready for the next adventure. The next battle.

One day soon, he would have to say goodbye to this woman. His Claire. He knew that would be the hardest one of his life.

Argos finally cleared his throat. She blinked out of the daze, her eyelashes chasing the spell away, and smiled at him apologetically. "Sorry, I was zoning out."

"It looked more like you were in love," he corrected, putting a word to the expression on her face. He watched as Claire's eyes widened and a red blush crawled up her neck. She looked shocked, afraid, and utterly confused. Yes, love was the right word.

"What are you—"

"With this place," he continued. "I'm not blind, Claire. You love this place."

Her color paled but the wild look in her eye tempered down. "The King Crab? Well, yeah. Of course I love it. This place is like a second home to me."

He nodded. "It looks similar to your own tavern."

She smiled. "Restaurant. It's called a restaurant. And I know it may sound silly—this place isn't the fanciest in Annapolis, but it definitely has the best food in the area. I used to work here every summer when I was a teen."

She gave a happy sigh, her gaze sliding back to the area around them.

He liked seeing her happy and relaxed. There had not been many times since they had met that she had been either of those things. Her guard was down, and without it Claire let herself talk. "I've always wanted a restaurant of my own just like this. A place that brings people together. Where I could choose the menu and what we serve. It's my dream to get that old shack up and running soon."

Claire laughed, but it was horribly forced. The restaurant she had left behind still haunted her, and he had been the one to remind her of it all. The one who'd forced her to run away. "But we have a long way until I'll get there. Now, where was I? Oh, Poseidon! Have you ever met him before? Is meeting a god something I should dress nice for? Because… I'm kind of limited."

"You look beautiful," Argos answered honestly. He did not think there was anything wrong with the compliment, except Claire now refused to meet his gaze.

"Thank you."

He'd said the wrong thing again. Somehow, communicating with women had gotten harder over the years, and he hated it. An apology croaked up his throat as he tried to make things right, but before it could come out, Laura appeared with her arms full of plates and beverages.

"You two look like you could use a drink." She beamed, setting down two large jugs of frothing beer. "Nothing like a cold one on a hot summer day, and to accompany it, our famous Crab Cake Sliders."

Argos stared at the food in front of him. It was unlike anything he had ever seen before. There were three small stacked pieces of bread on each plate. He had no idea what was between the bread, but the smell of meat was undeniable. "What is it?"

Laura was grinning victoriously, her eyes watching Argos. "That dish right there is Claire's own creation she made just for the restaurant."

Argos took in the strange combination of bread and meat and looked up at Claire. She was studying him intently. "You made this?" he asked.

"Years ago," Claire answered. "Laura wanted to add something to the menu. I'm surprised you still serve it."

"It's one of our best sellers," Laura grinned.

Argos picked one up and the smell of cooked meat hit his nostrils. The slider was tiny. He could practically fit the entire thing into his mouth. Biting down brought the meat's juice dribbling down his chin, but that was an afterthought as the flavor assaulted his senses.

It was as good as sex. Better, even. His throat was making noises as if he was caught in the middle of the action.

When he opened his eyes, both women were staring at him, mouths slightly ajar.

The older woman patted his shoulder. "I'll give you and the burger some privacy."

Argos picked up the second one and bit down. It was gone too fast, but he was still smiling. "Claire," he said excitedly, "this is it."

"The slider?"

"Yes, this is the perfect offering for Poseidon. I cannot think of anything better to offer him than your cooking."

V

"KEVIN ALREADY CHECKED all that. You were with him."

"I know. I just want to make sure I'll know the difference if something changes." The tone in Argos's voice made it sound as if it were the obvious answer. The three of them had spent the morning making sure *Sebastian* was seaworthy. Once Kevin headed up to the house for lunch, Argos poked at everything again.

Claire studied him. "Why?"

He popped his head up from where it was checking under the control deck. She expected to see annoyance at her prying questions, but instead there was just open honesty. "Because this boat means a lot to you, and I intend to take care of it. That was what you two were talking about, is it not?"

"Y-yes." Her words stumbled out of her mouth as she watched him go back to work. He wasn't tinkering with the machinery like Kevin had, just staring at it. Memorizing the old metal and aged wood. If anything so much as shifted out of place, he would be able to tell.

The effort touched her. She stood from her chair on the dock, where she had been supervising the men's work. It was a beautiful day, clear sky and a gentle breeze coming in off the water. There was nowhere else she wanted to be. Except maybe *on* her boat.

In one graceful leap, she joined Argos on *Sebastian*. His eyes followed her as she danced around him and took one of the boat's cushioned seats. "Take a break," she said. "The boat will still be here tomorrow."

Argos stared at her. "Will you take a break with me?"

"I was going to get back to reading *The Odyssey*. I have studying to do, remember?" He came forward, his eyes never leaving hers. "I'm just getting to the part where Penelope is talking to her son Tel…Telemakus?"

Argos settled beside her; the closeness of their bodies made syllables even harder to get out. "Telemachus," he corrected with perfect enunciation. On his tongue, the syllables sounded like a real name after her butchering attempt.

"I swear, all the men have ridiculous names. I don't even want to attempt saying any of them."

"Which ones are giving you trouble? Is it Antinous? Eurymachus? Aegyptius?"

"*Gesundheit.*" Claire laughed. "Argos is so much easier."

"It is the name my mother gave me, after the great city which many heroes called home. You know of Perseus?" He already knew the answer by her blank look and continued, "The man who killed Medusa?"

A jolt of joy shot through her. "Oh! I actually know that one."

If what she had gotten before was a jolt, the smile

awarded to her was simply electrifying. "His tale was my mother's favorite. She wanted me to grow into a great hero like him."

"And you did."

"I did."

"You know all these stories by heart, don't you?"

"We did not have books back then. The only way to tell it was from memory."

"Good." She wiggled into a comfortable position. "It just so happens I'm not much of a reader. I like things explained to me. So, explain away."

With her blessing, Argos picked up right where her reading left off. Claire told herself to pay close attention, to try to glean as much from his retelling as she could to utilize the information later, but within seconds she was entranced by the tale he wove. It was much faster than her snail's-pace reading and much more riveting than she had expected. He knew how to use his voice, the right moments to give a dramatic pause, and which tidbits to explain to her in grander detail. He painted a picture of his world for her, a place of temples and kings and trials of the sea.

As enticing as the story was, Claire also found herself staring at Argos himself. At how his face lit up with emotion as he recalled his history, the relaxed state of his body. This was not a man afflicted with a curse. For that brief time on her boat, he was just a man. Happy, comfortable, and dangerously handsome.

⚭

He talked, weaving the tale of Odysseus as he found himself stranded on the Isle of Lotus, when he fought off the

Cyclops, son of Poseidon, earning the god's wrath. The words fell from his lips with a flourish.

Claire was enraptured with the story, never tearing her eyes away. She was lost to the ancient poem, a poem that was often told at grand feasts and kings' palaces. He had never told it to a lone woman before. At some point, they both lay comfortably on the boat's deck as they talked, her body draped over his legs in the same way a cat sprawls out in sunlight. There was something intimate about it, and he never wanted to stop.

She made a noise of contentment as he finished another section of the poem. "You are very good at telling stories."

Argos laughed. "You are not the first to tell me such a thing. My men used to beg like children for a story during a feast. If there were no poets on hand, I would jump on the table and tell the stories with lips stained with wine."

She laughed, stretching her body and moving from his touch. At her absence, the evening chill settled into his bones, as did the curse.

It was an impossible problem to hide from the perceptive woman next to him. Claire glanced down, taking in his growing lust. She gave a smile he was beginning to recognize. "Have you ever had sex on a boat before?"

Heat enveloped him from head to groin at the look. "Eons ago. I barely remember the experience."

"That is a tragedy." She licked her lips and it was a beautiful sight, one Argos would want to remember even centuries from now.

There was no questioning that she wanted him and that he wanted her. This time, though, he would make the first move. His hand fell against her cheek, then moved down to the curve of her breasts. Claire's eyes widened as she gasped.

His hand kept moving, trailing down her stomach, pausing only to lift her garment and touch the soft skin underneath.

Claire sighed and pressed against him. "Going a little slow, aren't you?"

"Patience," he groaned, though it was killing him as well. He kissed the bend of her neck and felt her buckle under him. His hand slid lower until it cupped her mound. He was dying for her, but he would be damned if he let his curse rule this moment. This time he was in charge. "My curse makes me want to fuck you, Claire. Hard and fast."

"That—that sounds nice." She was panting now, her eyes hooded.

"But I say damn the curse. I'm going to take it slow." He flipped the button of her pants and slipped his fingers down the lace of her underwear. They slipped between her lips and, gods—she was wet.

He tugged at her pants and she assisted, casting a cautious eye to the house behind them. But the rail of the ship shielded their intimate moment from any prying eyes. "Not too slow, I hope," she said, tossing her pants aside.

"I believe I still owe you for what you did in the other day."

"The other day?" Claire smiled at him knowingly.

"The alley...," he explained.

She arched against him, raising her breasts near his mouth. "It was nothing."

"It was everything," he insisted. She was everything. Without her he would have lost his mind by now. And he intended to repay her kindness. "Come here." With one arm he tugged her up. Claire landed in his lap, her mound firmly against his aching erection. They both hissed in pleasure. He pawed at her underwear, pushing it aside and slipping a finger into her wetness.

"Argos," she moaned, kissing his chin, "w-wait a second."

He stilled as she bent over towards her pants and came back with a little wrapped square. She waved it in front of his face. "I've come prepared this time." Last night, she had explained the mechanics of modern protection. He understood it to an extent, but if it made Claire feel safer with him he would not complain.

"Good," he breathed, flicking his finger and bringing out a delicious moan from the woman in his lap. She lifted her hips and he slipped in the second finger, stretching her.

Claire began to move, fucking herself against his finger, rocking the boat as she did so. "I want you," she said.

And I want you, he almost replied, but not because of the curse or because she was helping him. Because she was a woman unlike any he had ever met, a woman with a warrior's heart who was winning his own.

He almost said all this, but her fingers against his pants made his mind go white hot. The moment his cock was in her hands he could not think anymore; the curse had him. All he wanted was to be in her, fucking her.

Claire ripped open the package and rolled the plastic over his cock head. He did not like it, but at least there was not much time to dwell on the discomfort. Claire grabbed his shaft and lined it up against her opening. Then she paused. She *paused*.

"Alright?" she breathed.

"I'm not going to break," he told her before pushing in. They both tensed as their bodies adjusted to one another and then it was pure relief. For a moment the water and everything around them was stilled. The only noise was their breaths intermingling.

Argos was trying to control his senses, but he was overwhelmed with the feel of her, the taste of her.

Something soft cupped his cheek, bringing him out of his daze. When he opened his eyes, Claire was searching his face for reassurance. He smiled and kissed her. "I told you I wouldn't break."

"I know," she said in the space between them.

Her pleasure clenched around his cock, making him lose what little control he had. He gripped her hips and thrust against her. Her hand gripped his shoulder, digging in with monstrous strength.

They were humans at the dawn of the gods, at their most primal state. Fucking, loving, moaning and roaring against each other.

"Oh, Argos." She buried her face into his shoulder, smothering a cry. He felt her body tremble against his own as her orgasm took her.

He fell right behind her, calling her name for the sea and all others to hear as he spent himself inside her. It was a pleasure unlike anything he had ever felt. Not in the times Claire helped him before, not with Circe, not with Hestia, or any mortal woman. This was different.

When the moment had passed, the world around them still shook from their lovemaking. *Sebastian* bumped the dock nearby, the waves sloshed against the shore, but the man and woman were utterly still.

Pulling back, he brushed the hair out of Claire's eyes. "You are a gift from the gods."

"I think that's the nicest thing a man has ever said to me after sex." She laughed, snuggling close to him.

There was more he wished to say. Blasphemy nearly fell from his lips. The gods did not hold a candle to her. Her compassion, her strength. He had once loved Hestia because of the stark difference between the goddess and mortal women. But no one compared to the woman he held in his arms.

Having lived hundreds of years did not mean he was wiser. And as he stroked Claire's back, what he said was, "Mortal women are incredible. I should have never trifled with the goddesses."

In his arms, Claire tensed. She pulled back and looked at him the same way she had when they had first met. In that instant, he knew he had said something wrong.

"I have upset you..."

"No, you haven't." But she did not meet his gaze.

She stood and reached for her pants, but Argos laid a hand on top of hers. "You can tell me anything, Claire. I never want to be the source of your distress." The words shocked her. They surprised him as well. The word *never* burned under his skin as if someone had lit it on fire. No one would harm her, especially him.

Claire's jaw was set in a determined line. She was still irritated with him. But then, with a sigh, all that tension eased out of her bones. "I just keep thinking about the other mortal women you've talked about..."

Argos blinked in surprise. "I have not talked about them much because it was so long ago."

"Exactly." She bit her bottom lip, considering her next words carefully. "You said you forgot them—your mother, the woman in Rome. What's to stop you from forgetting me as well?"

The pain she tried to conceal from him revealed itself

for a moment before Claire quickly schooled her features. His strong, beautiful Claire. He had not thought about how she would feel when he regained his immortality.

She tried to tug her hand back, but he twined his fingers with her own. "Claire." He moved closer to her and before she could assure him with false words, he put his mouth against her own. He waited a moment before she opened up to him, moaning as she leaned forward into the embrace. He deepened the kiss, taking the time to memorize every aspect of it. The feel of her lips, the noises she made, the smell of fresh soap that tickled his nose.

Claire broke the kiss, her face flushed in both pleasure and mild embarrassment. She still did not look convinced. Argos could not help himself. His hand reached up and cupped her cheek affectionately. "You are the woman who saved me, my partner in all this. I could never forget you, Claire."

Her mouth dropped open, uttering a small "Oh" in its wake. Concern no longer creased her brow. Instead a new emotion tugged at the features of her face. An emotion Argos could not quite place, and by the looks of things, neither could Claire.

She pulled away, breaking contact between their skin and the moment that had been shared. "We should talk about your plan for facing Circe. Isn't she immortal as well?"

Argos blinked at the sudden change in topic. "Yes, she is a demigoddess. Half of her blood belongs to Olympus. It means killing her will be incredibly difficult with her magic, and her island keeps her immortal."

Claire's lips mashed together as she considered this. "So, how did Odysseus escape her?"

"Do you want to hear that tale?"

"It would be smart to know what I'm up against."

He could agree with that. It was the basic principle warriors followed. But Claire would not be the one fighting Circe; he would. If all worked out well, once he received his immortality he would drop Claire off back at her tavern with a reward and his thanks. She would be safe, and he would be on to another dangerous adventure.

It was not a new plan, but for some reason his lungs ached at the thought of leaving Claire behind. He ran his fingers through his hair and forced himself not to think of it. Instead he thought of Circe, of the stories that surrounded her. "Circe...Circe wasn't always this cruel."

Claire's brows shot up. "Are you defending her?"

"No, never. The things she did to me and other men deserve a fate worse than death." His fingers reached up to rub his necklace, assuring himself that it was still firmly around his neck. "But in the stories, she was not cruel. Jealous, yes. But many of the gods were. I believe she was lonely. Capturing stray sailors and turning them into her companions with drink and witchcraft was how she dealt with that. Odysseus, with the blessing of the gods, did not fall under her spell and forced her to stop her mischief. She honored him with food and wine for days, and I believe she fell in love with the great hero. She tricked him into staying on her island for a whole year before he finally demanded to be let go."

Claire scoffed. "I bet she didn't like that."

"No, she told him to go to Hades."

"Seriously?"

"When Odysseus accomplished her request in the underworld, she finally let him go."

Her body shook with laughter. "You were serious!"

He nodded. "It may have been because in that year they spent together, she grew to love him, but Odysseus's heart remained with his wife, Penelope. In the end, Circe allowed him and his men to go. But she longed to fill the hole Odysseus left behind. That's when I arrived."

The rest of the story was too painful to speak of. How foolish he had been enjoying his time with Circe until the day she refused to let him leave and his captivity truly began.

"She will not be easy to defeat." The task was akin to taking on a god, but he had no choice. Circe would never stop looking for him, and he refused to live the rest of his life in fear.

Claire rested her head against his shoulder. "We all face difficult odds when it comes to the things we want. The hard part is to try anyway."

Argos closed his eyes and wrapped his arms around the woman. No one had ever understood him the way she did.

"And Odysseus…" Claire's lips moved against his skin, planting light kisses with the words.

"You wish to know the ending of his story?"

She pulled back and looked at him, searching for something. "He is one of your brothers, isn't he? Is he still alive today, as an immortal?"

His throat tightened, the way it always did when he recalled the old heroes, but she deserved to know the truth. "No, he is not."

Claire blinked in surprise. "What happened?"

"He did not die in battle, if that is what you are thinking. Nor fighting a great beast. Many heroes died that way before I was born. But it was Odysseus, along with a chosen few heroes, who established my Order. When the gods offered them immortality, all took it but he. He was old at that time and had spent much of his days fighting in wars. After his voyage, he finally found his way home, to his wife and son. He chose to spend the rest of his life as a mortal to die with Penelope.

"Once a year we hold a pyre in honor of our fallen brothers: Achilles, Ajax, Jason, and Herakles. The great men who died before their time."

"Except Odysseus." Her voice was soft. "The only hero who truly had a happy ending. He died with the woman he loved by his side."

He nodded and said nothing. He had never thought of it that way. He'd always been riddled with regret over the loss of Odysseus. It was a shame they did not have such a great man with them anymore, the knowledge they had lost. It pained him that he had never sailed with the great hero.

He used to wonder how the man had found the strength to turn down immortality, but now it was not so hard to imagine. With Claire in his arms, the same thoughts were creeping into his own mind. But without his immortality, he would never be able to defeat Circe, to protect the people he had come to care about. Occasionally Argos allowed himself to think of a time when he would be able to visit Claire in her tavern, of meeting with the Kings under different circumstances, but those thoughts belonged to a fool.

He would gain his immortality and defeat Circe, because that was what he was. A hero, a fighter, an immortal. And meanwhile Claire would grow old, the Kings would pass away, and the world would keep moving. It was best not to think about life as a mortal.

Because heroes never got happy endings.

❧

She was going on a journey. Maybe it wasn't the same as Odysseus's years at sea, but it was an adventure nonetheless, and Claire had no idea what would come of it. One thing was for certain—she would be going a couple days without a real shower, so it was best to enjoy the luxury now.

She ran her fingers under the warm water and smiled. *Alright, make that a bath. I'm giving into relaxation today.* Laura and Kevin had a large tub and a sleek bathroom. At one point they had talked of opening a bed and breakfast. People loved coming to Annapolis's historical homes, especially the ones located on the water. But their rooms were always filled with visiting friends and family, so the B&B idea had never taken off.

That didn't stop Laura from treating each and every houseguest like a paying customer. The bathroom was spotless, and she quickly found a bottle of bath bubbles on display. Claire dumped a healthy dose into the tub.

As the water filled, she took the time to stare at the exhausted face in front of her. Mirrors don't lie, and one lazy day out in the sun couldn't wipe away days of stress and fatigue. Her fingers danced along the solid tan line just along her collarbone, and the summer freckles that dotted her skin. Some people had complimented her complexion in the past and the natural wave of her chestnut hair. Her past boyfriends had called her beautiful, but she'd never really felt that way. Not in her old life, held hostage in a prestigious kitchen. She'd been a slave to its high expectations.

But when she was with Argos, that wasn't the case.

He thought her freckles and frizzy hair were attractive. He thought her food was good enough for a god.

Calm down, she told herself stubbornly. *Don't think too much about it. Don't think too much about him.*

The best way to do that was to enjoy her bubble-filled tub. She turned the water off and began to strip, but by the time she was naked the bubbles had disappeared. Frowning, Claire bent to stir the water. As soon as her hand touched the surface she jerked it back.

The water was ice cold.

Ripples from her touch extended out, ring after ring. She stared in fascination as the rings continued over the surface, growing in frequency and strength. Water sloshed over the side as a small hurricane seemed to take shape in the tub. Without a second thought, Claire dunked her hand into the water, reaching for the plug. Her teeth clenched as an icy chill raced up her skin. Fingers numb, she tried to drain the water, but the stopper refused to move.

And then she saw it—a woman's face reflected up at her from the water.

She was beautiful, with the eyes of a cat and lush lips. Her dark hair was slicked back as if the water she appeared in made it wet, and her bronze skin appeared to have a greenish tint. Claire couldn't tell which features were muddied by the water and which were enhanced by it. One thing she knew for certain, though, the woman wasn't human.

Forget the drain. She tried to just get her arm away from the cold, to pull it out of the water, but it was stuck. Eyes glued on the woman, she let out a frantic scream.

Beautiful lips twisted in a cruel smile as the creature laughed, and the noise actually rang up from the water. Clear as crystal and as alluring as a song, but the moment the laughter hit her ears, dread seeped into Claire's body. All at once she knew the face that stared back at her.

"I've found you and soon so will my Pets," Circe cooed, eyes flashing in hate.

Claire tried again to jerk her hand free and this time she managed, but the force of her pulling made her stumble backwards, slip on the water, and sprawl naked on the bathroom tile. Circe's laughter ended just as Argos opened the door.

"Claire!"

Argos was by her side, a towel in his hands as he tried to cover her up.

"She was here," Claire said, wrapping the towel tightly around herself. A feeling of vulnerability crushed her lungs; she hated that. She'd promised herself this wouldn't happen again.

Argos nodded, his eyes dark. He might have said something, but a sudden knock on their bedroom door gave him an excuse to put distance between their bodies. Distance she didn't want.

"That must be the Kings," he said. "I'll reassure them that everything is okay and then we'll talk."

"Everything isn't okay," Claire said, her voice weak. "She said she knows where we are. She's coming after us."

"Then we'll have to leave immediately," he said after a long silent moment. "Get dressed, Claire, we must act quickly."

XVI

H E NEEDED TO make sure Claire was safe and then he needed to whisk them as far away as possible. It seemed simple enough, but he'd made a mistake. He did not consider that Laura King had a higher capacity than him for trouble.

When he opened the door, the couple was clustered close to the frame, Kevin's hand raised in mid-knock and Laura holding an end table, ready to bust in if need be. Neither looked sheepish at being caught. Laura jutted out her jaw and gave him a hard look. "We heard a scream."

"Claire fell while she was washing up," he answered easily.

Her eyes glanced down, taking in the sword in his hand. "Is that a sword in your hand?"

He hesitated, unsure of what combination of words would be the correct answer. Laura did not let him explain. Her face was set in a vicious glare. "I'd like to see her."

You cannot, he nearly snapped, hand clenching into a tight fist on the weapon. If they saw her, there would be questions. Time would be wasted, they needed to leave, but that would not get him far with a woman like Laura. The quickest way to reassure people was usually to let them do so themselves. He stepped aside and the couple bustled in.

Kevin held back by the door, blocking any escape as Laura went directly to the bathroom. She nearly ran over a newly dressed Claire. "Claire! We heard you scream. Is everything alright?"

Claire's eyes widened at the sight of them before seeking out Argos. The desperate attempt she'd made to keep their two worlds separated was splintering apart. The fear was evident on her face. She could lie, but the Kings would ask questions. And now that Circe knew where they were, the couple was in danger as well.

The truth, he told her gaze, *tell the truth*. It had worked out for him, after all.

Claire closed her eyes; it was not what she wanted to do but still the truth spilled forth. "I'm not alright. We have to leave tonight."

"Tonight?" Laura repeated. "What's the rush?"

Claire shook her head. "Not just me. I mean all of us. You have to leave, you're in danger."

"What are you talking about?" Kevin's body pulled to attention, the solider in him ready to fight.

"You wouldn't believe me if I told you, but please—just trust me." The plea in her voice was heartbreaking. If she had given him that same look with the same request, he would bend to her will.

Kevin and Laura looked as if they would as well. Laura shook her head. "I may not believe it, but we deserve to hear your version of the truth. That's the only way you're going to leave here." She pinned Argos with a hard stare.

"Something tells me this has everything to do with your sudden romance."

It would not be easy to explain, but there was a way in which Kevin would accept the news easier.

"Kevin, everything in your stories is true," he said. "I know because I was trapped on Circe's island for centuries. Claire found me after I escaped, and now the Sea Witch has found us. We're in danger unless we leave now."

He faced the silence of the room, bracing himself. Gods help him, it had been hard enough getting one Atheos to believe him. What else could he say if his words did not work?

It was Kevin who recovered first, his face breaking into a grin. "*I knew it!*"

⋰

Claire was a bundle of nerves as she crouched in the study with Argos, her pocketknife in hand, as the plan they'd come up with played over and over in her mind. She was ready to prove herself. This time a bunch of oversized cats weren't going to get the better of her.

Besides, she had nearly two hundred pounds of muscles backing her up. With his new sword, Argos was armed and ready to slice the door down. "That worked out better than I thought," he said. They were so close his breath tickled the back of her neck.

"For you, you battle-hungry maniac," she said. Things did seem to work out after telling the Kings the truth. Her guilt about lying was lifted, and if all went according to plan, they wouldn't have to worry about the Pets anymore.

"They impressed me. They have a real warrior's spirit protecting their home."

"No one wants to leave their home behind," Claire said, thinking of the small building she'd abandoned. The terror of seeing the cats had forced her out once; she wouldn't let them do the same again.

Argos seemed to understand. In the kitchen, they heard Laura and Kevin preparing to guard the back door. Metal clanged as Laura picked out her most trustworthy pan. Her voice boomed back at them from across the house. "No blood will be spilt inside this home. These are the original floors, and I don't need those monsters staining them."

"Yes, dear," Kevin said without pause before his shotgun clicked.

Claire glanced back down the hallway towards the kitchen, where she could see the two huddled near the window. She'd never seen bookish Kevin as the military man he had once been, but now his experience showed in how he stood watch, assessing the yard outside. She remembered when she'd been younger, her father and the older man would go out shooting on the weekends. Ducks, targets, sometimes deer—a few of his trophies were hung around the house. Testaments to his accuracy.

They'll be fine, she told herself, but the idea of a normal middle-aged couple taking on a group of jungle cats didn't seem fine. And then there was Circe. Her body shivered at the memory of the woman.

Circe intimidated her on every level. As a woman, as a living being. An animal instinct inside of her knew that if something rivaled humans at the top of the food chain, Circe would be it.

"We might be able to fight off these Pets, but we're screwed if Circe shows up, aren't we?" she asked, voicing the fear that had crept into her thoughts.

Argos nodded. "Do not worry about that. Circe will not come. She never leaves her island."

"Like, *ever*?" It sounded like a lonely life, but Claire quickly rid herself of any pity. There was no excuse for her to turn wayward sailors into her servants, to hurt Argos the way she had.

"I do not know when she was exiled to the island, all I know is that she will not leave it. Whether it is a matter of cannot or will not, I do not know, but I suspect it is the latter."

"But in the bathroom...," she began to say, but Argos had followed her train of thought.

"Do not worry, Claire. I believe that was the most she could accomplish from the island. If she could hurt you, she would have." His tone dipped into a low growl at the thought. "For everything else she sends her men."

"You hate them?" She could hear it in his voice, anger mixed with pity.

"Hate them? No, I hate that they know her evil and do nothing to stop it. While I was there they certainly hated me. I was Circe's favorite toy for years. They saw me as competition. When they could, they crawled into my room and tore into my body as if it were a feast."

Claire gagged at the words. "They ate you?"

"My body grew back every night," he said, voice devoid of any realization of the horror he described. "Her island grants men immortality, but it has a price."

"That's not the point. They... they..." They were just as bad as Circe, maybe worse.

"If it makes you feel better, I got my revenge." He smiled. "At your tavern. Away from the island, they are mortal men like me."

"It doesn't, but thanks for trying." She sighed before realizing how close they were huddled together. It dawned on her that it had been hours since she'd last helped him with his curse. A reminder was beginning to poke her in the back.

"I don't mean to distract you, but are you going to be able to fight... like this?"

It took him a moment to figure out what she was alluding to. When he did, he shifted farther away. The grip on his sword whitened. "I will be fine. The upcoming battle will distract me."

"Gets the blood rushing somewhere else?" she guessed with a smile, but the joke went well over his head.

He was concentrating on the door now, eyes dark in concentration. His lips were wet as he licked them in anticipation, a nervous habit she'd never noticed until now. She wanted to kiss that sensual mouth, just in case they didn't get a chance after the fight, but that would be a distraction neither of them could afford right now.

"What's that?" Laura's idea of a hushed whisper echoed back through the house, and the tension around them spiked.

"Do you see something?" Argos called.

"I think so. There's something in the water, but it doesn't look like a cat." Laura shifted to get a better look by placing her body in front of the window. Her figure was outlined by the moon, dark and looming as she hunched near the glass. A gasp escaped her. "There's something in the water—my God!"

That didn't sound good. Claire and Argos both moved towards the back of the house to see what had caught her eye. All four squinted out into the darkness. It took a moment before they saw it. The slender tendrils waving in and out of the water. Long and large, it appeared to be an octopus, but there weren't any creatures like that in the Bay.

Another tendril peeked out and the two began to twine themselves around her boat. Claire's body jerked in realization. "They're trying to destroy *Sebastian*!"

"They will do no such thing," Argos growled as he tore the door open.

He was sprinting down to the dock before Kevin had time to shout, "Don't!" but it was too late. A wolf leapt out of the nearby foliage and slammed into him.

Claire clasped a hand over her mouth, muffling a scream. It was a trap. Kevin cursed beside her. "Idiot. I can't shoot it when it's on top of him."

"Worry about that later," Laura said. "We have company." More predators moved out of the brush towards them, a jaguar and a tiger. Their eyes had a haunting glow to them in the darkness, and their claws dug into the dirt.

Kevin didn't hesitate. He pulled the gun to the side and fired at the tiger. The shot echoed across the trees. The creature yelped, falling to its side as dark liquid stained the grass beneath him. The jaguar bared his teeth; his all-too-human eyes reflected new caution.

Laura shook her head. "Kevin, everyone in a mile radius is going to wake up and be wondering what that gunshot was."

"But I got him, didn't I?" Her husband grinned, his gun still focused on the jaguar. "Keep an eye on the tiger. Yell if it looks like he's getting up."

In the distance, she could hear Argos grunting as he threw the wolf to the side. Claire glanced to make sure he was alright, but her gaze snagged on the threat in the water.

Whatever it was knew exactly which boat was hers. Several dark tendrils encircled *Sebastian*, while *Queenie* sat perfectly still in the water. A low whine of fiberglass bending moaned from the water.

She'd be damned if she let Circe's creatures take her boat.

Clutching her pocketknife, she sprinted down the walkway. Laura's protest was lost to the wind. She was only concerned about getting to her boat. The pocketknife in her hand felt so small. It wouldn't do much damage against the creature she faced, but she would stab it a million times if it meant getting that thing off her boat.

Blood pounded in her ears as she got closer. The tendrils were much larger than they had looked from afar. A few were raised in the air like threatening columns. Power pulsed in their movements. It could destroy the boat and the dock with a single swing. Instead its tentacles twisted around the railings, holding the vessel hostage.

Climbing onto the boat was no easy task, but Claire managed it. *Sebastian* rocked back and forth, making it difficult to steady herself on board. She clutched her pocketknife in her hand and jabbed at the closest tendril she could find. The knife sunk into the meaty flesh up to the hilt, and when she jerked it out, dark blood sputtered from the wound. But the assault didn't ease up.

She jabbed again and again, clenching her teeth against the acidic smell of the creature's blood. "Let. Go. Of. My. Boat."

Finally, she saw the muscles tense in the arm she'd been attacking before the whole thing relaxed. It was a stupid assumption, but she thought maybe it was a good sign. Maybe she'd injured the arm into letting go.

She was wrong.

Instead it reeled back, the single arm withering and moving like an angry snake. It lashed down, cracking the railing Claire held on to. A loud crack filled the air as another tentacle punched a hole into the side.

She had just enough time to push herself back as everything tipped to one side. Water brushed against her fingertips as she scurried under the control cabin for shelter. *Now you've done it, Claire.* She cursed, watching as the other tentacles began to dive against her boat. Plastic and fragments flew in the darkness, slicing through the air and cutting her skin. It was a terrifying sight, but she had a weapon in the face of it, and anytime one tentacle dared to slither near her, she stabbed at it, determined to save her precious boat at any cost, even her life.

XVII

EVERYTHING HAPPENED SO quickly. Kevin's
gun let out a booming cry, causing the wolf he
struggled against to pause. Argos managed to throw
the animal off him just in time to see Claire dash across the
dark lawn. He called for her, but she was focused on her
boat, under siege by one of Circe's monsters. Growling, he
scooped up his fallen sword and slayed the wolf while it
was dazed.

His body screamed at him to give chase to Claire, but
the odds of battle were against them now. They were scattered and the enemy had the advantage. As if anticipating
his thoughts, the jaguar moved to sprint after Claire. He
did not get far before the ground beneath its feet exploded,
followed by the loud bang of Kevin's weapon. With a hiss,
the cat redirected itself and darted into the nearby foliage.

"What are you waiting for?" Kevin shouted behind
him. "Go after her. We have everything under control here!"

A loud cracking noise filled the air as a tentacle slammed
down on *Sebastian*. Claire's scream of anger followed the

noise, and it was all he needed before taking off in a dead sprint down the pathway.

The screams were good; they meant Claire was still alive. Yet they made his skin break out in a cold sweat of terror.

As he drew closer, the tentacles lashed out at him. Argos barely managed to dodge out of the way, his momentum urging him forward. The dock shook under his feet, its base unhinged by the struggle. The wood cracked and splintered under his weight as he lunged to grab *Sebastian*'s nearby railing.

An earsplitting noise rang out in the area around them. Not the cry of an injured Pet, but something that was neither animal nor man. Something inhuman. His basic instincts recognized the sound of a monster when he heard it, though it had been centuries since he had last faced one in battle. Now, one lay right under him, its body obscured by the dark waters.

Argos hoisted himself onto *Sebastian*'s body, eyes warily taking in the cruel-looking tentacles that were wound around it. Then he saw her, a small body huddled directly beside one of the coils. No, bracing against it, as Claire's hand pummeled against the creature.

His heart stopped at the sight. If the creature merely took a moment, it could bat Claire's body to the side as easily as a fly. It could break her bones, throw her into the water where no one would be able to find her. He rushed forward, sword slamming down on the tentacle the moment he was within reach.

The boat gave a hard shudder as the remaining tentacles released it and returned to the water. The ship groaned as the pressure on it gave. Water sloshed against his feet from its broken beams.

"Argos?"

He looked at Claire, really looked at her, and saw her body wet and covered in dark speckles. Blood, but not her blood. In her hand was the small pocket blade she claimed to have for protection. Today, it was no longer a claim.

"Gods above, Claire." He let out a low whistle of air from his teeth, relief flooding out of him at the sight of her in one piece. "You cannot run off like that."

The awe he saw in her eyes vanished as she stuck out her chin. "It's attacking my ship."

"A ship is not worth your life," he seethed. It was a lesson all sailors had to learn, no matter what era they lived in.

That brought her up short. Her face flushed at his raised voice, embarrassment and anger coloring the skin.

Though the creature had let the ship go, they could still see its tentacles skimming along the top of the water. It had no reason to hold on to the boat after the damage it had done. *Sebastian* was going nowhere.

"Is it running away?" Claire wondered.

Argos shook his head. "Worse, it's preparing the next attack." It wanted all its legs free for the next onslaught. Something glimmered in the water amongst the moving limbs. Two eyes caught the moonlight. Staring at him, daring him.

He had seen those dead eyes before, knew immediately it was a creation of Circe's own design. It would not stop until it accomplished what she wanted. There was no reason for it to fear humans, or the gods. It had no soul.

He turned to Claire. A million words in a hundred languages came to his mind, things he wanted to say. Needed to say. But the only thing that came out was, "I will slay it. I will avenge your boat."

Her expression broke him. They had not been the right words. Anger and fear still colored her expression, and he wanted nothing more than to make them go away. But the boat shuddered underneath their feet. Water licked against their shins. Time was running out.

Without another word, he turned and jumped into the water.

❧

The noise and chaos of the world above disappeared under the surface of the water. He swam with purpose, quickly working himself into an offensive position. The bay was not deep. Still, Circe's creature would have the advantage, its movements faster than Argos's own. But all he needed was one clear opening at the creature to finish it off.

Lights from the nearby homes flickered to life, illuminating the water. He could see the hulking figure, its octopus limbs just barely out of range from his toes as its body huddled on the murky ground. There, among the coiling tentacles, swayed the torso of a man. At the abdomen stretched a monstrous mouth that could have belonged to a Titan.

A single name echoed in his mind. Scylla. The woman turned creature at the hands of Circe's jealousy. With her numerous heads and sea creature body, she was feared across the seas for eating those who dared bypass Circe's island. This was not the same monster, but it created the same fear.

In a flash, the creature lunged towards him, kicking up dirt to shield its movements.

Argos clenched his teeth, feeling the need for air

burning his lungs as he prepared for the attack. Something slammed against his side, a large tentacle attempting to wrap around his abdomen before he sliced it off. Another wrapped around his foot, yanking him down. As soon as his foot touched the ground, it would be on him like a lion on its prey.

He slashed out, but cutting the hold on his foot meant bending into a more vulnerable position. The water pressure around him shifted as the twisted face of the creature appeared before him, its eyes wild from the hunt. It was the only thing he saw before the water around them was bathed in light. The creature's pupils dilated and it reeled back in surprise. *Claire.* Argos sent a silent prayer up to her quick thinking as he slashed down. His sword slid through the monster's skull like butter. It jerked in surprise; both of its mouths gaped open as it sank to the ground. The magic that shaped its body dissolved as blood filled the space.

Desperate for air, Argos kicked his way to the surface. He sent one last glance down to the well-lit floor below him and the skeletal monster that was left lying on it. Warm summer air hit his face as he broke the surface. He gasped, hair clinging to his eyes and momentarily blinded by the harsh light coming off a nearby boat. A familiar shriek filled the air before something splashed into the water beside him.

A small circle floated on top of the water, bumping against his chest as a soaking wet Claire pushed it at him. She should not be in the water, not when she had no way of knowing if the monster was defeated or not.

She knew that, though; she knew all the danger that was around them and yet she had jumped in to save him.

"Grab onto the lifesaver," she said. "The fight isn't over yet."

❦

"That spotted son of a bitch got away. He ran the moment you jumped into the water," Claire said as they climbed on the muddy bank. Her words burned with anger, not directed at anything but brewing nonetheless. Argos's body heaved in exhaustion and disappointment. She hated the sight of it, especially after what he'd done. Words continued to tumble out of her mouth in a half-hysterical, half-desperate attempt to give him comfort. "Kevin wounded one of Circe's men, though. We can question him."

"Ah," he hummed as they summited the hill. His sword was still clutched in his hand, dripping red. At the top they saw a man lying in grass, his bloody hands clamped across his side as Kevin held a gun to his head.

The marine's eyes didn't leave their captive even at their arrival. His body was taut, ready to react if any trouble stirred. "Good to see you two are still alive. Laura was about to rush in herself."

"Where is she?" Claire asked.

"Soothing the neighbors," Laura answered as she stepped out the back door. "Everyone is having a fit with all the noise. The Cowans were talking about calling the police." Claire's eyes widened as she looked down at the bleeding man. Laura spoke quickly to quiet her rising fear. "Don't worry. I told them a group of drunks vandalized your boat and we'd contact the police. They seemed to buy it."

"That's a lot better than what I would have come up with." Claire sighed.

"That's because you're a terrible liar, honey."

Argos bent near the Pet, his sword shoved threateningly against the man's scruffy neck. "Can you talk?"

The man lowered his eyes, his body weak from blood loss. His neck pressed uncaring against the sharp edge. "If I do not, you are going to kill me, right?"

Argos growled, twisting the Pet's hair in his fist and pulling the man's neck from his blade. "I am not going to kill you. I am giving you an option. Tell me what I need to know, and you can leave. You do not have to return to her. You can help me stop her."

Their captive shifted so he could meet Argos's gaze for the first time. He had eyes the color of melted gold, Claire realized, the eyes of an animal. "I cannot help you."

"Just tell me her weakness," Argos prompted. "Tell me and you can have your life back."

"What life?" The man's voice cracked in pain. "I had no life before Circe. Anyone I knew is long dead and the world has changed so much. She offers me power and paradise."

Argos sighed, laying the man down with gentle hands. "He is no good to us."

"Then I guess we'll have the police take him away. We can't just let him go," Laura said with a sad shake of her head.

"No!" An abrupt scream tore from the Pet's throat at her suggestion. His body sprung to life, fighting as much as his weakened muscles would allow. Argos held his sword up in another threat, but it did nothing to calm him. "No, you cannot put me away. You cannot put me away from her, please—I do not know this new world. I do not want to live in it."

His fear was real, and Argos seemed to soften at his plea. "Then tell me what I need to know."

"I will not," howled the Pet. His movements were frantic as he fought, and then he grabbed the edge of Argos's sword. Everyone tensed at the action, watching in stunned horror as the Pet pressed his neck against the blade in a clean sweep.

Argos's shout was too late as blood gushed onto the metal. The body fell into the grass, lifeless.

Kevin cursed, lowering his weapon to dole out directions out like a general. His voice was a vague noise in the background of Claire's mind as she stared at the body. "He killed himself," she whispered, awe and confusion mingling in her voice.

"No," Argos said, his voice cracking as he stared at the broken body. "Circe killed him."

⚓

There was no time to mourn. Kevin and Argos were already laying out tarps. With all the noise made, Laura would have to call the police shortly and come up with a good explanation for everything. Claire's mind struggled to conceive of reasonable excuse, but the older woman shook her head. "That's not for you to worry about. You and Argos need to get out of here."

Claire faltered at the offer. "But—"

Laura silenced her with a look. "No buts. I can handle the police, but you have a real living, breathing Sea Witch after you. That terrifies me. The sooner Argos stops her, the sooner I can relax."

Guilt constricted around Claire's heart. "I'm sorry I dragged you into this. I really didn't mean for any of this to happen."

The stern set of Laura's face dropped. "Oh honey, I didn't mean that I'm worried about myself. I'm worried about you. From the moment you washed up in my kitchen in your pajamas, I've been worried about you. I want you to be safe, and as much as it pains me to say this, your best bet is sticking with that man and helping him fight."

Claire couldn't meet her friend's gaze, touched by her words. "I'm just helping him get back his immortality. I doubt I would be much help to him in an actual fight."

"Now that is just nonsense. I saw you rush off and attack a sea monster to defend your boat. Scared twenty years off my life, but you and him both were a force to be reckoned with. That Circe woman should be afraid."

Laura smiled at her and Claire smiled back, until the words shocked her into realization. "My boat..." They turned to look at where the *Sebastian* used to be docked. The boat was in shambles, nearly split in half from the fight and filling with water. All her hard work and preparation was gone. Her beloved ship was destroyed.

Tears rolled down her cheeks at the sight. She forced herself to turn away, afraid that Argos would notice her grief. Large soft arms wrapped around her in a bear hug as she was brought to Laura's chest. "You'll have to take *Queenie*. Kevin can work on that ol' tugboat while you're gone. When you come back, he'll be like new."

"I couldn't. I've taken so much from you."

"You haven't taken enough in my opinion." Laura pulled back so their eyes could meet. "Besides, if I'm going to convince the police that there is a reason the neighbors heard gunshots in the morning, your boat will be pretty solid evidence."

"If Kevin was the one to give this the pep talk, he'd say something about this being my heroic quest."

"No, he'd compare himself to Gandalf giving the hobbit a sword."

Claire laughed, and it relieved a little bit of the weight on her chest.

"Now, let's get you two out of here so I can work my charm on this little story."

"What are you going to tell the police?"

Laura gave her a long look. Claire laughed and held her hands up in surrender. "You're right, I don't want to know."

XVIII

CLAIRE WASN'T SURE how they did it, but within the hour they had transferred everything from the ruins of *Sebastian* onto the Kings' larger boat.

Having *Queenie* turned out to be a blessing. The small yacht was much more comfortable than *Sebastian*, bigger in size and faster too, not that she would ever admit that out loud. There was no need to worry about maintenance or where they would sleep on the journey to the Atlantic. The deck had enough room for a small group of friends to enjoy an evening out at sea. Below deck was an intimate bedroom with wood-paneled walls, just big enough for two.

Leaving Laura and Kevin wasn't easy. It was almost as hard as leaving *Sebastian* behind. They'd left a mess for the older couple to clean up, but neither one would hear it. Laura practically started the engine herself as she ushered them onto the boat.

"We've got everything covered here," the older woman shushed. "Don't worry about us."

"A man just killed himself on a sword in your back-yard," Claire said with a meaningful look at Argos's weapon. "How can I not worry?"

"Because you have too much to think about already," Kevin said. "Focus on one thing at a time. When the two of you come back safe and sound, we'll have dealt with this whole thing and then we tackle the next obstacle."

"Like getting your restaurant up and running. So don't worry about us." Laura gave her one last hug that nearly squeezed the air from her lungs, but Claire hung on until the very last second.

∽

It took every ounce of concentration to take Laura's advice to heart. The quiet rumble of the engine in the morning hours reminded her of the angry growls of Circe's monsters. Claire swallowed hard against the memory and navigated back down the river they'd come up only a few nights ago.

It was necessary to submerge herself into navigating the twilight morning water. Doing so allowed her not to think about how she'd nearly been killed in the last couple hours or how she had endangered her closest friends, or the fact that Kevin expected her *and* Argos to return together. She fidgeted with *Queenie*'s speed, checked and double-checked the map with the navigation system, anything that kept her busy. If she stopped for even a second, she feared the tears would come.

Gentle fingers skimmed her arm, coaxing her out of dark thoughts. "Do you want me to take care of that?"

She huffed. "I can captain this ship."

"Gods forbid I tear you away from that wheel." Argos smiled. "I saw what you did to that monster."

Her smile was forced. "I told you I could hold my own."

"I have never doubted that," Argos said softly, his touch lingering to accentuate his words. Her arm suddenly felt hot at his touch; her whole body did. Argos continued, "But it was also incredibly foolish."

"Hey!" She turned to him, breaking the contact between their bodies. "If it was your coin, you would have done the same thing."

"Perhaps, but I've fought these kinds of monsters before. I know what I face."

She raised her chin. "So do I. I saw Circe in the water. I've faced her Pets twice now."

"That was just a display of her power." His face was grim. "On her island, she will be much stronger."

"You said she could be killed," she pointed out, only to have silence follow the accusation. "Didn't you?"

"Yes, but I also said it would not be easy. I could very well die doing it."

That got her attention. She yanked her arm out of his reach and smacked his shoulder. "Are you serious? Is this a suicide mission?"

"Not if I get my immortality back."

"And if you don't? What then?" She waited for his boastful answer, for him to assure her that would not happen. Instead there was hesitation.

"Then I will die a death worthy of a hero."

"That's crazy. Even if you don't get your immortality back, you don't have to fight Circe. You could still find your brothers, you could—" *Stay with me.* She almost said it but stopped herself in time. Clearly, he didn't want to stay with her and that hurt. Her blood sizzled at how willing he was to throw away his life. Her knuckles whitened on the steering wheel. "You don't have to die."

The man next to her didn't move. She hoped he might agree, might see what she meant and how his words had affected her. But those feelings were in vain.

Looking into his eyes, she saw she had said the wrong thing. When Argos spoke, his voice was the gentlest she had ever heard it. "You may know much about this world, Claire, but it will take more than a book to make you an expert in mine."

He stepped away then, moving to the back of the boat, out of her sight.

Good. She scowled at his retreating back. At least now she could concentrate on getting them to their destination. The Bay ran in one direction, the water taking them to where they needed to go, carrying them to the mouth of the Atlantic. The route was a straight shot, easy sailing but not enough to occupy her mind.

His absence didn't soothe her like she'd thought it would. Instead it left her body with several raw holes.

Argos's words echoed in her ears. She'd been working so hard to understand him, to understand his troubles. Circe's presence had shocked her back into reality. If he thought she was just going to let the man she loved die, he had another think coming.

Her eyes widened in realization.

No. Oh God.

She cared about him.

Bingo, her heart seemed to sing with a little flutter.

"Fuck," she seethed, laying her forehead against the wheel. She shouldn't have slept with him. That was her first mistake. Her second mistake—well, that she couldn't place.

She thought back on his smile when he'd eaten her food, the compliments that made her glow.

She lifted her head, sneaking a peek at the infuriating man, and found him staring at her, open concern written across his face until their eyes met. Then he went back to fiddling with their supplies as if nothing were wrong.

As she steered the boat, she began to do the thing she was second-best at. Planning.

~

"You don't have to die." That was what she had said, but she did not know. She did not understand.

He was a man that fought for what was right. Before joining the Order, he had protected his people, their land. His courage and bravery had impressed the gods and they had gifted him with immortality, with brothers with purpose.

What was a man that lived without purpose?

Claire silently steered the boat, ignoring him. This was a fresh kind of torture, the kind that happened when one lost the respect of his men. The feeling of your soul not being in sync with your body. This was not how he had planned this trip to go. He hoped to enjoy every second he had alone with her. Spend these little moments in joy instead of dread.

The sun had fallen below the treetops, painting the sky a dull pink before nightfall. Still he sat at the back of the boat, exiled.

He spared her a look and saw her head drooping at the controls. He was on his feet in an instant, putting a hand on the wheel and the other around her hip. That startled her awake. "Wha-what are you doing?"

"You have been awake for almost two days. You are exhausted."

A stubborn scowl flexed across her lips. "I am not."

"You were falling asleep. I think we should anchor for the evening."

He expected her to fight back and saw the deep inhale of what was guaranteed to be a long-winded protest. But the night air seemed to soothe Claire's anger. No protest left her lips. She nodded weakly and finally detached herself from the helm. Argos rewarded her with a warm smile.

They tiptoed around the small deck, setting up lights, as the sunset blanketed the surrounding area in dusk. Argos dropped anchor and secured *Queenie* just offshore. When he turned around, Claire stood on the boat's small deck, two sandwiches in hand.

"It's not much," she said. "Gotta save the good stuff for the god."

He took it as she sat down next to him, their arms just a hair away from each other. He thought about touching her, of issuing an apology. Though he was still unsure what an apology would mean. He had done nothing wrong— honesty was not a crime—but he could not forget the hurt on Claire's face. A chariot had trampled over her heart, and he had been the driver.

The sky was dotted in stars, the woodland shore blanketed in darkness. Claire reached into her cooler and brought out two beers. She snapped the caps off with quiet efficiency before handing him a bottle.

It was a silent peace offering, one he took with a gracious smile.

He watched her take a deep swig, her slender neck bobbing as she took one gulp, then two. The glass bottle pulled away with a soft pop and a softer sigh. "I'm sorry," she told the empty space between them, "I shouldn't have snapped at you."

"It is human to react to death," Argos said, taking a sip of beer. "I should apologize as well. I thought you understood my quest."

Claire hummed, staring at her uneaten sandwich. "I thought I did too. I just didn't realize what was at stake. Every time I've seen you fight off the monsters, you look unstoppable. I can't believe you could ever lose."

"I'm mortal, Claire, just like you," he said gently.

"I know." She took another drink. "How are you okay with death?"

Argos tilted his head back and stared up at the night sky, seeing the stars there. A few he recognized; it was good to know some things did not change. "If I cannot regain my immortality from the gods, then I can gain it the way heroes like Odysseus have."

Her brow furrowed and then realization sparked. "Through stories?"

"Yes, I hope my brothers would tell of my adventures and, if it is so, my falling." A bitter laugh shook him at the thought. "I could be a cautionary tale."

"Stop that," Claire said, her voice soft, and like magic he did. The hollow feeling eating at his gut eased a little at her command. She moved closer to him, curling against him. His curse flared at her touch, but he ignored it. Instead he wrapped his arm around her small body and accepted the warmth. "You will not be a cautionary tale. If I have to, I'll tell your story. I'll tell everyone about how brave you were fighting back monsters, and how kind you were taking Thalia's burden as your own."

"Thank you, Claire."

She nodded as silence fell between them. Water slapped against the boat, rocking it in an easy rhythm. The sounds of nature echoed around them and then Claire's soft voice. "Would it be so bad? Being mortal?"

He squeezed her shoulders. "I would grow old while my brothers remained young. My body and strength would disappear with age. It would be difficult to say goodbye to that life. They are my family."

"It is difficult to say goodbye to family."

He paused at the tone of her voice, the utter grief he heard there, and then Zeus's lightning struck him. Oh gods. "Your father...," he rasped.

She nodded weakly, not meeting his eyes. "You've probably seen a thousand men die in your lifetime, but that one was enough for me."

No matter how many men he saw die, it was never easy. Victory was a glorious feeling for a hero, but the bloodshed made his mouth bitter. "How did he die?"

A small sniffle came from his arms. "Cancer. It's a disease that weakens the body until there isn't anything left. It was hard to watch."

So that was why. He knew Claire's father had died, but now he understood why she had reacted that way.

He should have known. Guilt twisted in his throat, burning it from the inside out. "He sounds like a great man. You, Laura and Kevin speak very highly of him. With that, he'll live on forever."

"It doesn't make me miss him any less."

"I'm sorry," he said again, "I did not know." There was so much he did not know, and he felt a fool for it. He intended to change that. "Tell me, what will make this better?"

"What?" She snorted. "Argos, it's alright. You already promised me compensation."

"No, I mean—" He searched for the right words. In all his years he had never needed to comfort a woman like this. "What will make you smile again?"

Now. He wanted her to smile now. All day this distance between them had been insufferable.

She was quiet next to him, thinking. "Well, usually cooking makes me feel better, and—"

"And?"

"Nothing, it's stupid."

Curiosity grabbed him now. "I'm sure it is not. Tell me, Claire."

"I… like to dance when I'm feeling down. Nothing big or fancy. When I lived in the city, I would go out, but since I moved it's been nothing but solo dance sessions in the restaurant. There, it's stupid, huh?" She pulled back to look at him and stopped at the sight of his beaming grin. "Why are you smiling like that?"

"Because that's perfect." Dancing, of course. "You know, centuries ago when my people prayed to the gods, we would have feasts that lasted for days. There would be food and dancing." She would have loved it.

Claire tilted her head at him. "Oh really?"

He leaned his head in close and kept his voice low, his words a whispered secret between them. "I say we have our own festival."

"Here? Now?"

"Why not? Maybe it will persuade the gods to our cause"—he smiled—"and I would love to see you dance."

"Argos—" Her voice was a plea as he got to his feet. He did not want her to feel grief over the loss of her boat.

He wanted her to forget all their problems, just for a night, and enjoy herself.

"I will start," he told her, moving his body to the rhythm of the rocking boat. It had been a long time since he'd danced. The movement felt awkward and without any music it was difficult to find a beat. But when Claire suddenly laughed at his attempts, none of that mattered.

A brilliant smile lit up her face, Apollo's sun making an appearance in the nighttime hours. "You are so crazy. You can't dance without music." She stood and moved to the boat's control panel. There she turned on the engine and flicked on the small machine near the steering wheel.

A soft guitar filtered back to him. Under the boat's soft lighting, Claire beamed and sashayed back. "There we go."

She was right, the music helped. Claire's movements were small at first. She was smiling. Occasionally her eyelashes fluttered in a way that would make Aphrodite proud. He was mesmerized.

This reminded him of home. He recalled the sound of flutes, the dancing and the smell of cooked meat from deep in his memory. He tried to imagine what Claire would be like if she had been there, dressed in soft linen, her hair tousled from dancing and her fingers slick with fruit juice.

He moved towards her and she opened her arms to him. When he had last been in the world, dancing so close would have been unheard of, but he was not able to deny Claire anything. As a new song came on, one slower than the first, he allowed her to lead him in their dance.

"How are you not worried right now? Last night we were attacked by a sea monster and now we're spending a night on the water," Claire whispered against his skin.

"There is nowhere else in the world where I feel safer

than at sea. I grew up on boats and fought many battles on them as well. Circe is just one of the creatures who draws power from the water, but there are others who are kind as well."

"Like Poseidon?"

"Yes, even Poseidon. All the gods can be wrathful at times, but they also provided good winds to carry our sails to war. They gave us harvest and wine. I even think Poseidon sent you to me when I was on that boat. A true blessing in the disguise of a nymph."

Claire laughed at that. Her arms tightened around him. "I do feel better," she said, swaying with the music. Their movements made the boat rock more, causing her to stumble. Argos's arms held her tight as she laughed. The sound went directly to his soul.

"I'm glad." Their bodies pressed together, swaying in a steady rhythm, her in his arms. It was nearly perfect except for the inability to hide his growing attraction to her.

"Oh," she noticed. "Do you want me to—"

"No." His voice came out a little rougher than he intended. He swallowed a stone and tried again. "No, not tonight."

For a moment he had not been thinking about the curse, or the pleasures of the skin. It had just been him and Claire, a man and woman, enjoying each other's company. He wanted her to know he did not need the rest.

Understanding softened her features. "Alright, not tonight."

Tonight, there would be no more talk of monsters or death. For once, he wanted to be just a mortal man with his woman, his desire for her more than just a curse. Like this, it felt as if Eros's arrows had truly struck him.

XIX

THIS WAS A challenge. Claire gritted her teeth as she stared at the small grill. It was too small. There wasn't room to cook any side dishes or the crab cake. She'd have to do it one at a time. The lack of counter space was a problem too. She'd resorted to crouching next to the large cooler and using it as a tabletop.

Not for the first time, she cursed her arrogance at volunteering to cook. There was no way she could whip up a five-star meal in the middle of the water, certainly no meal fit for a god.

It was too late, though. Squaring her shoulders, she made the best out of the situation and went about her recipes. She lathered butter on burgers, flipping them and seasoning them until they were perfect. Smoke wafted in the air, filling it with the smell of cooked meat. When the meat was cooked, she flipped them onto a spare plate and moved on to phase two, the crab cakes.

Her hands were covered in sticky batter as she portioned out the small cakes and shaped them into perfect circles before slapping them on the grill. She inhaled the smell of crab meat with a smile. The hint of green onion and spices made her mouth water. Damn, she was good. Her concentration focused on the food in front of her, making sure the meat was properly cooked and not burned. These needed to be the best gods-damned sliders she'd ever made.

"If he does not show, I'll eat this offering myself," Argos huffed, eyeing the small food the same way he'd looked at Claire the night before. One hand uncrossed from his chest and reached to flick the side of the homemade crab dip before Claire smacked it away.

"Don't eat the feast," she tutted, placing the finished crab cakes on the plate. She got to work putting the sliders together, trying to make it look as visually appealing as possible. The plating wasn't her best work, but Argos assured her it would be enough. Three small crab meat sliders with her own pita dip on the side glistened under the summer sun. For the hundredth time she leaned forward and swiped the edges of the plate clean, making sure it was a feast fit for a god.

Insecurity clawed at her insides as she stared at the small offering. "Do you think it's enough?"

"Probably not," Argos said as he stepped away from the display and came up to her. One large arm encircled her waist and tugged her into a warm embrace. She felt his body shiver at the contact, calling out to her as the curse came alive. Claire melted into the touch, the strength and assurance it provided along with the lust. When he whispered in her ear, she was done for. "He'll probably want seconds."

She could empathize with that need. In their short time together, she'd gotten use to his frequent touches and kisses. At times it felt like they were the only two people in the world. It was becoming more and more difficult to keep her hands to herself. She could almost believe they were actually a regular couple, that there wasn't a curse urging him to touch her at every moment.

Claire shook her head of the thought. "Well maybe I can whip up some dessert."

Argos was quiet, and when she dared to look at him, there was a mixture of exasperation and warmth. Her breath caught at the sight. She'd seen it before. In the eyes of her father when her mother squeamishly stepped onto a boat. When Laura announced she wouldn't be cooking at home after a full day of running the restaurant and Kevin agreed. Even Thalia had given the look to her daughter.

It was a look that said, *I love all of you, wholly and completely.*

Maybe it wasn't all curses and sex.

She ached to believe that.

Despite her bad jokes and her hesitation to believe in the world Argos had introduced her to, he looked at her like that.

She stepped out of the embrace and towards the railing of the boat. "Alright, how do I do this?"

"Call out to him," Argos encouraged. "Tell the god you present him with an offering."

The smell of cooked meat wafted with the sharp tang of sea salt. There was no one else on the water; everything around them had gone quiet in anticipation. They were at the mouth of the bay, where small islands appeared sporadically, and the open water trickled out into a vast ocean. Goose bumps prickled up her arm as she took a deep breath, praying that they'd gone far enough. Then she let the words fall from her mouth. "Poseidon. Great God of the Sea, I have put my heart into an offering in your honor."

Argos stifled a groan behind her. "A simple name would do. Now you've gone and stroked his ego."

She turned to him. "I just said whatever came to mind. If there is an incantation you should probably let me know."

He looked amused. "Incantation?"

A blush scorched her face. "I sound like a moron."

"Don't listen to him, lovely, I liked how you did it just fine," a silky voice purred behind her, followed by the quiet dripping of water.

Claire jumped, unable to stifle a squeak as she whirled to meet the new guest. A man was propped against the railing as if he had always been there. When Thalia had first advised them on calling for Poseidon, Claire had envisioned a man with a long white beard. He'd been handsome in her mind; the imagination could never suggest an ugly god.

Poseidon's his hair was the color of wet rocks, dark and glistening as if he'd just walked out of the shower. It was clipped short against his scalp while a scraggy beard clung to his chin. His eyes were the bluest she'd ever seen; they could put the sky to shame. It was almost impossible to tear her own away. Unfortunately, his face was the only appealing thing about him.

He wore a shirt with cut-off sleeves and loose pants made of simple cotton. A strange woven bag was slung across his shoulder with the crumpled tips of paper sticking out of it. Even stranger was the metal pitchfork he held in one hand, a cheeseburger wrapper speared on one tip.

He wasn't at all what she'd imagined, but there was still something alluring about him. Her eyes were glued to the spots of his skin where water evaporated in midair. Poseidon smiled when he noticed her gaze. His eyes changed from Caribbean blue to rainfall, and her entire lower region quivered.

No, he wasn't what she was expecting, and by all accounts he looked like a homeless man. But he was still… beautiful. Impossibly so. It was difficult to sort out if her body was responding in intimidation or lust.

"Great God of the Sea," Poseidon repeated, and she realized he had the same accent as Argos. There was a pattern in the way he spoke that sounded like an old song. "It has been a long time since anyone has called me that. People just tend to call out for Poseidon."

Claire couldn't move. Seeing him felt as if something had been desperately missing in her life, and now she was getting it at last.

God, she was meeting God or… at least, a god.

"Poseidon," Argos said behind her. The name was bitten out in a growl. "My Claire has never met any of your kind before…"

"Ah, an Atheos." Poseidon grinned. "I have forgotten the effect we have on them. I'll try to tone it down."

And just like that, the ball of mixed emotions in Claire's stomach vanished. Her muscles sagged and she felt hollow, nearly brought to the edge of ecstasy and then denied. She blinked rapidly, trying to puzzle out what had happened. Argos's hand landed on the small of her back. "Claire?"

"I'm sorry," she murmured, voice shaky and lips dried. Her hand came up and patted her cheeks, trying to slap away the awe that still tingled across the skin. Cautiously she looked at Poseidon, who was taking in the small display of food. "What just happened?"

"You just met your first god."

"Is that normal?" She took a deep breath and tried not to dwell on the dull pain between her legs.

"There is nothing about a god that is normal."

"Right, okay." She took a couple more seconds to collect herself before daring to look at the Sea God again.

Poseidon's attention was back on them, his eyes focused on Argos. "Well, hero, it certainly has been a long time since I've seen you. I barely recognize you."

Argos held his body at full height, his jaw locked under the god's attention. "As do you. It appears the modern day has not treated you well."

"Well, I wouldn't say that," Poseidon said, lifting his metal stick and dispatching the piece of garbage into the bag around his shoulder. "I was just in Brazil cleaning up a beach when you summoned me. Hardly the glamorous position I was in a few centuries ago." He snapped his fingers and his clothes rippled like water, changing from hobo chic to something out of a boating magazine. A dark blue tailored jacket, white Dockers, and brand-new shoes decorated Poseidon. His trash pick shimmered as it transformed into a beautiful gold trident.

Claire gapped at the change, while Argos bowed his head. "We are honored that you have graced us with your presence, Poseidon. We present you with an offering in thanks."

"Oh, so you do learn," the god laughed. "I did hear your calls before, but you know how this works. I don't just appear for anybody. That includes ex-heroes."

"An honest mistake," Argos said. "It has been a long time since I've interacted with any of your siblings."

"Yes, apparently Circe has been keeping you occupied. There is little my waters don't hear, and they have been subjected to her howls of anger ever since you escaped," hummed Poseidon, a quiet smile sitting on his lips.

"Please"—Argos motioned to the small plate and wine—"enjoy your feast."

Claire felt the nerves flutter in her stomach. She'd seen senators and celebrities eat her dishes but never a god.

He looked down at the plate, eyes narrowed. "As far as feasts go, this is not the grandest," Poseidon picked up the plate and inspected it. "I suppose I'm expected to accept anything these days."

When he took the first bite of slider, she nearly closed her eyes when a hand reached out and cupped her own. She squeezed Argos's reassuring hand tightly when Poseidon swallowed. The god's mouth pursed, and she felt all the air leave her lungs. Then he took another bite.

"This is…" Poseidon started before he dunked a chunk of bread in the dip and popped it in his mouth. The low groan of pleasure he let out after that told Claire exactly what she needed to know. "*Divine!* And I would know."

Claire laughed in relief. "It tastes better with wine."

The god perked. "You have some, I assume."

"Of course." Thalia had been right. Wine appeared to be a vice for the gods. She poured some into the only cup they had, a red plastic Solo, and handed it to their guest.

Hungrily the man took another mouth full of the meal and chased it with a sip of red. He made the same rumbling noise of approval. "I must admit, this is the best offering I've had in nearly a century."

"The best cook in the area had a hand in it." Argos looked at her, and Poseidon followed his line of sight.

Claire blushed. "You should see what I can make in a proper kitchen."

Poseidon grinned, new interest flickering in his eyes. "Alright," he said, sitting on the small fold-out chair they had set up. Seeing him sprawled in it dressed like a millionaire holding a plastic cup of wine was an amusing sight, but she knew better than to point that out. Without a word, the cup turned into a proper wineglass and split into two more. "Pour yourself some of this wine and tell me why you called for me."

Claire was more than happy to pour both herself and Argos glasses. Her nerves were shot from meeting her first supreme being and having him enjoy her food. She gulped down half of her glass before Argos started on his explanation.

"As you can see, your sister has cursed me and taken my immortality. I need a god's blessing to get it back."

"And you want me to give you that blessing? To give you a quest?" Poseidon rubbed at his chin, contemplating.

Argos nodded. "I do not have any ill wishes towards Hestia—"

"You couldn't hurt her even if you did," Poseidon interrupted.

"But Circe is another story. I will avenge the years she took from me, the pain she put me through."

"You seemed to enjoy that pain those first hundred years."

Argos's face went ash white at the comment and Claire glared.

"She kept me for far more than a hundred years, and any enjoyment I felt has long since curdled into hatred." There was no hesitation in Argos's voice. Where before he'd sounded almost mild-mannered, he now spoke with calm determination. His next words came out as a vow. "I will kill the Sea Witch."

"The odds are not in your favor without your

immortality. And Hestia's touch is still on you," Poseidon noted. "Her curse will continue to turn your body against you even as an immortal."

"Take it from me, then," Argos growled. "Only one of her elder siblings would have the strength. Take this curse off me and give me back my life."

The god's features shifted, causing him to look much older. "This world is different from what you remember. It doesn't need you to protect it anymore, or your brothers for that matter." Poseidon paused at the words, holding Argos's gaze as if forcing the hero to come to the same realization, no matter how much it might hurt. Then those sea-blue eyes slid to Claire. "The monsters have been chased into hiding, and the Atheos state of mind has spread. You don't need your immortality back."

There was an undeniable sadness in his words and Claire couldn't help but feel like they were directed towards her as much as Argos.

"You're wrong," Argos seethed. His anger was barely contained by his own self-preservation.

Poseidon took his anger without complaint. Picking at the tip of his trident, he said, "You've lived through enough eras to know nothing can stay the same forever. Empires rise and fall, even those of immortals. Even my own father ruled the gods before Zeus dethroned him. I'm just grateful the humans would rather forget about us than doom me under a mountain."

"So, you're picking up garbage because mortals won't do it for you anymore?"

She watched emotion flicker across the god's face once again—a look of longing and resignation that didn't look right on such an ageless face. *Ah*, Claire thought to herself, *so you do feel emotion.*

"What would make you think gods don't feel emotions?" Poseidon pointed a knowing look at Claire, his voice as calm as the water surrounding them. "Humans have made it clear they feel they no longer need me or my siblings. And I don't need them either."

Claire tensed. *All-powerful being*, she reminded herself, *tread carefully*. "We've heard the gods haven't been as... involved as they used to be," she quickly clarified, flashing what she hoped was a charming smile. Just in case, she poured more wine and it seemed to do the trick. "But I know that can't be the case. You're here, after all, though I'm glad you aren't as scary as the Odysseus story made you out to be."

Poseidon snorted into his wineglass, then wiped away the red liquid dribbling down his chin. "Now that is a name I haven't heard in a long time. I admit, things have changed since then. I don't put nearly as much effort into torturing mortals now, even if they do deserve it."

"Why?" Claire pressed softly, keeping in mind who it was exactly she was talking to. A god with enough power to sink them if he wanted, who could easily decide not to help Argos if she annoyed him. But if he had so much power, why were the gods pulling back?

"I've never had to explain myself to a mortal before," Poseidon mused, pinning her with his changing eyes. Claire stared right back, watching as he plucked up another one of her hamburgers and tossed it into his mouth. He continued to talk around the crab meat. "After living for so many years, we've come to realize that the world wishes to change with or without the gods' wishes. It might not feel like that to you—your mortal lives are just specks in history while we are stone. We sit in the same place, do the same things, our abilities are ingrained in us. We do not like change, but mortals, they love it. My siblings and I blinked one day, and they were off, building new structures, communing with new gods." He took a deep swig of wine, as if the words burned the back of his throat. "We fought the progress at first, putting mortals in their place, but that never seemed to work for long. We helped build empires and soon they would fall, replaced by new leaders and new religions who had no place for us. That's when we decided to leave you to it."

"You're a god, though," Claire argued weakly. "If you wanted to, couldn't you do something to strike the fear into mortals again? Shouldn't Zeus or someone do something about that?" She thought about the words coming out of her mouth and quickly added, "Not that I'd want you to be angry with us."

"My brother has been missing for a long time," Poseidon said, letting his words sink in. "And when he disappeared, we had our own problems to address. I don't like Zeus very much, but somehow he managed to hold everyone in check. We all fought for his position and no one came out the victor. Some looked for him, are still looking for him, but to no avail. Eventually we all grew tired of the fighting, of being forgotten, and we've settled."

"Settled?" Argos frowned at the word but gave a pointed look to the god's attire.

Poseidon shrugged his shoulders. "Yes, settled. Mortals have taken our blessings and turned them into places even we wish not to attend to. Ares has lost all interest in war. Modern warfare has no rules, no armies to rally behind.

It's cruel, merciless, and senseless. Dionysus has lost interest in the feast, where people drink to lose themselves and commit atrocities towards each other. Last I saw Athena, she was passing out pamphlets at a university in Europe, trying to spread wisdom, but the voices of others drown her out. As for myself, the mortals spill their oily greed into my oceans and tarnish my beaches." He raised the bag by his side with a sigh. "Only Hades seems undeterred by the changes, but I suppose no matter how much time changes mortals must always die. So you see, this world does not belong to us anymore."

"That's not true," Argos said sternly. "I *need* to be immortal again. Circe is not the only creature I need to kill."

"Did you not hear me? The monsters are gone. Who else has wronged you so?" Poseidon looked unconcerned as he took a long swig of wine.

"Xanthus."

The god's glass cracked in his hand, wine spilling between his fingers. "What did you say?"

"You heard me," Argos said. "I know things have changed. I have heard the cry of those who have been wronged by my brother. I promised that I would track him down."

The boat rocked suddenly, hit by an angry wave. Claire staggered and clutched onto Argos to steady herself. Both men were glued in place, as if they hadn't felt a thing. "You don't think we have tried?"

"I thought the gods were minding their own business."

"Other heroes have already attempted to catch Xanthus, and they have either failed or joined him on his crusade."

"You have not sent the right men," Argos told the god easily. "I know him better than anyone."

"He can do it," Claire spoke up and suddenly she found herself the center of attention. She shook off the slight thrill her body felt at Poseidon's gaze and pushed on. "Argos is the best, even now as a mortal. He can take Xanthus down."

"Do you even know what he has done?" Poseidon asked.

"We saw evidence of his handiwork. A destroyed temple, disfavor from the gods." Argos raised a brow. "There is no need to punish those who unknowingly sheltered him."

"Ignorance is no excuse," Poseidon snapped. "That man has destroyed nearly two hundred temples in the last decade alone. They were already few in number and now even more so. Not even we know what he plans, and you think you can stop him?"

"I do."

"You'd do that? Without hearing his side of the story? You would kill a man who was once your brother in arms? Even if I didn't return your immortality?" Skepticism dripped from the god's voice and Argos hesitated.

It was just a heartbeat. Long enough that Claire could see the moment he realized this vow would mean killing a man he had once known. Enough that they both remembered seeing the broken shell of a temple underneath Thalia's wine shop, the way Xanthus had destroyed one family and probably hundreds more.

"I made a promise to someone he wronged," Argos repeated, his voice stone. "It matters not to me if I'm mortal or immortal when I do it."

Poseidon considered the two of them for a long moment before nodding. "Alright, I will lift Hestia's curse and give you a quest. Complete it and your immortality will be restored."

Claire sagged in relief. Argos turned to her and smiled

the brightest, most genuine expression of happiness she'd seen since meeting him. Things were finally looking up.

Face solemn in concentration, Poseidon raised a hand towards Argos and gracefully brought it down. A wordless gesture, but as his hand fell, Argos fell to the deck.

She followed him, worry clawing up her throat as her hands touched his shoulders. "Argos?"

He blinked slowly, a shaky breath coming out between his lips. "I feel it…"

"It's gone?" She couldn't help but glance down at his crotch, where the nearly constant evidence of the curse had always stood out to her. It wasn't there now.

Argos looked up to meet her; their eyes met and held each other. Claire didn't dare breathe as she searched for any sign of emotions. His hand gently cupped her cheek just as she saw it. The smallest hint of regret. "It should be gone."

Why are you sad? The question tugged at her, but the god did not spare them the moment.

"And now for your quest." Both hero and woman looked up as Poseidon spoke. "If you accept it, I will grant you your immortality once again and a place with your brothers."

Argos nodded, his body practically trembling in anticipation. "I'll do anything."

Poseidon smiled, slow and lazy, before finishing off his wine. "For your quest, you must receive Hestia's forgiveness for the wrong you have done her."

❦

Argos gaped at the man in front of him as the words echoed in his head. Silently he prayed this was another of the gods' jokes, their cruel sense of humor showing itself before presenting a proper quest.

The smug smile that stayed in place assured him the Sea God was deadly serious.

Acquire Hestia's forgiveness? Where was the honor in that? Where was the blood, the battle, the glory? He barely noticed voicing these concerns out loud until Poseidon laughed.

"Oh, I don't know. There might be a chance for a battle when Hestia lays eyes on you," mused the god.

"She will not have it," Argos said. "She will never forgive me my transgressions. I have tried…"

"Then try harder," replied Poseidon. "This is what I ask of you."

Anger ignited his blood along with the feeling of embarrassment. So close, he was so close to being reunited with his kin, and still the gods decided to play their games with him. "Then I will find another who will give me a quest."

"So quick to turn to someone else, even when I took my sister's curse off you." Poseidon stood, his body growing to a threatening height, looming two men high. His voice was still as calm as the Dead Sea. "I have never known a hero to refuse the quest given to them."

"You ask the impossible," snapped Argos.

"Then maybe you should wonder why I ask it."

Silence cut across the ship. There would be no changing the god's request; the firm look in Poseidon's gaze told him as much. Argos looked down at his clenched fists. The sharp shells of his wine glass cracked, cutting into his palm. The pain was nothing but a numb pulse against his skin.

The discussion was closed, and Poseidon had given them everything they had asked for, regardless if they liked the outcome our not.

XX

"I WILL TAKE THIS wine with me. It would be a waste to leave it," Poseidon declared, eyeing the wine bottle in approval. "Claire, it was truly a delight to eat your meal."

Claire scrambled to her feet, still feeling frazzled at what had just occurred around her. It was practically an afterthought for her to reply, "You're welcome." She couldn't stop herself from looking at Argos, the slump in his shoulders, the utter defeat on such a strong face. The tension between mortal and immortal had died away with Argos's silence. Poseidon seemed happy to pretend as if nothing had occurred.

Poseidon didn't move, his head tilted in consideration as he looked at her, and only her. After a moment he crooked a finger. "Come here for a second, young heart."

The request threw her. Maybe he sensed the irritation that had pierced her when he'd given the quest.

Good. She wouldn't hide it, not even for a god. It was an

unreasonable request. Just thinking about it made her skin crawl, imagining Argos asking that woman for forgiveness.

Claire took a deep breath and did as requested, moving closer until there was just the plate between them. Her instincts went haywire the closer she got. The smell of salt and sunlight clung to the god like perfume, and she inhaled it greedily.

He had everything working for him, filling all the senses and every space with his essence. It would be easy to become infatuated with him. Claire made sure to keep herself in check.

Even though he gave her charming smiles and complimented her food, he had still broken the man she had come to care for dearly. Had destroyed Argos's dreams without batting an eye. He was Hestia's brother, and the fickle way he handled their lives proved it.

"I am not bad, Claire," Poseidon said.

She raised her chin. "I never said you were."

"And yet you're glaring at me after I have showered your offering in compliments." He pushed the empty plate into her hands and she took it. "It has to be like this."

"Why?" She dared to stare into his fathomless eyes. "Do your cosmic powers allow you to see into the future or something?"

The question got a laugh that would melt a million hearts. "It doesn't exactly work like that."

"Then why put him through this?"

"The hero's gift is one from the gods," Poseidon explained. "All of us. We must all bless the individual, to help prevent someone unworthy from acquiring the power." His eyes drifted away from her in a look of guilt. She realized that even with this requirement, Xanthus had become a hero. Poseidon's fingers trailed down his beard as he continued, "Hestia must accept him before he can join his brothers again."

She felt helpless, realizing there was no other way. "And if she doesn't?"

Poseidon's smile was weak but no less handsome. "Your man is strong. He doesn't need the gods to defeat Circe."

In a swift movement, he bent forward and brushed his lips against her forehead. They felt cool as water against feverish skin. "I hope this was not the last time I feast on your delicious food."

"Well, then, you better hope we survive this," she said before her lips pursed on the words.

We? What would she do if Argos didn't get Hestia's help, or if Circe killed him? She couldn't go back to a normal life, could she? Go back to trying to pick up her restaurant and forget everything? She couldn't do that.

Poseidon must have known what she was thinking. "This is why I don't come here anymore," he mumbled. There was pity in his voice. "I get attached too easily."

He leaned back over *Queenie*'s railing and gracefully tipped over the side. No splash followed him. When Claire rushed over to look, there was no sign of the god. Just the gentle waters massaging the boat's side.

She took a deep shuddering breath, knowing deep in her bones that they were in trouble.

❧

In times of doubt and despair, wine was always a dear friend. Claire knew this from recent challenges regarding her restaurant, and she had learned that it was healthy to indulge, but just for a day.

She knew this, but she didn't know how Argos handled failure. He hadn't said a word since Poseidon's departure, just sat against the bench, his head leaning against the ship's wall. Deep in concentration, trying to figure out his next step.

But Claire already knew. Gently, she nudged him with her hand. When his grass-green eyes opened, she held up the wine bottle and two plastic cups. "Here's what we're going to do," she told him. "We're going to drink this bottle and come up with a game plan."

"I thought Thalia only gave us one bottle."

"She did. I bought another to thank her for the help. It's important to establish good relationships with local businesses." She nudged him again with the bottle. "Here, it's the good stuff."

His lips quirked up and he didn't deny her as she filled the glasses. "Hestia will never forgive me. A goddess's anger is impossible to temper."

"Even so, that doesn't mean we're completely screwed," Claire told him as he put his lips against the bottle. "Look, you told me that your goal was to get revenge on Circe. We still can, but it's going to be a lot harder without the gods' blessing."

Argos looked at her. The embers of determination that always sparked in his eyes were gone. Her stomach pinched at the sight, but she kept talking. "We have nothing to lose by trying to gain Hestia's forgiveness, and if we don't, then we'll come up with a way to fight Circe."

"No, Claire," he interrupted. His voice was firm, back to its usual commanding tone. "I will not involve you in this any longer. You've already offered too much."

Something difficult lodged itself in her throat.

Rejection. Claire pushed down the feeling with a ferociousness and kept talking. "What I'm saying is we have to give Hestia a try. What do we have to lose?"

"She could punish me again. Her anger reawakened."

Claire blinked, feeling cold. "She can do that?"

Argos's held her gaze. "Finish that book of yours and you'll know the extent of a god's rage. Poseidon was gentle enough to you, but he made Odysseus suffer for years because of a slight."

"And Odysseus still made it home to Penelope," Claire shot back and felt a smug slither of satisfaction when he had nothing to counter with. Her hand reached out for his arm, giving him as much reassurance as she could. "You have to try."

He shrugged the touch away and said nothing.

Another twisted feeling of rejection fluttered through her. Something had changed between them since Poseidon's visit. The air had shifted; the warm familiarity was gone. He could barely look at her. Since Poseidon had lifted the curse, there had been cold dismissal.

Claire frowned and nudged the hero hard in the ribs, noticing his recoil at her touch. There was no way she'd hurt him; something was seriously off. "Hey, what's the matter with you? If you really don't want my opinion here, I won't give it. And you can just get the hell off my boat."

"What?" His attention focused back on her and she rewarded it with a no-kidding glare.

"Usually the brooding hero thing is attractive, but right now I need to make sure you're alright."

"Of course I am alright."

"Then why won't you let me touch you?"

"Because of the curse!" The shout was unexpected,

causing Claire's mouth to shut with an audible click as she watched the visible frustration twist Argos's features.

She didn't know what to say. "I thought he took away the curse."

"I thought he did…" He groaned and looked at her, looking more anguished than she'd ever seen him. "I felt his power. I felt it wash through me and I was left empty. Then you came to me, touched me… and it was back. In that moment all I wanted was you, Claire."

Relief pulsed through her like a heartbeat, and Claire nearly dropped her glass of wine at the news. "You do?" Her voice was barely above a whisper. Anything louder and she feared her excitement would bleed through.

"My body still… the curse… I want you so badly. I'm sorry, Claire. I do not think the curse was lifted."

The look of apology that he wore did her in. "You delusional man." She couldn't hold it back any longer. She laughed, placing the wine bottle on the floor before lunging at him. The look of apology that he wore did her in. Kisses were planted along his jawline until they fell upon his mouth. "Don't apologize for wanting me."

"But the curse…"

"Argos, the curse is gone," she said slowly, grinning like an idiot. "Did you ever consider that those feelings are your own?"

"I…" He trailed off quickly, brows narrowing as he considered her words.

"If you're still afraid you're cursed, then I think it's contagious," she murmured, dragging her lips down his throat and licking the tender skin. "Because I want you as well."

"Claire," he growled, body tense under her touch as he clung for control.

She pressed her body down against his erection and said, "Take me."

"Gods, woman," he bit out before his large arms wrapped around her and hoisted her up. She squeaked in surprise as he carried her downstairs to the bedroom. Her body bounced on the mattress when he dropped her. There wasn't much time to say anything more before Argos was on her. Their lips met, and the air was stolen from her lungs.

Argos kissed her with a passion that hadn't been there before. Where there was once just pure lust, now there was something else. He took his time, his tongue making velvety strokes along her neck and down between her breasts, dipping towards her navel as he hiked up her shirt.

Claire's hands greedily tried to undo her pants while he performed his silent worship, moaning and arching when he found a particularly sensitive spot. "Oh," she whined. "This is all very nice, but do you think we could pick up the pace?"

"No," hummed the man on top of her, and he pulled away long enough for her to see the wicked gleam in his eyes. "Claire, I have wanted you for so long, but this is the first time I feel in control. I plan on taking my time with this."

Her head fell back, a groan of dismay silenced by another kiss. His hands massaged her breasts until her nipples were tender peaks. Claire panted, feeling the way her body tensed at his skillful touch. An orgasm was already building, and she didn't even have her clothes off.

"Argos," she pleaded again but he shook his head.

"I will give you pleasure, Claire. Slowly."

But he had some small mercy on her by tugging her pants down. Eagerly she kicked her legs out and shivered as his hands stroked her folds. The underwear she still wore created sensuous friction with his touch. When he bent down to lick at a rosy nipple, she bucked uncontrollably.

The orgasm came suddenly and quickly, but it shook her entire body for eternity. A cry spilled from her lips as she curled into his touch, shaking while his free hand cradled her head. "Oh God," Claire breathed, blinking past the sensation. "Oh God."

"Do not pray to any gods here, Claire," Argos said. "They have no place between you and me."

"You mean there is no sex god I can pray to?" She smiled, eyes lighting up. "Or is that you?"

"Hush," came the gentle reply as his head dipped between her legs and planted a kiss against her underwear.

She shivered and obeyed. Forgetting the names of Greek gods wouldn't be a problem, but it meant something to her that even Argos seemed to want to forget about them. His attention was solely focused on her. All the other times, he had been lost to his own lust, and while she had enjoyed it, she had known something was missing. This time it was different.

This wasn't stress relief; this was passion.

His lips were tasting her, moaning as if she were a delicacy. Heat touched Claire's face at the sinful sight, but she couldn't look away. Anticipation built in the pit of her stomach when she noticed his large hands clasp around her thin panties, pulling them down. The warm heat of his tongue licked at her bare skin, sliding between her pussy's lips with ease.

Her body, still buzzing from the recent orgasm, seized at the touch. She moaned. After disposing of her underwear on the floor those hands found their way back to her breasts, rolling the nipples between thumb and forefingers. One hand kept up its frenzied attention on her nipple while the other came down to her thigh, holding her legs spread open.

The edge of a second orgasm tickled her senses and she began pumping her hips to get as much of his tongue's lavish touches as possible. At her encouragement, his efforts picked up. Argos was eating her out with the same frenzy she'd seen him eat her meals. The moans of pleasure coming from him went straight to her gut. The sight was unbelievably sexy, and when she caught a peek of his green eyes glancing up to catch her expression, it pushed her over the edge.

She screamed, throwing her head back as her body crumpled in on itself. To her astonishment, Argos didn't stop. He kept darting his tongue in and out, holding her as she came undone. As the last shivers calmed down, he finally pulled back, placing kisses on her naked trembling thighs, up her stomach and towards her neck.

Her body refused to move after the exertion he'd put her through. She was spent after the day of excitement. Luckily, Argos seemed to know exactly what to do to accommodate her. He got up, shuffling around the cabin before returning with a blanket. Claire smiled at him. "I haven't had that many orgasms since college. Give me a moment and I'll return the favor."

He shook his head. "I do not require it. Tonight was all about you. Your pleasure is mine."

"Don't you want to celebrate? I mean, we lifted your curse! We are one step closer to getting your immortality back." Somehow, she found the strength to sit up and made room on the bed for him. He crawled on the mattress and together they nestled under the blanket. Outside the sun was setting over the water, casting the sky in colors of bright pink and pastel blue. It was beautiful, romantic.

"Did this not feel like a celebration to you?" he asked her softly.

Oddly enough, it did. Their lovemaking had been a moment of freedom for them both. The cloud of the curse was gone. For the first time, they could take their time with each other, enjoy the act of making love without any precursors. Argos could touch a woman without shame. He could give his lover his undivided attention, and she could relish being at the center of that attention.

She laid her head on his shoulder and smiled when she heard the steady rhythm of his heart. When he became immortal, would that sound go away? The thought burned at the edge of her mind before she forced herself to push it away. Questioning his immortality would lead down a dark path, revealing answers she was not yet ready to discover.

*

For the first time in a long time, his body felt at ease. Even lying on the boat's small bed, he was content. With Claire draped over him like a warm blanket, his limbs boneless from exhaustion, there was nowhere else he would rather be. Her small body barely covered his own, but he did not dare change their position. They had spent a whole day anchored in the exact same spot, nested in the small bed below deck, doing everything their bodies would allow them to do. Claire had given him pleasure before, and he the same, but this time it was different. He felt as if he could breathe again. Finally, his body was satisfied, and Claire had been the one to bring him to his point.

"I do not think I will be able to move tomorrow," Argos murmured into her soft locks.

He felt Claire's lips move against his skin. "Really? Did little old me do that? I don't think I've ever been the one to exhaust a man." She pulled back, her body arching gracefully, like a cat, as she looked at him. "You must be getting old."

"Gods," Argos laughed, "I suppose I am."

Lazy strokes up and down her back occupied his hand, the skin smooth and free of scars. She hummed at the touches and snuggled back against him. "So where can we find Hestia?"

"Hestia is the goddess of the hearth. A person's home. We should be able to beseech her there," he answered.

The body in his arms pulled back, allowing Claire to blink her large eyes at him. "That's it? No 'I will deal with Hestia myself.' You're going to let me help you?"

"I have tried that before and it did not work. Unless, of course, you do want to leave the rest to me." He raised his brows, causing Claire to laugh.

"As if. I'd like to give your goddess ex-girlfriend a piece of my mind."

The idea of the two of them on a quest together warmed his heart. There were few lovers who made such an incredible duo—fighting off monsters together, confronting the gods. He could not ask for a better partner. He laughed softly. "I fear I have corrupted your simple Atheos life past the point of repair."

"You have," Claire sighed, sounding happy, "gods, you have."

Argos ran his fingers through her hair, brushing down

its tangled waves. Claire felt her body purr in pleasure. "So, tomorrow we'll head back home," she said.

"Home," he repeated thinking of the tiny building just off the water. There had been a time when he'd had no home but the sea. His men and brothers had been family, and his bed had been different in every city. He had been young and restless back then. So eager to prove himself a hero, and after that to find the next fight.

Even Hestia could not tie him to one place, though she'd tried to persuade him to stay in the city of Rome, where the people had built the biggest and most extravagant temple in her honor.

So much had changed since then.

So much had changed in just a few short days. All since he'd met Claire.

Over the years, he had forgotten what it was like to be mortal, to be a man. The fear of uncertainty, the adrenaline of living for each moment, the relief that came when one met people who cared enough to help. His brothers were his family and he still yearned to be reunited with them, but suddenly, facing a life without them did not seem impossible.

XXI

ON THE OUTSIDE, The Saucy Leg looked much the same. The white paint was visible from the shoreline. It looked like a picture from the water, reminding Claire how much she loved her quaint little restaurant. The door was closed, and light glowed against the windows, making it look as if someone were home. The weather had washed away any paw prints scarring the ground. It was as if that first night had been a dream.

Walking inside was where dream became nightmare. Claire had to bite back a gasp when she stepped into the broken building. The night she'd woken up to pack of wild animals in the small space felt like eons ago, and the late-night hour made her memories dark and haunted. Like a bad dream. A really, really bad dream.

By seeing it now in the light of day, she was forced to accept reality. The overthrown tables and the claw marks etched into floorboards, her newly purchased televisions in shambles on the ground. All the time, all the money, ruined in one night.

Tears burned her eyes, but she was quick to blink them back. *You knew it would be bad*, she told herself, *you can't run away from it.*

Still, the thought of cleaning the place up was daunting. She wouldn't be opening her restaurant anytime soon—and that was a hard pill to swallow.

"Do not worry, Claire," Argos said, jaw clenched as he took in the room. "I will help make things right."

She nodded mutely, recalling the promise of treasure that he'd made. Without the blessing of the gods, would he be able to make good on that promise? It was selfish to think such a thing, but Claire could allow herself this brief moment to grieve.

"Claire." Argos stepped towards her, but she moved away. He didn't need to see her like this. There was enough on both their minds. Trying to survive Circe and appeasing Hestia were more important than a few broken tables.

They had a job to do. After it was all done, when Argos left, she would let the tears come.

"I'll go see if there's anything in the kitchen we can give to Hestia." She offered up a weak smile before fleeing towards the kitchen.

Even the back kitchen was a mess. The cats had spared nothing. Cabinets lay open, their contents spilled across the floor: damaged food, scratched-up pots and pans. She closed her eyes; there was little to salvage. With a sigh, Claire settled on a simple bag of chips and dip. The idea of serving dip that wasn't freshly made was abhorrent to her, but the situation called for it and, if she was honest, she didn't feel like wasting too much effort on Hestia.

Plating the food was therapy, though. It helped calm her nerves and gave her time to organize her thoughts. *So, your restaurant won't open anytime soon*, she told herself. *It will happen. It will. Right now, things are crazy, but it will all work out. Besides...* The voice in her head grew thoughtful. *If you opened the restaurant, you wouldn't be able to help him.*

Her restaurant or the man. She couldn't have it both ways.

Claire had sacrificed so much to make this dream a reality: money, relationships, even her career. She'd never been willing to give up her future for any boyfriend or any man. Period. But now it wasn't about her. It was about Thalia who had been hurt so terribly by Xanthus, and Argos who'd been tortured for years at the hands of Circe. Helping them was more important than getting her restaurant off the ground. Her father would never forgive her if she put food before people.

She sighed and brought the chips out to the dining hall. Argos had straightened some of the debris, moving bits of the smashed tables aside and opening the windows of the restaurant. The salty air from outside filled the space, making it smell cleaner.

"Is that Hestia's offering?" He took in the chips and dip with amusement.

"We won't tell her what Poseidon got, right?"

"Agreed." He took the plate out of her hand and placed a quick kiss against her lips. The offering was set on a table that was still intact and moved to the center of the room.

Argos's head swiveled around the room, checking and double-checking things before his eyes finally landed on Claire. He paused for a moment, staring at her, considering her before saying, "I hate to ask this of you, but you have to be the one to summon her."

"What? Why me?"

"It is your home. Hestia responds better if the owner of the hearth summons her."

"Okay."

"And after she arrives, you'll need to leave."

"Excuse me?" She frowned at him, but he was quick to ease her annoyance.

"I do not know how she will react to you, Claire."

"And what about how she'll react to you? She could curse you again or zap you somewhere without me knowing?"

He didn't deny it, but his voice dipped low in a plea. "Please, let me speak to her alone."

Claire swallowed hard. She wasn't blind; she knew exactly where his need to speak in private came from. The idea of meeting one of her ex-boyfriends in the presence of Argos was both terrifying and thrilling, but discussing dirty laundry in the same meeting was downright horrifying.

This was a private affair.

"Alright," she agreed, "but if something happens, let me know."

"If something happens, I want you to go to the water," he countered. "Poseidon likes you. He will not let your blood be spilled there."

"Good to know." She smiled sweetly. "But I'm not going to leave my restaurant behind ever again."

⁕

Argos felt calm as Claire stood before the offering and called upon Hestia. It was a feeling he had not experienced in a long time. The calm before the storm, his soul coming to accept whatever might happen.

Forgiveness, that was all he was looking for. Not to fight with the goddess or to place blame, but to get her blessing so that he could once again become immortal.

This was the task that he had been given, and he would not back down. Not when so much depended on him. Claire's treasure. Thalia's revenge. His own.

None of it would be possible if he failed.

"Hestia, Goddess of the Hearth. I beseech you with an offering." Claire stood tense as the wood around them creaked. She repeated, "Hestia, Goddess of the Hearth…"

Glass from the opened window broke and Claire unleashed a string of curses as dust kicked up around their feet. A voice, light as air, came from the sudden gust. "Who summons me? And in such an untidy little hovel?"

Argos looked up and sucked in a breath. It had been difficult for him to recall her features after so many years apart, but now, one glance dazzled him. When he had first stepped outside of Circe's palace, he had looked up and felt the sun against his skin for the first time in centuries. Seeing Hestia was like seeing the sun again.

Long golden curls tumbled down her shoulders and back, casting a halo around her head. She was tall and slender, shaped like a young tree. The smile on her face was not the one he usually saw, filled with kind politeness. It was tense, barely hiding disdain.

"Hovel?" Claire hissed, bringing Hestia's gaze towards them.

The goddess tilted her head. "Yes, dear. Next time you summon me, make sure to clean up first. And what's this?" Her ring-clad fingers glittered as she picked up a chip delicately. "Is this my offering? I can't eat this. It came out of a *bag*."

Claire's face flushed red. "Oh, you are making it really easy not to like you."

"Claire, would you mind giving us privacy?"

Both women swung to look at him. He stared back, facing their ferocity head on.

"I'll be outside if you need me," she said, voice coming out in a gruff mumble, before the door slammed behind her.

Hestia preened in victory as her eyes raked over the room. They lingered on the chipped wooden floors and broken window. "How could I have been summoned here? Surely somebody doesn't live here."

"Somebody does," Argos answered curtly, feeling his own irritation arise at the way she looked at Claire's home.

His voice caused the goddess to regard him. "And who would that be? You?" she hummed, placing a pale, slender hand against the wood. "No, it's that woman. The hearth here is fond of her, though I don't know why. She's keeping it in a shabby state. And the thought of someone sleeping here, ugh. I don't think I can last another moment, so speak of what you want before I decide to leave."

Leave? He wished she would. Seeing her had reopened an old wound. He had faced down the worst kinds of monsters, but there was no fear like facing the wrath of the gods. Now he did so willingly—defenseless, mortal, and alone. Foolish. He wished he could have given Claire a proper goodbye at least.

"It has been a long time, Hestia."

Her eyes narrowed as they roamed over him, taking in his fine new clothing and his new scars. Argos waited, watching for the moment when she finally placed him.

Then the real trouble would begin. He could see it on her face, the way her delicate brows turned up and her nose pinched. She recognized him, she—

"Don't mock me." Hestia crossed her arms over her breasts. "I know I am not often summoned now, but that doesn't mean my time isn't valuable. Explain yourself to me, mortal."

Argos gawked at her. "Hestia, it is me."

"Me?" she repeated. "I have seen many men in my lifetime. *Me* simply won't do. I need a name."

"Argos." He waited for her recoil.

She blinked. "Argos. That is an old name, but a good one. You won't believe what some mothers name their children these days. Well, what do you want Argos?" She said his name as if it was the first time. As if there hadn't been a hundred years where she had cooed, laughed, and praised his name.

Surely this was a jest.

"I have come to ask for your forgiveness."

"Forgiveness for what?"

She did not remember him.

"For betraying you," he said, the words coming out as a gasp. A painful vise squeezed in his chest as though she had struck him. Argos had been prepared for so much, but not this. The need to make her remember burned like hot coals in his stomach. "For giving myself to another woman when I had sworn myself to you."

Hestia's lips pursed at the thought, but still there was no familiarity in her gaze. "I see."

Five hundred years he had waited to see her again. Five hundred years he had suffered because she'd claimed that he had betrayed her, and she had forgotten him. His fear dissolved into anger; he could not stop the words from tumbling out. "You cursed me, tricked me. Sent me to Circe's island, where I suffered, all because I had caused you a grave offense."

Hestia sniffed, her mouth tight. "It sounds as if you have."

"But you do not remember me?" The question burned his throat raw. As soon as it was out, he wished he could take it back. Shouting at the gods was asking for a smiting. She could easily curse him again or kill him on the spot, but his anger had won. His body tensed for whatever would happen next, but Hestia was not a fighter, not in the same sense he was. She fought like a woman, slashing the air with her words. Cutting him with the truth.

"I do not."

He had known confronting her would be difficult, but never in all his years could he have imagined this scenario.

That she would not remember him.

The pain behind the truth was staggering. Pieces of his heart chipped away, shedding the skin of an old love. It ached, but that was nothing compared to his broken pride. The ashes of its pyre floated to the tip of his tongue.

It had been so many years. Of course she had forgotten him. He had clung to her memory and his own revenge for centuries to keep sane, to keep fighting. But she was a goddess, and the world kept changing.

A memory of Claire hit him hard. Her hair windblown, her face pursed in grim determination. "*You might have loved Hestia once, but when you cheated on her, you definitely weren't in love,*" she had said. "*I'd be willing to bet that Hestia didn't really love you either.*"

Could his brothers have suffered the same changes?

Had they all forgotten him? The idea was too horrible to entertain. Maybe the threads of time were stronger than their bond. He could not remember the name of the girl whom he had slept with so long ago, Hestia could not remember him, and Xanthus was no longer the man he had known.

Argos had seen curses up close, and now he knew enough to admit immortality was its own kind of curse.

"You have a handsome face, but a goddess can't be expected to remember all of her grudges. If you wronged me, then tell me why you summoned me."

Immortality. To be the man I once was. But was that really what he wanted? The man he used to be deceived the gods; he had run off on monster hunts without a care in the world.

He was not that man any longer.

He did not want to be an immortal hero. Just a hero. A hero did not put his pride before the emotions of others. "I wanted to apologize."

Hestia blinked a look no man had ever seen on the goddess's face before: surprise. "Apologize?"

"Yes, I realize now that what I did to you was wrong and I never told you I was sorry."

Argos watched as her mouth opened and shut several times, but words refused to depart. It was a miracle. He had driven the goddess speechless.

Finally, Hestia gathered her wits. "But you said I cursed you. I tricked you and sent you away."

"Yes, and I suppose you'll have to live with that for the rest of eternity."

She said nothing to his gibe. "Why would you apologize to me?"

"I will be honest," Argos said. "I talked to your brother, hoping he would give me the opportunity to regain my immortality. The quest he gave me was to gain your forgiveness for the wrongs I have committed."

He watched her face and saw no emotion, no surprise there.

"I remember a time when the gods ruled the known world with an iron fist. People and creatures feared them and loved them, but time has changed that. It has been changing for a long time."

"Get to the point." Hestia shivered, as if suddenly cold.

"You're lonely," Argos said. "Even back when we were together you were lonely. Hestia of the Hearth, guardian of the family. Yet families are torn apart by war and envy. Women leave their children and never come back; men bring mistresses into their home." He took in her luminescent eyes, the same as her brothers and saw how they were slightly sunken. Apparently not even gods could escape eternity looking undisturbed. They faded with time, just like everything else. "The world was changing and you only had me. I was not loyal. For that I'm sorry."

Hestia's narrowed at him. "So, you want me to forgive you."

"No," he answered honestly, "not anymore."

Poseidon wanted him to ask for forgiveness. If he never asked, he would never become immortal. It was throwing away his best chance to destroy Circe and he knew that, but the cost was too high. Losing Claire, never seeing her achieve her dream, he could give up forever for that. Before immortality, he had managed to accomplish the impossible. Surely it could not be hard to do it again.

Hestia was as still as a statue, her face marble white.

Only her eyes moved, roaming over the room, giving it a second assessment. With a deep inhale she declared, "I was wrong. Your home isn't as musty as I first observed."

"It is not my home."

"No? The wood welcomes you like family." She tilted her head towards the door. "And the beams are soaked with that woman's love. The floorboards are mangled, but they tell me they weren't always like that. This place is filled with love."

His heart jumped at the words. "I hope so."

"Thank you for your apology," Hestia said with a gentle smile. "My followers always used to ask me for favors in return for their prayers, but I've never received an apology before. Are you sure you don't want anything in return for your apology?"

"It was enough just to say those words." He knew without a doubt that she would have granted him the forgiveness he sought, but he could not ask for it anymore. There were more important things.

Hestia touched her hand against the wood of the wall, her body shimmering translucent as she began her ascension to Olympia. She gave him a sad smile, one that could say nothing but goodbye. "How could I have forgotten a man like you?"

◆

Turning down Poseidon's quest might have been the stupidest thing he had ever done, and that list ran as long as the River Styx. Yet it felt so right.

Claire might be cross with him when she found out. She liked her plans, after all, but they would make it work. He did not need his immortality to defeat Circe. There were other options. They could think of other options.

But first he needed to tell her. Tell her that he had given up his immortality for her. Tell her that an eternity without her love, her food, her stubbornness was not an eternity worth living. That he would rather see her restaurant filled with happy patrons than see all the wonders of the world. The words burned in his soul as he placed a hand on the clawed-up floorboards, silently thanking the old building for trusting him, before bounding outside.

A grin broke out across his face when he saw her standing by the water. She stood tense, angry probably, but he would soon kiss away her concerns.

Thoughts of what else he wanted to do to her distracted him so that he did not notice the eyes watching him from the bushes.

Fear bit into him at the same moment he heard Claire scream his name in the distance, but it was too late. A wolf collided with him and together they rolled onto the soft ground. He saw a blur of black fur and vaguely recognized the creature attacking him as the Alpha among Circe's wolfpack. The right eye was missing from the shifter's socket, giving a fierce look to an already predatory personality. Circe had rallied her strongest men this time, leaving nothing to chance.

Instinct took over as Argos raised his fist and slammed it into the wolf's snout. A pained yelped escaped the animal. He raised his hand, reaching for his sword to deliver the final blow, when another heavy shadow fell over him.

Claire screamed as a bear's large paw caught him in the chest. His ribs screamed as he fell facefirst into the ground. Before he could attempt to get up, one massive paw pressed firmly into his back, pinning him in place. Its claws dug into the sensitive skin at the same time Argos looked up and stared into the hungry eyes of Circe's Pets.

XXII

CLAIRE WAS TOO late. She watched as Etros's men tackled Argos to the ground and pinned him there. Despair dug its talons into her gut as she stood helpless, watching Argos tussle with the wild beast. He matched the wolf's claws with his own furious movements. When he landed a solid blow to the snout, she felt a smile break out across her face.

Things were different this time. Argos was a true hero now; he was immortal. He would beat the creatures back with ease. They'd win and then they'd...

A bear charged from the sidelines, landing on Argos's back and clawing at it until the man fell to one knee. Red stained the back of his cotton button-down.

Claire's hope froze at the sight.

Blood. Did immortals bleed? Air refused to leave her lungs as she watched, waiting for the gory wounds to close.

They didn't.

"Argos." His name broke on her tongue. She stepped forward, but Etros's nails dug into her wrists.

"Do not fight us, hero. If you do, we will not hesitate to maim your pretty companion." Etros sneered.

The fighting ceased immediately. Argos's chest heaved in deep panting breaths; his clothes were torn and bloody, making him look like a wild man. He would have kept fighting, she realized, all the way to his dying breath. Because he was mortal.

Hestia hadn't forgiven him.

Despair dug its talons into Claire's gut, but she forced herself to meet his gaze. There he confirmed her worst fears. His lips moved in a silent, "*I'm sorry.*"

She shook her head, trying to relay a message back. *It's not your fault.*

He didn't look reassured.

"Grab him," Etros commanded, "and bring them to the ship. It's time to go home."

The tiger and wolf shifted into their human forms. One was a big man, his biceps threateningly large, making Argos look small in comparison. He hefted the hero to his feet and pinned his arms behind his back. Blood dripped from Argos's wounds onto the shifter's own hand as they tore Xanthus's sword from his hip.

Etros roughly pulled Claire to *Queenie*. The small boat they'd used to reach her restaurant was tied next to the yacht, but they ignored it. Etros's eyes shined bright as he climbed onto the boat, excited for the upgrade. "This will do nicely."

The Pets grabbed some spare rope and quickly went about securing their captives. Argos grunted as his wounds were treated with little regard. Etros paced in front of them, his smile crooked as he took in his prize. "We have a lot to talk about before we get back to the island. I'd like to personally tell you how much of a pain in the ass you've been."

"Fine," Argos spat, "but let Claire go. She did not do anything to you."

Etros rolled his eyes. "The mistress was not pleased when you ran off with another female. You should know better than to cheat on a powerful woman."

To her horror, his hands began to pat down her clothes. Claire squawked at the harassment and Argos let out a string of Greek curses. Etros laughed at the foreign words. "Do not worry, hero. She's not really my type." His hands reached her hips and stopped, extracting the *Queenie*'s key from her pocket.

"Let her go," Argos growled. This time his voice held the promise of violence. It sent the hair on Claire's arms standing on end.

Etros moved towards him, accepting the challenge of his words. "You really think you can protect her? You can't do anything." He tore his eyes away from Argos and smiled at Claire. "You will not be returning to the life you had before, pretty little thing." Etros waved one of the Pets towards him and announced, "Go torch that shack. She will not be needing it."

Claire froze. "Please, no."

She had her pride when it came to many things, but for her restaurant, she would throw it to the sidelines without a thought. Even if it meant begging. Even if it meant begging a man like Etros. "You can't…"

"I can." Etros looked at her, his expression an open canvas of triumph at his own power.

The slender warrior who transformed into the wolf leapt over the side of the boat and headed towards the restaurant. Claire moved to follow after him, her arms bound behind her back. Her legs were willing to fly in an attempt to stop him. Etros's hand snagged the back of her neck and gave a squeeze of warning.

Icy numbness filled her veins as she stared at the building. The outside looked unchanged. No one could imagine the years and money spent to transform it into what it had become. A place where she had imagined her dream coming true, the place where she had sheltered Argos those first few nights, where he had saved her life and she his.

The smoke came first, then the low crackle of the fire grew until she could hear it from the water. All her life savings had gone into the restaurant. All her time and energy. It all went up in smoke that turned into blazing flames in just a few minutes.

From the boat she could feel the heat of the fire. Her eyes ached as she stared into the flames, watching them devour the wood. She dared not breathe, fearing the moment air slid back into her lungs would allow the sobs to break out.

A loud bang echoed across the trees as the wood broke and the roof collapsed. The only thing louder was Argos's howl of fury as he struggled against the bear.

The hand around her neck held it steady, forcing her to watch as her dreams were destroyed.

As tears flowed down her cheeks and a wrecked sob escaped her, she kept looking. Only when Etros gave the order to set sail did she dare close her eyes. Everything was wrong, so wrong, and her body didn't know how to deal with the shock. In the distance she could hear the sirens of the firefighters arriving at the scene, but the boat had pulled away and the wreckage of her dreams was nothing but smoke in the distance.

They were too late.

XXIII

THE BOAT WAS crowded with the five of them. Claire was shoved down in the lower cabin, falling facefirst into the floor as the door slammed behind her. Her nose throbbed painfully from the hard landing and her eyes ached with the need to cry.

Her restaurant was gone. She and Argos had failed.

She took a slow steady breath to make sure it didn't break her completely. Above, the sound of men jeering was muffled by the hum of the engine. She forced herself to take deliberate breaths and not think about what was to come. She needed a plan. There wasn't much give in the ropes binding her, but she could feel the solid lump in her back pocket; her pocketknife. Etros hadn't found it.

Her arms ached as she fished the blade out of the pocket, awkwardly feeling the weapon until she felt comfortable with it in her hands. It would come in handy when they got closer to Circe's island. The hard feel of it clutched in her fist gave her some reassurance. She could do this. She was not going to die.

But to make that happen, she would need more than her tiny blade. At times like these, people usually said their last prayers. Claire had never really been one to pray when things didn't go her way, but this time was different. Now she knew gods were listening, or at least one of them.

"Poseidon," she whispered against the floor. "Please, Poseidon. I could really use your help right now." There was no offering, nothing but what she could promise. She hoped that would be enough. "Poseidon. I swear if I live through this, I'll make you a meal every day for the rest of my life. Just answer me."

Only the waves crashing against the side of the boat responded, Claire let her head fall forward against the cool floor. Well, she couldn't be surprised. She'd said her prayer and the god had turned his back on her.

"Did I come at a bad time?"

She raised her gaze, breath catching as she once again laid eyes on Poseidon in all his glory. His pitchfork was clutched in one hand while he wore a bright yellow shirt that read VOLUNTEER with a happy dolphin. A smug smile pulled at his lips as he stared down at her. "I came because I heard you'd cook for me, but maybe I've come too early. Is this how your hero likes you?"

Claire flushed at the insinuation, but it wasn't enough to cover her relief. She smiled at him. "Argos and I need your help."

Poseidon's eyes flashed. "Food and some mortal fun? I'm honored, I don't usually partake in these kinds of offerings."

Jeez, gods really did only think of one thing. "I'm not the offering here! We're in trouble. Circe's hunters are taking us back to her island. Hestia wouldn't forgive him."

She watched as Poseidon's amusement fell. "It isn't that

she wouldn't forgive him. He could have gotten her forgiveness if he'd wanted. He just didn't ask."

"What?" The words threw her. "What do you mean he didn't ask?"

"I talked to my sister. Argos didn't ask for her forgiveness." Poseidon lowered himself beside her. "He chose to stay mortal."

"But why would he…?" Her question trailed off at the god's raised eyebrow. She stilled. "Because of me?"

"It appears so. Love does make mortals do foolish things. I suppose your man didn't think through his plan if you two ended up like this."

"Can't you help us?" she said, irritated that he seemed to be giving her up for dead so easily. "Just, use your god powers. Smite them or something."

The amusement was completely gone from his face now, and for the first time she saw the kind of being people would truly fear. One who held life and death in his hands and felt indifferent about it. "Smite? You expect me to kill because you made me a burger once?"

Claire didn't know what to say to that. Yes! No! That wasn't what she'd meant, but at the same time, these men had taken everything from her.

Poseidon's tone softened a degree. "I cannot get too involved in the deeds of immortals and men. I'm afraid I can't help you."

"So, you're going to let them kill us?" She demanded.

He shook his head. "I shouldn't even listen to your plea. If you are not my offering, then I have no need to hear your request."

An offering. That was what this was about again? Of

course. He'd nearly let Argos starve in a boat because he hadn't offered anything.

"I have an offering," she blurted out, pleased when it stopped the god in his tracks.

Ice-blue eyes narrowed in suspicion as he looked down at her prone body. "Oh?"

There are some people the gods favor. That was what Argos had told her. "You liked my food, didn't you? My deal stands if you grant me this request." *Poseidon favors you; he won't let your blood spill.*

A low, interested hum came from god's throat as he looked at her with newfound respect. "Go on."

⚓

The lush piece of land in front of them looked like paradise. Green treetops rolled over the island's hills, and white sand decorated its skirt. It was out of place, drifting between two ends of the Bay with their rocky edges and dense forests. Yet if anyone were to look at Circe's island, their confusion over its appearance would quickly shift to curiosity, and their fates would be sealed. When Argos caught sight of the island, his gut burned with dread. Eyes focused on the stark white mansion visible on a hilltop, he knew only pain awaited there.

"Home, sweet home," Etros said with a feral grin. His eyes gave an appraising look at Argos's new injuries. His skin was shredded with deep cuts, and his chest ached with the possibility of a broken rib. They had worked hard to make sure the injuries would not be life-threatening. Not until they reached Circe. "You there, go grab the girl from downstairs. We're almost at the island."

One of the lesser Pets scrambled away from the boat's

railing to do as commanded. When he returned, Claire was held in his firm grip, her face grim but otherwise unharmed. Cool relief touched him at the sight. Her eyes squinted against the sun as she took in their surroundings. When they landed on him, she visibly paled.

Argos flashed her a smile he hoped looked reassuring. To his surprise, Claire returned it. She did not seem as rattled as he had thought she would be. The Pet dropped her beside Argos with little care.

"Cannot wait to sink my teeth into you once we get home." The wolf shifter sneered down at her.

Claire glared as he stalked away. Once he was on the other side of the boat, her face shifted to concern. "Are you okay? You look like hell." Her arms moved instinctively towards him, but the rope kept them in place. Argos could see the ache in her eyes as she took in the deep gouges across his chest.

"I should be the one saying that to you." He sighed.

"I was just uncomfortable for a few hours. They hurt you." Claire leveled him with a stern glare.

It was amazing how unconcerned she seemed about their situation; her bravery would match any of the men he called his brothers. She had lost everything because of him, and still her jaw was set in defiance. But sometimes boundless bravery only ended in tragedy. "I'm sorry, Claire."

He saw tears gather in her eyes and regretted the words. She leaned in and pressed her lips against his. The kiss held all the beauty and strength he saw in this woman. His Claire. He felt her kiss in his heart. As she pulled away, she softly whispered, "Help is coming."

He wondered if he'd misheard as the bear shifter pulled

her away. Etros scoffed at them. "I did not bring you two together for a final kiss. I want you to look."

The shores of the island were visible now. From the boat, Argos could see the long winding stairway that led from the beach up to Circe's mansion. He could also see the small dock where he had once untied a little rowboat and escaped against all odds.

Then he saw her, the lone figure of a woman walking along the beach, the wind catching the green ends of her thin dress. A wolf prowled by her side, adding to the ethereal appearance. Circe had always been a figure who could make even the gods look bleak in comparison.

A Pet forced Claire and Argos to their feet as the boat docked. His limbs were sore, moving stiffly as he prepared himself for what was to come. He gave Claire a long look, drinking in her appearance and the stubborn line of her lips as her eyes settled on his sword, lying propped against the control room.

He knew that determined look in her eyes. Recognized the pursed lips and the words she said into their kiss. His Claire, his beautiful, smart, talented Claire, had a plan.

His body moved closer. Their arms touched as he said, "I will protect you."

"I love you, too," Claire told him with a meaningful nudge of her shoulder.

The words were exactly what he needed to hear, a balm that could ease any wound on heart or body. A newfound energy surged through his veins, a need to protect this woman as she intended to protect him. As they stood together, facing down whatever might come, he felt as if he could welcome life and death. As long as Claire decided to stand next to him through it all.

They docked, and Etros helped Circe step up onto the boat. Claire sucked in a sharp gasp at the sight of her. Seeing the water image of Circe before was nothing compared to seeing the actual being. Her eyes were dark voids, unable to hold warmth, only cruelty. The hands she clasped next to her breasts, looking like a woman longing for the return of her lover after war.

Circe gave them a smile, one that could almost be sweet. "Well, you two sure did give my men a lot of trouble. It was fun at first, Argos, but you should have tried harder to get away from me."

"I was not trying to get away from you," he said, bracing as she stepped closer. "I was preparing to kill you."

"And how did that work out?"

"This is bold, even for you, Circe. No Atheos can ignore an island like this popping up here. People will start asking questions."

"And the gods will do nothing. That has become their game for these past centuries. Besides, I could use a few more Pets added to my collection. I seem to be short recently." She shrugged her slender shoulders. Without the gods, she had grown cocky, dangerous. His heart beat faster at this information.

In two steps, Circe was in front of him, her body pressed against his. A cold hand crept up to his chest, fingers dancing close to the inflamed skin around his new wounds. He worked to keep his breathing even, but the pain flared up sharp when she dug one of her nails into a fresh wound. He hissed and Circe pressed down harder in response. "Still putty in my hands. You have not changed."

"Stop it." Claire's voice cut through the pain, her entire body shaking in either anger or fear.

Circe refused to look at her. "I do not think I will. We have played this game before, you see, and he loves it."

Without warning, she leaned close, capturing his lips with her own. Not long ago her kisses had felt as if Hades's flames were licking at his body. His lips would have parted for her without hesitation. Now her touch could not bring even a spark of interest from him. Her tongue tried to slip into his mouth, but it was furiously denied. She froze at the realization, reeling back as if he had bitten her. The anger and shock in her eyes was a sweet taste of the revenge he craved.

"I would not say I have not changed at all," he told her. "Poseidon was generous enough to lift Hestia's curse off me while I was away."

"You..." Her face was pale with anger. It had been ages since a man had turned her down. Her gaze fell to Claire, who was unable to hide a smile on Argos's behalf. "You dare turn me down for *this*?"

He stepped forward in an effort to draw her ire away from Claire.

There was so much he wanted to tell Circe, that he had grown tired of her long ago, that he had never really been hers to begin with. That when it came to Claire, there was no competition. All his words gathered in a deep breath, about to be free when suddenly the air was gone from his lungs. Something sharp slid across his neck, enough to silence him.

The cut burned, and something slick dribbled down his neck. It was not until Circe was looking at him with her cold stare, her nails dripping red, that he realized she had attacked him. An attempt to swallow made the blood gush more, and his feet fell from underneath him. Claire screamed, horrified as she tried to move towards him, but the wolf kept her firmly in place.

Circe knelt slowly, smoothing her dress and pulling her dark hair around her neck like a shy maiden. Bloodied fingers cupped his chin in a harsh grip. "We're not on my island yet, Argos. It would not be such a loss to kill you here and watch the life drain from your eyes. For a man who once tasted immortality, it would be a terrible way to die. Tied like a hog, powerless."

From the look in her eyes, she was serious.

He had miscalculated. All this time he'd assumed she would continue to play the same sick game, keeping him alive to torture for another five hundred years. Really, she just wanted to be the one to kill him. Once he was dead, there would be no one to protect Claire. Circe was still talking, but her words were fading in and out. Looking past her, his eyes found the bright blueness of the sky and Claire staring down at him. Her face broken, tears falling.

There was still time for one last word. A dying breath. "Run."

⸎

She'd thought seeing her restaurant burn down had been the worst kind of pain. But that sorrow was nothing compared to watching Argos bleed out on the ground. For a solid minute, Claire felt as if the water had turned to ice and swallowed her whole. She couldn't stop staring at the blood that stained the boat's white surface.

He stared at her, eyes still burning with life. His lips moved and even though the words were barely above a whisper, she knew the message. The metal from her knife burned against her palm. It had nicked her skin numerous times in her frantic attempt to cut the rope, but it hadn't been fast enough.

"Mistress, someone is coming," Etros announced. Claire blinked through the tears to look out and spot a small white object making its way around the bend of the Bay, coming towards them. Argos was right—it hadn't taken the locals long to notice the new island. Soon those curious sailors would find themselves with much more then they'd bargained for if she didn't do something.

Circe stood in one graceful movement, a pleased smile on her lips. "Have someone greet them and lead them up to my temple."

"And what about him?"

"Bring his body to the island. I'm not done with him yet."

Etros frowned at the command. "Yes, Mistress."

Those words drew Claire's spinning thoughts up short. Not done with him? Argos's eyes were closed. He looked dead except for the shallow rise and fall of his chest. In a few moments there would be no saving him, except...

Except Circe's island wasn't subject to the same laws of reality that she knew. Immortality, that was the secret to Circe's island. How Argos had lived on it for hundreds of years without aging. Hopeful tears stung her eyes. There was a chance.

If the island granted everyone immortality, then it was her best chance to fight back. Her fingers went back to sawing the rope while Circe pinned her with a cold look. "When that is settled, you can tear into this one. I do not want to look at that face again."

The Pets all licked their lips, eyeing Claire like a newly opened buffet. One moved forward, the same young wolf who had tied her up. In his eagerness he didn't hear the quiet snap of the rope cutting, and his greed put him closer to her than any of the others. Claire swiped out, her knife digging into his side. It sunk in nearly to the hilt. The young man fell to the ground and so did her knife.

A look of surprise settled over Circe's face. It was a pleasure to see the surprise shift into fear as the Sea Witch realized her own weakness. Off the island, she was just as vulnerable as her Pets.

There was still a chance. Claire's body propelled forward with just one thought, attack. Kill her before the island granted Circe her immortality. She jumped towards the control room and grabbed Argos's sword. The weight of it was a surprise, dragging down her speed.

Circe lifted her hand and thrust it forward. A powerful gust of wind hit Claire in the chest, causing her to fly backwards. Her back hit the railing of the boat hard before she tumbled over the side.

Cold water shocked her system as the pain from the railing continued to ripple down her spine. Claire clutched the sword knowing that if it fell, she would have no other way to protect herself. *Run*, Argos had whispered. He wanted her to escape, and in some way Circe's attack gave her the perfect opening to do just that.

Get to the island, regroup, attack.

She swam as far as she could, pumping her legs and holding her breath until her lungs burned. Fear drove her towards the shore, and when her head finally broke the water's surface, Circe's screams filled the air. Claire pushed forward. As her feet hit the sandy bottom, she took off towards the jungle, trying to concentrate on her own speedy getaway and not on the man she'd left behind.

XXIV

IT TURNED OUT regrouping wasn't such a simple task when one was on the run.

The movies always made it look easy: leaping over fallen trees, swiping vines out of the way. Reality was much worse. Branches snagged Claire's soaked clothes, trying to hold her in place as if commanded by Circe's magic. She felt mud splash against her leg from a new hole in her pants. Dragging the sword along was a problem all on its own. Its weight was foreign to her, and already her arms were numb from using it to cut a path.

The dense jungle she stomped through was the exact place where a jaguar had the upper hand. Occasionally she spared a look at the dense foliage above her, expecting to see a flash of yellow before claws ripped her throat out.

Her only concern was finding a safe spot to hide out until Circe's Pets gave up looking for her. Not that finding a hiding place would be easy. The plants were so thick she could barely see where she was stepping. Only one thing helped orient her: the large protruding hillside where

Circe's mansion decorated the top. The hill was more like a cliff, one that bulged out of the island. Claire made sure to stick close to its rocky edges, knowing that eventually she'd have to make her way to the top. Maybe if she kept walking, she'd make it around to the back of the hillside. Everything had a back door, right?

She'd been running for so long her lungs felt like crumpled paper. A few minutes had always felt like hours when she'd gone for jogs before; now every second carried the weight of a year. In the distance she heard the yowl of a very large, very angry jaguar. The noise propelled her legs onward faster.

The wall of rock climbed higher beside her as she traveled, and through the treetops she was unable to make out the exact shape of it. Surely it would start dipping down soon. The island couldn't be that large.

Her thoughts came to an abrupt halt as water splashed into her shoes. Pushing an oversized vine out of the way, a beam of sunlight penetrated the dark jungle. Claire squinted against it, her mouth pursed as she took in the shallow beach in front of her.

There was little sand. As she stared, she realized it wasn't a beach at all but a lagoon. The tree line of the jungle stretched out on her right, and on her left the hillside stood over the water like a stone wall.

Claire shook her head in disbelief. There was no back door. There was nowhere else to run.

Across the bay she saw the edge of civilization, a forestry ledge so different from where she stood. So close, yet so far. She couldn't swim across, not as exhausted as she was, and even if she did make it, there was no guarantee that anyone would be able to help her. Circe would likely move the island before Claire could get help, and then Argos would be gone forever.

She stood frozen at the thought. In the span of a few days, he'd turned her life completely upside down, but the idea of him being cut out of it so violently would tear her world apart.

Her fingers clenched around the sword. She would not leave him again.

Claire turned on her heel and marched back the way she had come.

The sound of a twig snapping was the only warning she had before something heavy slammed into her from above. Her lungs seized at the impact, leaving Claire gasping as she fell to the muddy ground. A tingling sensation burned against the skin of her back and grew more intense by the second. When the cat on top of her flexed his claws, her back tore open.

Claire screamed, trying desperately to buck the creature off her. The weight shifted slightly as the cat let out a low growl. Out of the corner of her eye, she saw dark spots against golden fur. A jaguar.

The piercing claws hooked as they quickly changed into human hands and Etros pinned her in place. "You should not have run. Men love the thrill of the chase."

The hands twisted into her shirt and turned her onto her back. Mud and leaves painted her wet clothes, but Etros didn't seem to mind. He flashed his teeth, looking sharp and dangerous even in human form. "Do not worry. It will not be so bad; the island will heal you the minute my teeth sink in. I will probably finish a leg or two before I get full."

Panic crawled up her throat as her limbs flailed. She tried to hit him with her sword, but the angle was all wrong.

She couldn't get a good hit in. A line of red cut across his arm and side, but it did little to weaken Etros. His hands quickly pinned her arms to her sides.

The sound of a branch snapping broke their tension. Etros looked up, eyes alert, mouth still hanging open in hunger. Claire strained to hear more, hopeful that Argos would come bursting out of the foliage. She heard a soft whoosh of air above her head before a long spear impaled Etros.

The man made a startled noise, his body jerking back as the bronze end of the spear was buried deep into his chest. They both stared at the weapon in shock. More movement rustled in the jungle around them, with no attempt to be quiet. Etros's head snapped up, searching for the source of the spear, and Claire saw her chance.

She put all her strength into twisting her body and managed to knock Etros off. Panting, she scrambled to her feet and prepared herself for what would come next. They were still on the island. Etros would heal and then he would come after her. This time there would be no gloating. Just teeth and blood.

More twigs snapped behind her. Whoever had thrown the spear was coming. Claire's ears rang in fear as she realized she'd soon be surrounded. But she refused to take her eyes off the shifter.

He was standing now, teeth gritted in annoyance as he pulled the spear out. The jagged hole began to heal before her eyes. An animal growl escaped Etros's throat. "Who threw that?"

A rustle of leaves to the right caught both their attention. Etros snarled, eyes tracking the slightest movement. He didn't think she was a threat, and maybe while they were on the island she couldn't kill him, but she could still slow him down.

With a scream, Claire ran forward, sword up and ready.

Etros startled at the noise, brows narrowed in confusion when she dug the metal deep into his gut. She kept moving forward, putting every ounce of adrenaline and fear into her arms and legs as she pushed the man against a tree. His skin collapsed under the blade tip, sucking the weapon deeper inside.

Blood dripped from Etros's teeth as he smiled. "You whore, you cannot kill me."

"But I can pin you to this tree like a shish kabob," she hissed back. The anger in her voice took her aback. *Who was this woman?*

It didn't matter. This was the man who'd burned down her restaurant, who'd threatened everything she loved. Somehow, she managed to give the sword a vicious twist.

She watched Etros's smile fall. He looked down at his stomach, eyes wide. Claire looked as well. The wound wasn't healing. She held her breath and kept her grip steady, watching the blood seep out. Nothing. The hole in his chest had closed up in a matter of seconds, but this wound and the ones she'd inflicted earlier were still open.

"What did you do?" Etros gasped, his fingers clawing at her arm. "What did you do?"

His nails left long cuts across her skin that healed as soon as they appeared. Claire watched in awe.

Her sword, the sword Xanthus had thrown away, had magic in it. Thank the gods. She yanked her arm back, pulling the sword with it. Etros slid to the ground, leaving a bloody trail against the tree. His hands were pawing at his stomach, trying to close the wound.

"She cut you with the *Theres* Blade," a new voice called out.

Looking up, Claire saw a man step out from a dense patch of vines. He looked just as out of place as she was. Light blue jeans and a loose cotton T-shirt covered in mud, blond hair clinging to his head with sweat. But there was an ease about him as he bent down and picked up the bloody spear lying on the ground. Around his neck something sparkled in the summer light.

Claire stared at the necklace, hope tightening her throat. It was a coin.

He spared a look in her direction, eyes focused on the weapon in Claire's hand. "That sword is cursed by the blood of beasts. It was forged to kill monsters like you."

Etros's eyes widened. "Th-there's no such thing."

"You tell yourself that when you see Hades," the man said before he turned to Claire. "Well… aren't you going to finish him off?"

Claire sucked in a deep breath at the words. "What?"

He raised a brow at her. "You're the one who stabbed him, right?"

She looked back to the bloody man on the ground. Etros's face had gone white; he was close to death. She shook her head. "He'll die soon. There's no need for me to land a killing blow."

To her surprise the man smiled at her. "An Amazon who doesn't enjoy the killing blow? Interesting."

"I'm not an Amazon," she told him, watching as Etros's labored breathing began to slow. She wouldn't land the finishing blow, but she did need to make sure he was dead. She couldn't risk any more surprises on the island. Her stomach squeezed in nausea, but she held strong. When his eyes glazed over and his head slumped to the side, she finally allowed herself a sigh of relief.

Her own aches and pains faded as the island worked its magic. She turned to the newcomer. He'd moved closer, allowing a better look at the coin around his neck. It was identical to Argos's. "So, you're a hero?"

A small smile pulled at his lips as he answered, "That's generally what people call someone when they are saved from certain death."

"No, I mean... you don't look like a member of the Order." He was so different from Argos, who still had the aura of timelessness about him. This man looked like he could be a model for *GQ*. Perfectly at ease in the world around him.

He raised a handsome brow. "And you don't act like any Atheos I've ever met. Are you sure you're mortal?"

It wouldn't be the first time a hero had mistaken her mortality. It was almost flattering. "Yes, I'm Claire."

"And I'm Barcus."

Her smile froze. "Barcus?"

His head tilted as suspicion set back into his features. "You've heard of me?"

This was Barcus. *The* Barcus.

She smiled so hard her mouth hurt as she took in the man in front of her. There was the same arrogance about him that had clung to Argos when they'd first met, one cultivated from years of experiences. "Argos told me about you."

The smile was gone. His eyes seemed to take her in with new attention. Claire didn't miss how his gaze lingered on the sword in her hand. "How do you know that name?"

She clutched the weapon tighter. "Didn't you receive my message?"

"Message?"

"I sent an SOS with Poseidon," Claire explained. "Did you not get it?"

A loud barking laugh made her jump. "*You* sent one of the big three to us? How? These days the gods rarely answer to mortals, and they most definitely don't deliver messages for them."

"I made him an offer he couldn't refuse."

"Poseidon came and told us Argos was trapped here." His voice was soft; the hope in it was impossible to miss. "I haven't seen any of the gods in centuries. I was so surprised I thought it was a trick. But at the very least I wanted to investigate." When they met each other's gaze, the cocky hero she'd first laid eyes on was gone. What stood before her was a man looking for his friend. "Do you know where Argos is?"

Claire grabbed his hand and gave it a meaningful squeeze. They were in this together now. "I do, but he's in trouble."

❧

It was pointless. No matter what, Circe's touch revolted him and thank the gods for that.

Every time she danced her fingers along his skin or slid their lips together, he felt nothing. Nothing but cold contempt for the woman in front of him. *I'll kill you*, his nerves screamed, *I'll kill you, I'll kill you*. It was a primal chant rattling inside his skull.

He was so close, it would be easy to wrap his fingers around her neck and break it. Again and again, he would watch the light drain from her eyes the same way her Pets had done to him. But he could not move. Her magic was ice in his veins, freezing his fingers as they gripped the grooved wooden chairs at her table while she whispered soft seductions in his ears.

"Love me," she commanded. "Love me and I will grant you immortality."

The weight of a quest thrummed in his ears as he remembered—yes, Circe had a god's blood in her veins, but the cost was too great. He was back at the beginning, a hero under the command of a goddess whom he did not care for. "I will not," he said, her fingers digging into his skin at the words.

"Why?" Her voice lost its sweet edge, turning into venom that she pushed into his mouth with a desperate kiss. When she pulled back, her teeth sunk viciously into his bottom lip, drawing blood. "I am offering you everything. I just need you to be here. With me."

He narrowed his eyes at the hesitation in her voice. His torturer had always been confident in everything she did, but for a moment she almost sounded as if she might beg him to stay. "You have plenty of other men here with you, Circe."

"Yes, but none of them are like *him*." She emphasized the word while draping her body over his lap, her fingers and eyes focused on the necklace around his neck. "Nothing will satisfy me like a hero. Ohhh—" Her lips leaned in and touched the coin, her moan echoed against the palace walls. "Odysseus. He was my first hero."

"And then he left you."

A sharp burst of pain blossomed across his cheek, not a slap but a taloned scratch. Circe had tensed in his lap, her eyes cold. "He did not leave. I let him go."

"Why?" he growled back. "Why let him go but not me?"

"Because I loved him. Is that not what you are supposed to do when you love someone? You let them go." She leaned her head forward against his chest. "And if they love you back, they will return…"

It was almost laughable. The gods did not love; they were incapable of understanding human emotions. But Circe was not fully a god. She was just another creature of power. Forgotten by the person she loved. He would not laugh at the misery he heard in her voice because he knew it well.

"You do not love me, though."

Her reply was quick. "And you did not love Hestia. We are bound to settle for each other."

"I cannot. I love someone else."

She reeled back as if he had dealt a vicious blow, her face ashen. Hurt rippled over her eyes like water before it vanished, icing over into something darker. "I could give you everything you wanted. The immortality you crave, the power you desire. Yet you turn it away?" Circe climbed off him, standing with her fists clenched. Outside, the trees shuddered against her rolling power. "You wish to remain nothing for her. Fine, I will turn you into nothing."

The power weighing him down disappeared at her words, but before he could react, something else hit him. A pain that started low in his chest, right under his heart. He doubled over, his arms grabbing the table as he bit back a scream. A roaring sound echoed between his ears, but still he could hear Circe's words of hatred being directed at him, each syllable punctuated with a stab of magic.

"The question is what does nothing look like? A pig? A flea?" She clucked her tongue and something inside of him broke free. "Or a monster."

XXV

THE ONCE-SERENE BEACH was no more. Claire heard the shouts of war before stepping onto the shore, where a battle played out in front of her. Ordinary-looking men fought against a pack of Circe's animals. Their numbers weren't large, only six heroes total, but that hardly seemed to faze them. The moment blood spilled on either side, the island began the healing process.

"Should we tell them about the island's magic?" she wondered, watching one man kick off a pair of combat boots, grinning as his toes met the sand before charging towards a wolf.

Barcus shook his head, eyes focused in the direction of Circe's palace. "Nah, look at how much fun they're having. Some of these men haven't had a real battle in centuries. I'll tell them after we deal with Circe, or they'll figure it out themselves. Just don't get caught in the middle."

They moved along the tree line towards the stone steps leading up the hill, watching the battle in awe. One large and scruffy-looking hero was fighting a bear with his fists. These were Argos's brothers. Dressed in modern-day clothes, looking like everyday men. There was a definite resemblance in the fierce smiles on their faces, the gleam in their eyes, the coins around their necks.

She caught Barcus up on her side of the story as they walked, telling him all she knew about Argos's captivity and his battle for immortality, glossing over certain details of the curse. When she neared the end, Barcus wore a deep scowl on his face.

"I had forgotten how cruel the gods can be," he sighed.

"Not all of them are cruel. At least Poseidon doesn't seem that way," Claire defended. "He did lead you all here."

"That's because Poseidon had centuries to take his anger out on other people," Barcus pointed out. "It is a good thing they have learned not to interact with mortals anymore. Before the seventeenth century, gods just caused more trouble than they were worth sometimes."

"But the gods still give your Order the gift of immortality."

Barcus became quiet for a moment. "Not in the last century they haven't. The gods rarely interact with our Order now."

"Oh." Claire turned this news over. "Did you try giving them wine?"

That got a small laugh. "Indeed. It is not that they ignore us completely, but our numbers have grown too large. Once, only a few immortal men helped keep people's spirits up while fighting back the monsters. But now, the people don't believe and the monsters are nearly extinct. There is no need for an army anymore."

"I don't think that's true," Claire answered, nodding meaningfully towards the jungle around them.

His smile faltered, eyes falling to the sword in Claire's hand. "These days we are more often fighting amongst ourselves than against the monsters of old, so maybe the gods had a point."

Claire blinked as the words sunk in. Barcus paused on the steps, refusing to look at her. "So, Claire, where did you get that sword?" he asked, voice so low she almost missed the question.

"Argos received it from a woman named Thalia," Claire said slowly. She didn't know much about what had happened between Barcus and Xanthus, but whatever it had been, there was undeniably bad blood. She added, "He recognized it, too. We heard about the things Xanthus has done."

Barcus turned to her. "You don't know the half of it. He is not the man Argos and I once knew. The years have changed all of us in different ways, but his transformation has been the worst."

It was clear the memory still hurt. Claire looked down at the sword in her hand. There were still remnants of blood etched into the groves of the pommel. "You called it something, the *Theres* Blade. What is that?"

"The Beast Blade," he answered. "In our last years together, Xanthus was on a spree slaughtering monsters. They are immortal too, that is, until you cut their heads off. He was using their blood to create a weapon that would kill a true immortal."

And he had done it. Claire looked back down at the weapon. They'd had the key to killing Circe all this time. So why had Xanthus thrown it away? It didn't make sense.

Something that powerful belonged with a real hero, not a woman who could barely use it. She lifted her arm, offering it to Barcus. "This would be more useful in the hands of someone who knows how to use it," she said, holding out the weapon.

Barcus stared at her, face pale in the summer light. To her surprise he shook his head. "No, I couldn't. That sword…" His voice trailed off. "It does not belong to me."

She pulled the sword back to her side. "I could barely stab a jaguar sitting on top of me. How can I possibly defeat Circe?"

The hero next to her offered no answers. She sniffed and tried to fight back the mounting panic building in her chest. Barcus shifted on his feet, stones crunching under his thick hiking boots. "You can beat her."

"You can't know that," Claire said.

The man came down the steps until their eyes were level. His hand reached up as if to touch the sword but stopped just short. "Trust me," he said. "You have a magical sword and convinced a god to do your bidding. Don't sell yourself short."

She swallowed hard and nodded. His words both terrified her and ignited something within her. The heat of the steel in her hands now felt like a rekindled fire. She could do this. She *had* to do this.

A scream pierced through the air, one she knew intimately. "Argos…" Fear burned her lungs, propelling her up the steps behind Barcus.

Barcus wasn't waiting for her anymore as he leapt over steps with the agility of a deer. He would have made it to the palace in seconds when something darted out of the jungle towards him. Claire saw a blur of movement a second too late; if it had been her, she would have been engulfed by the large snake that had darted onto their path.

Barcus managed to jump to the side just as the snake dug its fangs into the stone steps. The rocks cracked under the creature's powerful jaws.

Lions and tigers had been enough of a shock, but this was new. This was an anaconda the size of a car. There wasn't a doubt in her mind it could and would eat a man whole. Its large body easily covered their path as the rest disappeared into the foliage of the jungle.

Claire stared as the creature's body thrashed about. Its fangs appeared to be stuck in the bedrock of the steps, buying them a precious few seconds to get a head start. Desperately she looked towards the palace, where Argos's screams continued to spill out. There was no other choice. They would have to cut through the monster in their path.

"I'll take care of this. You need to go to him." Barcus unhooked his spear from his back and pointed its deadly tip at the snake in front of them.

Heart hammering, she scrambled over the creature's torso, still blocking much of the stairway. As she sprinted up the hill she heard him muse, "Besides, I've never fought a giant snake before. This will be new."

The white vaulted ceiling of Circe's palace came into view as she reached the top. The building was much bigger than it had seemed from the shore. The front had no doors, just rows of columns that disappeared into the darkness of the building. White marble glistened against the summer sky. Animals and naked figures were carved into the stone, telling stories that were lost to time. Claire stared into the darkness, hoping to catch a glimpse of Argos, racking her brain for a plan.

There's no time, she realized in horror. The screams had

stopped. She refused to think about what that might mean. Clutching her sword, she sprinted into the darkness.

A torch flickered to life in the distance, carving a path for her to follow. The columns wreaked havoc on her nerves. Anything could be hiding behind them. There were too many places to look at once.

A taunting laugh bounced off the ceiling, coming from nowhere in particular but still sending her hairs on end. Circe was trying to rattle her more. Claire thought of Argos, of the monsters he'd faced in the past, and continued on.

Finally she came to a large room with a grand table in the middle. At the end of the table stood Circe, and crumpled on the floor next to her…

"Argos!" The name ripped from her mouth in a gasp. Her eyes fell on the man doubled over in pain, his body quivering with each heavy breath.

She had hoped her voice would reassure him, but it seemed to cause him more pain. His fists scraped at the marble floor, the skin blackening as fingers turned to talons. A scream of pain gurgled into something inhuman. Claire watched in horror as the man she loved transformed into an unrecognizable beast.

Circe looked up. Their eyes met from across the hall, and she laughed.

The creature's eyes opened, still green but with no traces of the human he had once been. There wasn't anything recognizable about him. His form was bigger. Midnight fur covered his body. The screams had stopped, but his mouth was now full of massive canines.

Fear tempted Claire to step back, but her feet refused to move. She couldn't keep the horror out of her voice. "What did you do to him?"

"He was having a hard time obeying my orders. So, I turned him into my new Pet," Circe crooned as she cradled the beast's head. "I think he is better like this."

"Give him back," Claire demanded, her voice steel even as her heart shattered.

Circe's smile widened. "I do not think so. A beast like this needs to be punished. I have a dark little cave where he will spend the rest of his life craving my touch. As for you, you will spend the rest of eternity down there with him as he gnaws on your bones. In a few years you will not even remember what the man looked like. A few centuries and you will be cursing his name before you will eventually forget how you even ended up here to begin with."

The hate in her words stole the air from the room. Claire felt her fingers tingle with fear. Under them, the sword was a solid presence that kept her anchored. She raised her hand, pointing the bloody tip at Circe, and demanded again, "Give. Him. Back."

Her words brought a frown to Circe's perfect lips. "Argos," she said, "go to your woman."

The creature pounced, fast as black lightning. In three large strides, his talons dug into Claire's skin and threw her to the floor. Her head cracked against the stone. Stars burst behind her eyes, leaving her stunned.

A hooked claw pressed down on her chest, digging painfully against her breast bone. Heat from the creature's mouth breathed down against her throat. Its eyes dilated in hunger.

"Argos." His name was a whimper. For him she would let the fear show. "I'm sorry, I'm so sorry. I was too late."

The talons clenched, breaking skin, and the mouth opened to reveal fangs that would tear into her like paper.

Her fingers squeezed the metal handle of the sword. She could raise it if she wanted to, but that would mean hurting him, and she wouldn't give Circe the satisfaction. With a shaky breath, she let go of the metal and threaded her hands into the creature's short fur.

"You probably hate me for leaving you, for letting this happen. I'm sorry, I tried…"

The creature growled, and she opened her eyes. There, the same pain she felt reflected back at her. Another noise escaped Argos, and she realized it wasn't a growl. It was a groan, one that dragged with pain. The talons that had pinned her to the floor began to shift. He was transforming, for her. The same way Circe's Pets had used her magic to transform for their mistress.

Claire tilted her head up, desperate to touch his human self. Her lips brushed against the creature's forehead in a chaste kiss. Magic filled the air, deflating from his body and leaving behind the man she loved.

Circe must have felt it too. Her voice boomed across the hall, one order. "Kill her!"

Claire hugged him, turning them both so she shielded his body with her own.

Circe's snarl died midsentence. "What did you do?" An unnatural light flickered in the witch's eyes, something that could only be magic.

"I didn't do anything. Argos did." Claire watched those words sink in.

Argos stirred at her voice, his movement sluggish at first, but worth it when his face lifted. He smiled and all was right in the world of gods and mortals. "You came for me."

A bout of nearly hysterical laughter bubbled out of her chest. "Of course I did."

"My hero," he deadpanned, unaware of what an ironic and stupid thing it was to say, and that was exactly the reason why she loved him.

A glass-shattering scream rippled through the air, destroying the moment.

Claire had anticipated an outburst, but the magic still caught her by surprise. It slammed into both of them like a truck, sending their bodies flying. Her arms came up to protect her head again, positive that the attack was meant to crack her skull open. Another pair of hands cradled her protectively as she and Argos slid across the floor and slammed against the nearby wall.

Every part of her body ached, but the island was already fixing that as the hissing pain of scraped skin began to fade away. It was easy then to focus her worry on Argos. On her hands and knees, she bent over his prone body, stroking his jawline. "Argos? Are you alright?"

His hands found hers in a hold that one would only use when facing their final moment, but there was something else there. Her fallen sword. Somehow he'd grabbed it before Circe's attack.

Both their hands gripped the cold steel. She was exhausted, Argos was exhausted. Together they were just two mortals standing in the way of a divine being, but still they could fight.

Circe was coming towards them, her movements celestial as she crossed the span of the hall in a blink. Claire scrambled to get a good grip on the man in her arms, knowing she looked every inch like a child unwilling to give up their favorite doll. With Argos's help she managed to lift the blade.

Circe was just a step away from them. Her lean form

towered over them as if they were ants. Claire was growing used to the look of utter contempt on Circe's face, but it was mixed with something else. A scrutinizing eye. "What are you?"

Claire had faced that question more times then she could count in the past week, and each time the answer came with more and more confidence. She raised Xanthus's sword at the witch's chest. "I'm a woman."

Circe's lips pressed into a thin line. "No, you did something to him."

Argos was tense in Claire's arms, awaiting the witch's wrath, but he was still looking at Claire. As if he couldn't believe she was there sitting next to him.

"Odysseus used to look at me the same way," Circe continued, voice devoid of any warmth or ice. It was flat, quiet like snow. Her gaze settled on Claire. "It's also how he looked at his wife when I let him return home."

Claire's throat grew tight. She knew the story now but hadn't realized that they had fallen into the web of tragedies it contained. She kept her voice calm. "Odysseus had a wife and child. Did you think he would return?"

"Yes," Circe answered, chin raised. "A wife and child? I could have given him gods for children. He was supposed to come back. He picked her over me. He died a mortal man instead of living as an immortal with me."

The irony of it held a bitter taste as she realized how Odysseus had made the same decision Argos had. Pity washed over Claire at the confession. The first time she had seen Circe, the woman had seemed untouchable, ethereal in every aspect. Now looking at her, Claire saw just another woman. One with wants and needs, who lashed out in her loneliness.

"Do I not deserve a hero?" Circe asked softly.

"Everyone does," Claire answered, her grip tightening on the man in her arms, "but you can't have mine."

True shock graced Circe's face. Her chest heaved on a sob as she let out a powerful scream. Argos grunted and Claire flinched as her eardrums protested against the noise.

Circe flung her arms out, hurtling her magic at them again. Her words were barely heard under the thunderous pressure. "If you want to live with your mortal, you can die with her too."

Argos gripped Claire painfully as the wind lashed around them. He steadied her as Claire raised the sword in defense and swung it forward with all her strength. The blade bit into Circe's stomach, just below her heart.

The witch smiled at her attempt, but then the smile fell. Blood stained the sheer fabric of her dress. A small noise of pain choked out of her throat as she staggered back.

Shocked, Claire pulled the sword back, dislodging it from the other woman's body. She could see the hole cut into Circe's stomach. She had done that. Claire's stomach squeezed painfully at the sight, waiting for the island's healing magic.

It didn't come, but she wasn't dead either.

Circe stared at her wound, eyes wide, mouth twisted in agony. When her eyes finally turned back to Claire, there was nothing but pure hatred there. "*You*," she seethed, and with the word, the magic was back pressing down on Argos and Claire with suffocating strength. "*You* hurt *me*."

The wind invaded the space between their bodies and threatened to tear them apart, but she refused to let go. Circe fell to her knees, blood still pooling around her as the magic stayed strong.

Claire swung again, hoping to land another hit, but the wind caught the blade and tore it from her hands. It howled around them, pushing their bodies against the stone wall until the air squeezed out of their lungs. The only thing they could do was close their eyes against the assault and wait for the inevitable.

She felt Argos's body shift and the wind nearly sweep it up, but his lips brushed against the shell of her ear. He didn't scream the words, but they made it to her safely. "I love you, Claire."

"I love you too," she said, trusting the words to find their mark. The sword clattered to the ground as she used both arms to grip him tighter. They were going to die, but at least it would be together.

XXVI

CLAIRE HAD FALLEN asleep many times in Argos's arms, but it was still a surprise to wake up in them. Mostly because she assumed they were both dead. She opened her eyes to make sure it wasn't a dream. Miraculously, they hadn't budged from their place against the wall. The rest of the palace was a disaster.

The blue sky shined through a gaping hole that opened the walls to the surrounding waters. Seabirds squawked in the distance. Columns and debris lay in toppled ruins. Circe was nowhere to be seen, but there was a man.

She immediately recognized the three-pronged trident in his hand.

Poseidon stood near the cliffside, where the palace overlooked the water. In that moment, she saw the true God of the Sea that Poseidon was. The water stretched out before him, head bowed in silent reflection. The sight was mesmerizing.

"You're both alive." Poseidon's voice carried back to them, but he didn't turn around. "I'm surprised."

"We are," Argos answered, shifting beside Claire. She hadn't even realized he had woken up. Turning in his arms, she met his gaze. He gave her a soft smile and touched his lips against her hair before turning his full attention to the god. "What happened to Circe?"

"Well, you didn't defeat her, if that's what you're wondering," Poseidon snorted. "But you almost did. I wonder how you managed that?" He eyed them with a look a parent might give their deceitful child.

How indeed? Claire didn't dare look for the sword that had done the damage. She looked back at Argos and smiled at him so wide her cheeks hurt.

Not even Poseidon's exasperated eye roll could ruin the mood.

"Her magic must have backfired." Argos shrugged, looking very at ease, all things considered.

"Perhaps." Poseidon stroked his beard. Claire thought he might push the subject, but his broad shoulders relaxed into an easy shrug. "It doesn't matter. I intercepted her before she could kill you. My ocean carried her away, back to her mother. She'll remain with her own kind for a few hundred years. I think integrating herself so closely with the humans has harmed her mind."

Claire nodded. It was hard to forget the unsettling look in Circe's eyes when she talked about her lost lover. Argos had once said the gods didn't understand human emotions, but she wasn't sure that was true. They felt things, love and hatred and jealousy; they just felt them stronger than humans.

"May I ask why you assisted us?" Argos asked, mouth dipping in a frown.

"I couldn't let my new follower die before she made

good on her offering." Poseidon gave Claire a meaningful look. "I doubt Hades would let you cook for me while you're in the underworld. He would snatch you up for himself."

He wasn't kidding, and Claire felt a swell of pride warm her chest that the god considered her so highly.

"Follower?" Argos asked.

She shrugged. "I asked Poseidon for a favor while we were on *Queenie*. Oh, don't give me that look. You should be thanking me... and him."

"What was the favor? What did you offer him?"

It was easy to see that Argos's alpha male personality was raising its serpent head. She pinched him on the chest. "It was nothing. I just offered my restaurant as a temple—"

"You *what*?"

"And said that I'd cook him a meal every day for the rest of my life."

Argos's mouth moved but no words came out. He looked from her to Poseidon, then back to her. His voice was low when he finally found it, tucking the words between them in a private conversation. "Claire, are you sure? Owning the temple of a god—it's a great honor and a great responsibility. Taking care of it will have to be your first responsibility for the rest of your life."

"It already is my responsibility. The deal is done. Besides, that isn't why I did it, you delusional man," she said softly. "I did it to save you. I'd do the same thing again if given the chance."

Argos shook his head, body sagging against the wall. "Gods above, you are such an incredible woman."

Claire watched him as he sat there, soaking in the information with his eyes cast at the sky. He was pale, but whole. He'd been through a lot in the past twenty-four hours; both of them had. Now was the first time they could breathe a sigh of relief. Circe was gone. Argos was finally free. She reached up, stroking the spot on his neck where it had been slashed earlier. There was no sign of the wound. The skin was perfect.

At her touch, Argos tilted his head and took a hold of her hand, placing a gentle kiss on the back. Claire felt tears burn at the edges of her eyes. She had thought they would never get to hold each other again. For a moment, she'd thought him lost to her forever. With the gods' blessing, they had survived.

Claire leaned against him to get a proper kiss from the man she loved when Poseidon loudly cleared his throat. "Claire, I expect my first meal tomorrow and the temple to be built as quickly as possible."

She bit back a groan and gave a stiff nod. "Of course." Argos squeezed her fingers in agreement.

Poseidon nodded.

Together, she and Argos stood respectfully as a tower of water rose from the bay to meet its master. Poseidon stepped on top of it and disappeared once again from the land of mortals.

✦

Since the moment he'd first laid eyes on Claire, he had underestimated her. "Never again," he promised as they walked down the steps of Circe's mansion. His body felt numb from all the pain inflicted against it and the rapid healing of the island. He walked like a man who had ridden a horse for too long, legs wobbling as Claire's arm braced him against her side. In her other hand was Xanthus's sword. She'd insisted that they find it before leaving the ruins of the palace. He had to admit, though, he liked seeing her carrying it.

"Never again what?" she asked conversationally, but the knowing smile on her lips told him she knew exactly what he was thinking.

"I'm never letting you leave my side again." There would never be a time where he would deny his woman anything.

"Ever?" she inquired softly. The word attached itself to another question. One with a simple answer.

It died on his lips the minute their feet touched the sand. In front of him lay the aftermath of what appeared to be an epic battle. Spears and swords stuck out of the ground, marking the sands as claimed territory. There were two types of men on the beach. Circe's survivors, recognizable by their bare chests and wild appearance, and men dressed in more modern attire. The only thing that revealed their true nature was the golden coins hanging around their necks.

One of the men turned from where he was barking orders, his face breaking out in a too-wide smile. "Argos! You son of a bitch."

Argos recognized the voice immediately. Joy overrode his confusion as the man collected him in a suffocating embrace. "Barcus?"

Barcus grinned, pulling back so they could both get a good look at one another. As expected, his friend had not aged a day since they had last seen each other, but he had changed in other ways. The long locks his friend used to wear as a source of pride were gone, cut into a short style that most modern men wore. As if by magic, it made Barcus look younger.

A new scar peeked from under his torn clothes. A deep

cut that started at the collarbone and disappeared under fabric. The stark whiteness of the wound against Barcus's tan skin revealed how deep the cut had been. Even if it had not been a different color, he would have noticed it. Immortals did not scar unless touched by something sacred. "You have changed much since the last time we met," he said, clasping Barcus's arm and speaking in their mother tongue.

"And you look the same. Claire told me everything that has happened. I've been looking for you for so long. I had no idea you were on Circe's island." Barcus tried to use his easy laugh, but there was something else under it. Worry. Uncertainty.

Argos shook off the concern and brought his brother in for an embrace. "I told no one, do not worry about it."

Barcus let out a huff of air. His arms tightened around Argos. "'Do not worry about it,' he says." Sarcasm laced the words as he switched to common tongue for Claire's sake. Her eyes had been darting between the two of them as they spoke. "We have much to catch up on."

"Yes," Argos agreed, "we certainly do." Now that Barcus was here there were so many questions he could get answered—the state of their Order, the truth behind Xanthus's betrayal—but for now he let his eyes linger on his friend's new scar and left the questions for later.

Barcus looked at Claire. "And Circe?"

"Gone. We do not have to worry about her anymore."

"Is that so…?" Admiration outshined the surprise in Barcus's eye as he nodded. "I told you there was nothing to worry about. The gods have blessed you with a fine warrior, Argos."

"Indeed, they have," he said, grinning at the blush that touched Claire's cheeks.

With the pleasantries of their reunion out of the way, Barcus turned and led them to the large boat that dwarfed the small dock. It was not anything like the trireme war ships they once traveled on, and it resembled nothing of the smaller modern boats Argos had become accustomed to. It easily dwarfed *Queenie*. The contraption was stacked like a house, a palace built for the sea.

Claire's mouth dropped as they drew closer to it. "This is one of the nicest yachts I've ever seen. It must have cost over a million dollars."

"I don't remember." Barcus shrugged as he climbed the steps. "I bought it because it's big enough to house the men, stay out at sea for long periods of time, and it has a wine cellar."

"All those men are of the Order?" Argos asked, looking back at the young men who were tying up the remains of Circe's small army. He recognized only a few of them. The Order was still alive. Relief rolled over his exhausted body at the sight surrounding him.

"Yeah, I'll introduce all of you later," Barcus said distractedly. "Right now, you both look like hell. Let us clean up the battlefield. There's some spare clothes downstairs. We'll be done shortly and then we'll set sail. Where do we need to drop you off, Claire?"

Claire startled out of her appreciation of the boat. Her smile vanished at the question. "Drop me off?"

Argos's stomach tightened thinking about the small wooden house she had planned to make her tavern, burnt to nothing but ash by now. "She'll be coming with us. I owe her a debt."

Barcus looked between them. "Alright, I get it. We'll talk more after everything is done here. I'm going to check on the men. In the meantime, why don't you two clean up? We'll cast out as soon as possible."

The joy that had been in Claire's eyes was gone. She stared quietly at her feet until Argos clasped her hand and steered them towards the stairs. There were four rooms and a large bathroom below deck. The wonders of the modern world sometimes left him speechless, but now Argos was nothing but grateful for the comfort. He started a hot bath and shed his clothes. The expensive shirt Claire had bought him was torn to shreds, coated in sand and dried blood. His blood. It was unsalvageable. He threw it in the trash.

When he looked back, he saw that Claire had not taken off her dirty clothes. They were almost in worse shape than his own, torn and covered in mud. Her eyes would not meet his. They darted from the floor to the cabinets. Anywhere but his naked body.

Something tightened in his chest as he asked, "Is there something wrong? Are you hurt?"

"No, it's just…" She stopped, took a deep breath and met his eye. There was the fierce, stubborn woman he loved. "So, what happens now?"

"We'll get my treasure," he said slowly, unsure what to make of the emotions changing across her face. "I'll pay you—"

"And then we part ways?" Claire interrupted. Her breath stuttered over the words.

Ah. That was what this was about. He stared at her, watching her chest rise and fall, the rapid fluttering of her eyelashes. "Are you done with me so easily, Claire? After all we've been though?" he kept his voice level. If that was what she wanted, then he would let her go, but back in Circe's mansion, he recalled the echo of her voice among the howling winds. Had he imagined those last words, that *I love you*?

Claire shook her head. "No, of course not. But... you are back with your Order. I would understand if you wanted to join them again..." Her voice broke off.

"I will not become an immortal."

"What?" She sniffed, shaking her head. "No, don't say that. Of course you will. There has to be some god who will help you regain your immortality."

"I mean, I do not want to be immortal anymore, Claire."

"Argos." A look of undeniable happiness and hope brightened Claire's face, even as tears began to fall down her cheeks. "You've been looking for your brothers all this time. You shouldn't have to give up your dream for me."

Argos stepped up to her and thumbed away the track of tears on her cheeks. "I do not intend to give up anything. At least not the important things. I have found my brothers again, and I have found you." He kissed her forehead gently. "Being with the woman I love for the rest of my mortal life. Watching you cook and be happy. That is my new dream."

"You...you love me?"

"I said so in Circe's palace, did I not?" Back when they'd held each other so desperately, sure it would be the last time. He'd said the words thinking they would be his last. That was his fault. He should have told her the truth sooner, every chance he got. It was a mistake he never intended to make again. For the rest of eternity, he would say those words as many times as it took to convince her.

"When I spoke with Hestia, I realized you were right. What I felt for the goddess was not love. But the feeling between you and me, that is something I am not willing to give up on, not to please the gods, and not even to rejoin my brothers." He grinned at her. "I love you, Claire. I choose you."

Her wide eyes took him in. "You're serious?"

"I am very serious." He nodded. "But if you do not love me back, I will reconsider my answer…" The air jumped out of his lungs as Claire threw herself against his chest. The force of her body and soul said everything it needed to, but he wanted to hear the words anyway. "Does this mean you love me as well?"

"Yes," came the muffled reply as she started planting kisses against any piece of skin she could reach. "Gods, yes." Her small hands cupped his cheeks and brought their lips together for a passionate kiss.

He groaned against the feeling of her teeth nipping at his lip. A warm bath and the large bed sat nearby, patiently waiting for them, but he was not so patient. His fingers busied themselves, working to take the ruined clothes off Claire's body. When the blouse would not come off fast enough, he tore it.

Claire laughed at the sound. "Are you seriously tearing my clothes off right now?"

"If it means getting you naked faster, then yes," he murmured, looking at her naked figure. He grinned at her and she back at him. "You saved my life in more ways than one, Claire Winters. A hero of your caliber deserves her own kind of worship." She gave him a smile that only a nymph could possess as she twined her legs around his waist and allowed him to carry her. He planted kisses along her skin, thrilled by the noises she made and encouraged to bring out more.

Together they climbed into the large bath, both sighing

blissfully as the water washed away the day. "I think I like being worshiped." Claire smiled, shifting just enough to turn and give him another kiss. "I love you, Argos. For all our meager mortal lives and more, I will always love you."

He laughed and kissed her forehead. "For all of my mortal life and beyond it."

"*There is nothing more admirable than when two people who see eye to eye keep house as man and wife, confounding their enemies and delighting their friends.*"

—Homer, *The Odyssey*

EPILOGUE

ONE YEAR LATER

COVERED IN BATTER, grease, and things she couldn't begin to list off, Claire smiled to herself as she pushed into the main foyer of her restaurant. A restless noise greeted her: the clatter of dishes, the low rumble of conversation. As always, the sight gave her pause as she soaked it in, one thought reverberating through her head. *This is mine.*

No matter how many days passed or how many times she stepped out of the kitchen, somehow the sight still managed to take her breath away.

It had taken a couple months longer than intended, but the end result was well worth it. The Saucy Leg was no more, but the new building had its perks. New floors, sleek wooden tables, a second floor that wasn't hosting her laundry—it had plenty of space for guests. Argos's treasure was enough to fund all of the construction, giving them both a new building and an actual house within walking distance. Where it lacked the history of the old building, Claire had made up for it by decorating the walls with the remaining bits of treasure. Polished armor, weathered maps, and a single marble statue of a god greeting all who entered. It was a historian's dream and had quickly earned them a loyal customer base.

Within months, Poseidon's Place had become a favorite hangout for the locals.

With a deep inhale, she crossed the floor to a nearby table where Thalia sat with Laura King. "Shall I get you all another bottle?" Claire asked, eyeing the empty bottle of wine between them.

"Please." Laura smiled. "I'm not driving tonight, so fill me up."

Thalia nodded in agreement. "And let me know how your stash is doing, Claire. I think you're due for another shipment soon."

Claire traded the empty wine bottle for a newly opened one. Laura clapped cheerfully at the sight. "Will do. Where is the rest of your table?"

"Where do you think?" Thalia's lips pursed in a familiar disgruntled look that had softened over the months. She inclined her head towards the back of the building, where the nosiest group was gathered around a table.

Claire gave them a smile in thanks and headed towards the crowd. As the owner of the restaurant, it was her job to make sure all the customers were happy and satisfied with their food. As she neared, she caught sight of a few familiar faces. The men Argos still called brothers, though he had given up his place in their Order, surrounded him. Even as a mortal, Argos's past had been unwilling to simply let him go. Heroes flocked to their home and restaurant, looking for a warm meal and a good story.

It was normal to have a crowd of them gathered around

one table, wine and beer covering every available surface as their laughter floated to the ceiling. The group burst into another roar of approval at whatever tale was being told. One voice, feminine and high-pitched in annoyance, cried out, "I can't believe you didn't kill anybody!"

Helen.

"There's enough tales full of bloodshed and death," Kevin's voice followed. "I'm pleased to hear this one kept it at a minimum."

"I like Claire's version better. She killed someone."

"Please don't say that so loud," Claire pleaded as she approached.

The table swiveled towards her, faces both familiar and new, all smiling. In the center of it all was her fiancé, dressed in a loose cotton shirt and fitted pants. Another sight she would never be able to get over. Argos had adjusted to the modern world quickly with his easy confidence and clever mind. Even in the moments when something strange slipped past his lips, no one seemed to pay it any attention. He had been eager to adapt, which meant late nights watching modern-day movies and dinner lectures from Kevin. He still managed to look like a man out of place in time, just the way she liked it.

Argos stood from the table and came to her side. The intent in his eyes immediately told Claire what he planned to do. Her hand came up to stop in him midstride. "Not in front of my customers."

He looked at the eyes surrounding them and smiled. "Why not?"

"Because I smell like fish."

"I do not smell anything."

"I'm a mess," she protested before his lips came down to hers.

When he pulled back, his tongue was licking the edges of his mouth. "You taste delicious. As always."

The men around the table gave a drunk cheer while Helen smirked.

Claire cleared her throat, trying to compose herself in front of the crowd. Argos's kisses still left her flustered. If she didn't know better, she'd think his curse never really left, just split between the two of them. "I take it you enjoyed your food?"

"Always. Right, men?"

Another drunk cheer and a cry for more beer made Claire stifle a laugh. "I'll see what I can do." She pulled away from Argos and saw that her messy clothes had spread the stains to his shirt. Argos beamed, as if the stains were their own reward.

The hostess's peppy voice welcomed a new diner to the restaurant. By the swoon of the young girl's voice, Claire could guess another hero had entered her sacred place. When she looked, her feet staggered to a stop. The ruckus behind her witnessed a quick death.

Barcus stood in the doorway. Looking the same as the day she'd first met him, standing in the space as if were a normal occurrence. As if he hadn't been gone for nearly six months.

His disappearance had been the only hole in her and Argos's perfect life. It was difficult not to worry about him, even more so for Argos. Claire knew it was only a matter of time before her lover decided to go looking for their friend and that her new responsibility at her restaurant wouldn't allow her to go off on another adventure. Now she didn't have to worry, but the needling in her throat had refused to go away.

Barcus waved the hostess off with a smile that melted women to the ground before making a beeline for the table.

He held the smile as his friends patted him on the back and welcomed him, but it appeared strained. Argos stood without a word and together the two headed out the back door.

Nerves prickled up her spine as she followed. If either of the men thought she would let them plot behind her back, they were wrong.

Darting to the kitchen, she told her staff she'd be back in a few minutes. She smiled at customers as she headed out the door and requested another round of beer for the heroes. It wouldn't do to have them grow curious either.

She didn't try to be subtle as she exited out the back door. Chin held high, she followed the path to their home. If Argos took their conversation to the house, that must mean it was something their guests weren't meant to hear.

And maybe he didn't want her to hear either.

A lump of worry formed itself in her throat at the thought, but she shook it aside and opened the front door.

Argos's most treasured items greeted her in the foyer. Swords and artifacts he couldn't bear to part with. Juxtaposed next to them were new pictures of the two of them, smiling as they built their new life together. Opening the restaurant, visiting the nearby cities, sailing the Bay on their new boat. It had only been a year since she'd first found Argos, but the life they had now felt as if it was always meant to be.

And now she might be in danger of losing it.

She found them in the living room, both men staring back at her, unsurprised.

"That didn't take any time at all," Barcus said, the tension ebbing away from his face the tiniest bit.

"You didn't say hello," Claire admonished, giving him a tight hug. "Besides, you made both of us worry, disappearing like that. The least you can do is tell me where you've been."

When she pulled back, a dark expression crossed Barcus's face. His answer was grim. "I was hunting down Xanthus."

Tension filled the room at the confession. It had only been a few months ago that Claire had drunkenly confided in Barcus about her worries about Argos's unfulfilled promises. That he would soon leave her, that he wouldn't be able to survive another quest as a mortal. Especially not against the man Xanthus had become. Shortly after that, their friend had disappeared.

"And?" Argos pressed his lips into a somber line.

"I found him—at least a trail I believe leads to him."

Claire tried to catch the gasp of surprise before it left her mouth, but it was too late. Joy and anxiety hit her gut in a confusing swirl of emotion. This was it. Argos had the clue he was looking for. He could avenge Thalia.

And what of her? She had the restaurant to run now, a god to appease. There was once a time when she would have been willing and able to follow him on another crazy adventure, but now…

Could she leave behind her business after everything was finally falling into place?

Her heart squeezed at the answer. *Yes.*

When she glanced at Argos, she saw the same emotions echoed on his face as well. "Where?"

Barcus shook his head. "I'm not saying. This isn't your concern anymore."

The good humor that always marked Argos's face disappeared. "What?"

The other hero didn't flinch. "This is Order business and I will handle it."

"I am the one who made the promise," Argos argued in a

harsh whisper. "I know I gave up my place in the Order, but I cannot let Xanthus go."

"You think you are the only one who has something against Xanthus?" Barcus spat the words with such ferocity they made Argos straighten. "I know you have your pride invested into this, but so do I and it's been hung on the string for much longer than yours. Think of Claire. You are a mortal now, with a mortal life. Don't throw away what you fought so hard for just to fulfill a promise that I can keep."

Claire looked between the two men. Argos had gone quiet at the confession. For months he and Barcus had been catching up on the years that they'd missed, but there were still things neither of them discussed. Barcus didn't know the true horror Argos had undergone at Circe's hands, and neither Argos nor Claire knew exactly what had transpired between Xanthus and Barcus.

All they knew was that they'd had a fight the night Xanthus had left the Order, and Barcus had the scars to prove it.

Argos shook his head, running his fingers through his long hair. For a moment it looked as if he would still refuse, but when he looked up, there was only resignation on his face. "Then you'll need this." He turned to the fireplace, where the sword gifted by Thalia hung on display, ready for the moment it would be wielded again. With a grave expression, he handed the weapon to his friend. "Do not tell Thalia I gave this to you."

Barcus stared at the sword, his easy posture gone. Claire remembered the way he had looked at it in the jungle. The sword held memories for the hero, but in order to defeat the monster Xanthus had become, he would need it. For his friend, he forced a smile. "Why? Am I not worthy of her quest?"

He reached slowly for the sword, but Argos was patient. The two men held each other's gaze. To Claire, it looked as if they were making an ancient promise. A ritual older than the stories Argos told.

"If anyone can defeat him, you can," Argos said quietly. With a nod, he released the sword to his best friend. "But Thalia will have my head if she knew I passed my promise on to someone else, and Helen would run to join you if she knew."

"Are you sure they aren't related to Amazons?"

The two men laughed as they embraced. Over the shoulder Barcus gave Claire a reassuring smile. She mouthed a silent "thank you" to him before moving in and wrapping her arms around the heroes. Her heroes. Barcus was taking on this quest for his own reasons, yes, but he was also doing it for her, for them.

"Take care of yourself," Argos said.

"Call if you need anything," Claire added.

Barcus rolled his eyes. "Thanks, Mom."

Out loud she gave the stern, reasonable speech she gave every hero who walked into her restaurant. "Be careful out there. I know you're immortal, but everything is perishable." She shared a look with Argos. "Even immortality."

Instead of the dismissive understanding she got from some of the younger heroes, Barcus nodded, eyes set in deep focus. "I know, but I swear to you, I'm going to kill him."

Thank you for reading Holding Out For A Hero! If you are interested in first looks, giveaways, and more for the Order of Olympus Series, please consider subscribing to my newsletter!

ACKNOWLEDGMENTS

There are a lot of people I'd like to thank for helping me make this book into a reality. I'll start with my husband, Nathan, who encouraged me in my dreams since day one. He always understood never to bother me when the door was closed and the true meaning of writing time. He helped so much with the pets, the house, and all other things when my day job, writing, and hosting writing groups took me away.

I'd like to thank my oldest friends who always told me to write my own stories. They helped edit my terrible fanfiction and the early versions of this story. A few joined me doing NaNoWriMo, staying up late in the coffee shops and getting the words written. Thank you, Melissa, Kelly, Jessica, Alicia, and Anastasia for all the support.

Next my newest friends, who I met through writing groups and romance novel book clubs. You were all my beta and critique readers. You were my cheerleaders and reality checkers. I've moved to two different states while writing this book and we've stayed in touch through it all. Special shout out to the Carnal in Columbia Book Club (Columbia, Maryland) and the girls there for being my cheerleaders: Heather, Leah, and Pam! To the Columbia Writer's Group and Shut Up and Write Honolulu gang: Amy, Sue, Gemma, Helen, and Casey. Thank you all!

Without friends and writing buddies, I truly don't think this book would have ever been published.

ABOUT THE AUTHOR

Maria Shield writes adult fantasy, romance, and science fiction. She was raised in Kansas but has since lived all over the world, from Korea to Japan, finally ending up in her current location in Hawaii with her husband and pets. She is passionate about Japanese culture, ancient history, and feminist activism. She also loves helping other writers find their communities and sharing craft tips and tricks. This often means she's participating in a critique group somewhere or starting one herself.

When she isn't writing, Maria can often be found doing the three R's: Reading, Running, and Researching.

You can also reach out to Maria at:
Email: mariashield.author@gmail.com
Twitter: @Mariashieldlady
Website: Maria-Shield.com

CPSIA information can be obtained
at www.ICGtesting.com
Printed in the USA
FSHW010505070220
66718FS